SAVED

GARRISON EARTH

V. K. LUDWIG

INK HEART PUBLISHING

ONE

Sophie

Sweet and decadent, the scent of Cultum winter rose barely masked the tang of sex lingering on my skin. It crept into my nose, potent, turning more and more bitter each time I braced against a thrust.

"Your cunt is the best in all of Odheim, *leska*," the Vetusian grunted, stirring his cock through my womb as if to underline his point. "If I had the credits, I would seed you every night. Would you like that?"

"Yes..." The word came hollow. As empty on the inside as me, but he grunted in satisfaction at the breathy qualities around it.

Fingers freshly manicured, I wrapped them around the elaborately carved poster of my canopy bed, silver *Ayura* silk valance caressing my knuckles.

The bed was a replica of the one Queen Elizabeth I used to sleep in. The Virgin Queen. Go figure.

It was grand. Opulent.

A priceless possession just like everything else this cage

afforded — including me. Except, of course, that I had a price. The Vetusian rutting behind me, who stabbed his shaft so deep inside me his balls slapped against my ass, had paid it.

If I could have remembered his name, I would have moaned it... help speed things up. Instead, I said, "Mmm... you feel so good."

With a throaty groan, he pulled out and turned me around by my shoulder. "Suck me, *leska*. Show me how you spread the taste of you and me across your gums."

A suppressed laugh expanded against my sternum, and I clasped my lips around his crown. Tasting him. Tasting me. Tasting the other two who had fucked me before him. Or three?

I stared up at the guy, knees braced against silken sheets which would be changed after this. Create the illusion for the next client that I was, indeed, precious. Not something used more often than a toothbrush.

Hands I knew belonged to a high-ranking warrior fisted my hair, ripping a whimper from me as he pulled on my roots. "I love you, *leska*."

Equal parts of impatience and faked affection fleeted over lustrous green eyes. He expected me to say it back, but I twirled my tongue around his cock head instead.

"*Sert*," he groaned, expectations replaced with the urge to ram his cock down my throat. "Beautiful *leska*, you're going to be the death of me."

I wish...

If blowjobs killed, I would have handed them out to every Vetusian free of charge. But they didn't, so I kept sucking his thick length, harder, white cream rimming around my lips.

One might have thought I enjoyed this, letting him

bump my throat so hard I almost gagged. If one year at *Taigh Arosh* had taught me anything, it was that defiance got you beaten or worse. Worse meaning that Sehrin, head of the compound guards, got to split you in two until your ovaries exploded.

Not that I had any — courtesy of that thing we *didn't* call invasion.

"Enough..." He pushed me onto my back and climbed between my thighs, bullying back inside me with one, merciless thrust that ripped a gasp from my chest. With STD's nothing but a minor inconvenience and easily treated, no barrier between us urged him to be less rough.

Lifting my thigh so he could penetrate deeper, he rutted me hard once more, squinted eyes demanding victory.

Rule number five: the client *always* makes you climax.

Like the starlet they advertised me as, I delivered a splendid act, bucking against him like a maniac. Vetusians were more inclined to slip me an extra credit if my screams praised their performance for all of Odheim to hear.

"Oh, baby," I moaned, arching my back. "I'm so close. Please make me come."

"*T'kam.*"

With honor. Such a warrior thing to say...

As he dragged his lips over my collarbone, the tip of his tongue lapping at me, his cock expanded with imminent release.

I lifted my pelvis toward him, meeting him beat for beat. I moaned, then grunted, then screamed, watching his eyes clench shut as he pretended he wanted to hold back.

Sharp and unforgiving, I dug my nails into his back. Next came that rapid inhale, almost hissed through clenched teeth, my entire body tensing up at the push of a mental button.

Faking an orgasm wasn't particularly difficult if one put some effort into it. With Vetusians, not even that was required. Clueless bunch.

I threw my head back, blonde tresses shoving over the pillow. "I... I... uh... I'm coming."

"*Sert, leska.*" He dropped onto his underarms, his chin digging into my skull as he grunted through his orgasm. "By the Three Suns... I swear I love you *an leska.*"

They all apparently loved me.

None of them enough to help me escape.

I ran the edge of my fingernail down his spine, caressing his trembling body which slowly sunk onto mine. He pressed sweaty pectorals against flawless, young skin.

My eyes trailed along the outline of the ceiling like a racetrack, following the scalloped edging which framed the reproductions of Earth's greatest artwork. The Birth of Venus. The Creation of Adam. Plus a bunch of others I couldn't name, but that didn't make them any less haunting at night when they stared down at me.

Judged me.

Whatever his name was pulled out, ran a finger along his shaft, and sniffed it. "That was beautiful, *leska.*"

I gifted him a studied smile and got up, the mix of lubricant, semen, and friction itching between my legs. With the edge of the sheet, I wiped myself clean and left the bed.

"I'm going to escort a convoy to Heliar in two suns." An expectant gaze followed me to the center of the room, the air cool around my searing crotch. "There will be hazard pay, and I have every intention to return and invest it in a night with you."

I stepped into the sunken tub at the center of my room, the splash of warm water camouflaging my sigh. Being used by these guys was bad but spending a night in their arms while they whispered sweet nothings into my ears was worse.

If there was hazard pay involved, perhaps I'd get lucky and he wouldn't return at all. "That would be lovely."

"You are lovely," he murmured and leaned over, trying to place a kiss onto my lips which ended on my cheek as I turned my head. "And I want you to be mine for an entire night."

Labia puffy from all the fuckings of that shift, I swiped my fingers through them and cleaned myself as best as I could. Outside, the solar pits drilled into Odheim illuminated the gardens a bit more with each breath as the night faded away.

Never clean but at least less filthy, I stepped out of the tub, which gulped away the water only to replace it a moment later. I dried myself off, masking the stench of hundreds with another pump of perfume before I stepped into a new floor-length dress.

"May the Three Suns watch over you during the convoy," I said, turning my back to him so he could snap the elaborately embroidered dress shut in the back. "This was very special to me, and I can't wait to see you again."

Rule number four: a fuck was *always* special and luring them back to *Taigh Arosh* was my job.

He swung me around by my waist, his eyes slipping to my lips, but he knew better than to try again. Instead, he placed a too gentle kiss onto my forehead. The threat of tears burned behind my eyes.

"I love you," he said, perfectly timed with the way he clasped my chin hard and pulled so I would meet his eyes. "Say it. Say that you love me too."

His demand crackled through my wall of hard-earned

numbness, striking an out-of-tune cord on my petrified heart.

I hated him.

Him and all of his kind.

I stroked my palm over the side of his face and cupped it around his hand until he eased his grip on my cheeks. "I love you."

Even as he squeezed it out of me, he gave me nothing else but a satisfied smile playing around a set of petty lips. No fingers lifted into my palm to place an extra credit. Fucking asshole.

Rule number three: patrons are not allowed to tip.

If there was one thing warriors loved more than following orders, it was sticking to the rules.

After he left, I slipped into my high heels, and twirled my hair into a loose updo with the moonstone-decorated hair claw from the Queen Anne vanity next to me.

I made my way to the hallway and toward the staircase, glancing over the railing to the atrium lying below. Vetusian scholars harmonized musical instruments, sophisticated arias reverberating the entire building, overwhelming the screams, sobs, and savagery hiding behind gold-plated doors.

Polished marble glided along my palm on my way down, the elegantly placed *tap... tap... taps* of my heels on the stone turning heads even from the orchestra.

The atrium held the only bar in this building along with several seating areas, from where patrons ogled the available females. Except for whenever I entered, and all eyes turned to me. Like now, the hungry stares of Vetusians no longer sending shudders over my body like they had a year ago. Over time, those reactions had fizzled into nothing but a quick tingle inside my ribcage.

I sat down next to Izara, one of the three Jal'zar females living and working at *Taigh Arosh*. Every sex slave working here had something special about her. Izara was a master at breath play. I... was simply human.

"I thought that guy would never finish," I snarled.

Beside her, one of the three healers of this establishment sat crookedly on a barstool. All of them *sgu'dals*, souldust addicted junkies, but this one had the habit of rocking back and forth without a break whenever he needed another fix. Fucking annoying.

Izara sighed and took a sip of her champagne, one slender leg elegantly crossed over the other, draped in expensive silk. "I had a Vetusian cradled in my arms and suckling on my tits for the last argos, pretending I was nursing him."

"Scholar Joleas?"

"Uh-huh."

"Sick fuck," I said, snapping my fingers toward the bartender.

The old warrior everyone called Ashrider limped over, twisting a split lip into that lovely snarl reserved for me. "What do you want, *leska*?"

"Campo Viejo," I said, tapping a fingernail against the frosted glass counter. "And don't you fucking dare pour it from that two-day-old bottle. Open up a fresh one."

Just as he turned away with a grunt, a Vetusian engineer walked up with a smile that would have looked charming on a man. "Put it on my account. And whatever else *leska* wishes to drink tonight."

"The night is almost over," I said, my legs crossing all on their own. "I'm afraid I am no longer available tonight."

He scoffed and rested his arm on the counter, his

hungry gaze roving me over. "Even if you were, I could not possibly afford you, Earth female."

Earth female.

The words had Vetusians turning their heads all over again, as if it wasn't known across Odheim that *Taigh Arosh* had purchased one of however many abducted women enslaved on this planet.

"Then why am I talking to you?"

I turned away from him and toward Izara, who watched the situation unfold with amusement etched onto her features. As the starlet, I got away with things other workers wouldn't dare. A depressing advantage, really.

The engineer strolled around me and squeezed himself between me and my friend, a knuckle stroking down my cheek. "I will offer two-thousand credits for a kiss."

As if his offer meant anything to me, considering I would never see any of those credits. Whatever meager tips I made I had to hide because, god forbid, I might save up enough to pay my way out of this hell.

I grabbed the glass of red wine Ashrider handed me and took a sip, the acid clinging chalky to my teeth. "I don't kiss."

"So I've heard," he said, twirling a lose strand of mine and weaving it underneath another. "That makes it all the more precious, and I enjoy precious things."

"And yet you can't afford them."

Cockiness at its finest, he leaned over, his whisper like poison against my ear. "After my next promotion, I will come straight here and pay for an entire night with you. I will fuck the arrogance out of your tight little ass before I shove my cock down your throat and drown that smug smile of yours in my seed."

A surge of panic tightened its fist around my neck, and I

swallowed the leftover bouquet in a lump of wine-flavored saliva. My clasp tightened around the stem of my glass, fingers itchy to shatter it against the edge of the counter before I'd ram it into his throat.

"Such expensive fabric," he mumbled, trailing his hand over the shiny surface covering my thigh. "And yet it doesn't hide that you're nothing but a whore. One I will make good use of when I return. Do you hear me, *leska*?"

Yes, I hear you.

I heard every single word like yet another shadow crossing over my heart.

Tension and hostility crept through my ribcage, the aftertaste of wine turning bitter at the back of my tongue. My mouth had gotten me into trouble more than once, and yet I refused to hide my disgust for his kind.

I stared over his shoulder and into the tense face of Izara, her tail already flicking behind in a defensive reflex she couldn't control. Then I whispered, "A whore you have yet to be able to afford, so get the fuck out of my sight and quit wasting my time."

Something menacing twisted around his lips as he slowly turned away. A creeping sense of discomfort infested my chest.

"You're making more enemies than you need," Izara mumbled into her glass.

As if the Vetusians had ever been anything else...

"Hate f-feeds on your s-soul, you know." The meek tone of the healer's voice was as unexpected as his lecture was infuriating, his eyes so bleached his irises had turned into a dirty, grayish white. "It keeps eating even after there's n... no... nothing left, turning you into a shell without a spirit."

He sat there like a pile of misery, tugging on a light brown strand while he nervously glanced over to me. Each time he rocked, flares of anger shot up from my guts. Who was he to give me a lesson on hate, considering it was his kind that had landed me here?

Arms flat on the counter, I leaned over and stared him down, enjoying the way he flinched. "Look! It talks."

Shoulders stiff, he immediately lowered his gaze and turned his head away from me like a beaten stray, mumbling, "You're a fucking bitch."

"What?"

"Come on, *leska*," Izara sighed, letting a finger squeak over one of her fangs. "You know he's not in his right mind."

I slipped off the stool and walked over to him, taking another gum-shriveling sip of my wine. His neck shortened by a few inches the moment I lifted the glass over his head. Tipping it, I poured the red liquid over his head, the occasional sprinkle landing cold and sour against my collarbone.

Back and forth, back and forth he rocked, and I swayed the glass to follow his motion, his brain already so fried he didn't even close his eyes. That guy just sat there, rubbing his hands like a mad person as he stared at the counter.

No, I wasn't a bitch.

Bitches fucked for fun or in the name of sexual empowerment. I had neither of those because I was nothing but a whore. A filthy prostitute. Because of him. His kind.

I slammed the glass next to him on the counter, and he jumped in his stool at the *clink*. "*Sgu'dal.*"

Izara held an arm out for me but I pushed it away, making my way back upstairs. Tears rolled off my cheeks and dripped mascara-tinted onto the white marble steps, my stomach roiling with rock-hard convulsions.

"What's wrong, *leska*?" Another Jal'zar female worker asked who passed me in the hallway.

Leska. Leska. Leska.

I swatted her away and fell into a sprint.

Palms to the golden double doors, I pushed back into my gilded cage and turned the lock behind me. There, I sunk to the ground, the silk of my dress slipping so easily along the metal.

I used to have a name, but nobody spoke it in this hell-hole. A name made you a person, but I was only a thing used by many. Everything I was, a male could buy, including the chipping pieces of my soul.

I was nothing but a possession.

I was just... *leska*.

TWO

Adeas

The human female paraded away with more sway in her hips than usual — if that was even possible.

Long legs extended into heels which hurried up the marble staircase, lustrous blonde hair caressing exposed shoulder blades.

Everyone stared after her, looking their fill of her bouncing breasts and her perfectly shaped behind as they adjusted hard-ons too desperate to recede anytime soon. Some checked their accounts, frowning when they realized they couldn't afford the human beauty. A beauty which truly resonated in the way she held her chin high even as she carried the scent of many males on her pallid skin.

Leska was the sun of *Taigh Arosh,* which rose alongside the night. She was a force of nature. Unpredictable and elusive. With the ability to burn deeper than the red wine stinging my eyeball.

"She h-hates me." My stammer matched the uncontrollable tremble ravaging my body, only slightly consoled by how I rocked back and forth.

"*Leska* doesn't care enough to hate you. Probably doesn't even remember your name." Black claw extending from one of the Jal'zar's digits, Izara scratched a curved line into the glass counter. "It's your kind she hates," she said with a sigh before she added, "and perhaps herself."

One, two, three puddles of wine on the counter, and my scalp still tingled from where *leska* had poured her drink over me. I reeked of alcohol, and my dark gray shirt clung soaked to my shoulders and stomach.

"What the fuck are you doing here?" The shove of the compound guard had me sway in my stool, nausea bubbling in my throat at the unexpected motion. "Nasty shits like you got no business loitering around in the atrium. Get your sorry ass off that stool before you accidentally shit your pants and ruin it." Something slung around the back of my neck, pulled me onto my feet, and pushed me into the hallway beside the bar. "Get back into the maze before patrons see you."

The maze.

Service hallways stretching across the entire compound, some underground, connected *Taigh Arosh* with the sweat-mines and the Casino. It was the clockwork behind all this, ensuring operations ran smoothly. I was a smudged gear.

"Calm down, Sehrin," Izara snarled. "He just sat here at the edge, minding his own business."

The warrior let out a grunt, the golden iris of his bionic eye focusing in on me. "This *sgu'dal* can mind his own business where patrons don't have to smell him. What the fuck happened to you anyway? All wet."

I wiped a trickle of wine from my forehead. "*Leska*."

A grisly scar running from his forehead over his eye

and down to his jawline stretched taut at his lopsided grin. "That female needs a hard fuck to put her in her place."

And he might have been right, considering the human female was the one who got him that bionic eye. First day at *Taigh Arosh*. Bam. Broke a bottle on the counter and stabbed it right into his face. I might have loathed *leska*, but he fucking hated her.

"Levear will have you killed if you touch her," Izara stated like the fact it was.

Nobody touched *leska*.

Unless that nobody paid.

"He can fucking try," Sehrin scoffed, large hand shoving me against the paneled wall. "That guy's too soft with the human female. As if she'd break if you put her on a nice, fat cock. I'd have her beg for mercy while I stretch that little mating cleft."

"Whatever, Sehrin." Izara slipped off her stool, gesturing me to follow her. "Come with me, Adeas. I need you to take a look at a tear I got."

I slouched behind her, my shoulder somehow bumping into every corner we turned, my mind dizzy with the urge to get my hands on some souldust.

Not because I needed to.

I didn't.

Using it was a conscious choice; souldust the only thing that kept my nerve damage under control.

"When was the last time you ate something?" Izara asked over her shoulder as we climbed one of the narrow staircases in the back.

I only shrugged and followed into the hallway, which accessed the rooms of the females from hidden doors, allowing healers like me to move about the building out of the patrons' eyes. Torn labia, sore nipples, and bruised thighs — I took care of them all and more.

Izara pushed against the door which turned into framed tapestry on the other side, waiting until I slipped through before she closed it.

A set of claws waved at the bowl of fruits standing on the sideboard next to her. "Are you hungry?"

"No." *I don't think I am...*

Luxurious fabric gathered on the ground as she slipped out of her dress, exposing the small breasts typical for a Jal'zar female.

She thrust her chest out, a pinkish-gray nipple pushed into view. "Joleas tore my nipple he sucked so hard earlier. You see that?"

"Sit down," I said, guiding her to the white couch in front of her bed, the *bullhabou* leather soft as I sunk into the cushion.

"He offered a hundred extra credits if I would nurse him."

After working at *Taigh Arosh* for over two solar cycles, I didn't bother to shake my head at the patron's request. Guys got off on the weirdest stuff — me included.

"We could split," she said. "If you induce lactation —"

"I'd rather not mess with hormones."

"*Leska* gets pumped full of hormones each day."

"That's different," I said. "She requires hormone treatment since something's off with hers for some reason."

Trembling fingers reached for her nipple, prodding the stiff bud aside. My eyes blinked the tear into focus. A deep crack ran vertically along the flesh, the skin around it bruised purple.

"I have to stitch that up," I sighed and walked over to the sideboard. "Which drawer?"

"Second left."

I retrieved one of the healer packs each room had stored and placed it onto the small table in front of the couch. Taking a sterilized cloth from a wrapper, I saturated the fabric in enzyme solution.

"Press that onto your breast. The enzymes will remove whatever crusted blood and germs have collected in there."

Her hand stalled a mere finger width from mine, purple eyes focused on the violent shake of my hand. "There's some counselor coming to the Odheim infirmary, you know. A Vetusian healer from Earth."

"Uh-huh."

She took the cloth and pressed it against her flesh, soaking her nipple in the solution. "Apparently, they opened a new rehab facility on Earth. He's going to talk about the program. The hologram said everyone affected by souldust is *encouraged* to attend."

Flashes of white light flickered behind my eyes, sending a dull throb into my temples. Great timing for a migraine. Why did everyone give me shit about this?

Thumbs pressing against my temples, their circles gave only minimal relief. "Why are you telling me this?"

"Maybe you could talk to him, and —"

"I could stop if I wanted to." *I know I can...*

Her lips pressed into a thin line, her eyes watching me prepare thread and needle. "Have you looked at yourself in a mirror lately? Your eyes?"

"That means nothing," I snarled, sitting back down on the couch with a needle clasped between fingers I couldn't always trust anymore. But I could trust them more than ever before after I got my hands on souldust. "A side effect. Like I said, if I wanted to stop, I'd do it."

"Why aren't you then?"

Because I don't want to.

Through the haze of the migraine, I reached for the cloth and tossed it onto the table. Then I leaned in close, the tiny hook needle throwing a glistening blur into my vision with the way it shook.

"Wait a second." Izara got up with a sigh and strolled over to her sleeping pod, retrieving something from deep within a pillowcase. "No way am I going to let you work on my nipple like that. Why didn't you stop at the Sweatmines in the afternoon like Levear wants you to?"

"I forgot."

When she sat back down, she held a tiny silver sphere in her palm, the sight alone making me grow hard against the zipper of my jeans. Like I said... getting off on the weirdest stuff.

I watched the sphere click open, the blue dust waiting inside sending an all-devouring shame across my body, which quickly transformed into excitement.

The moment her fingertip approached the sphere, I placed my hand onto her wrist and held her back, a whisper grinding at the back of my skull. *Choke on it, Vetusian.* "Uh-uh... I don't take that stuff from others."

Especially not from Jal'zar females, although I considered Izara as something as close to a friend as one might get in a place like this.

"Suit yourself," she said, holding the sphere a mere click from my face, making me want to spill my seed inside my pants. "Go easy, okay? I sure won't be the one helping you to get off if you take too much."

"Easy. Yeah. Yeah. Easy..."

I dipped my fingertip into the sphere, and a zap of electricity struck my skull. Blue and sparkling, the powder dusted my chewed-up nail.

Easy... Just a little.

Dipping thumb and index finger into the sphere, I took a pinch of souldust and brought it to my nostrils.

I sucked it in.

My body hardened.

The souldust burned from my nostrils up into my sinus cavity, from where it pounded against my eardrums.

Another snort.

I rubbed my fingertips inside my nostrils, making sure not to waste a single particle. A tingle rushed over my head, infesting my heart with adrenaline as it spread through my veins as liquified invincibility.

Across my body, muscles tensed, and the haze of the migraine disappeared as if it had never existed. For a brief moment, I wondered if I was still alive as everything around me fell away. Then it all returned brighter.

My ears pricked even before the sphere snapped shut, my perception sharper than it had been in suns. I sensed Izara's breath moving the air around us, smelled the *vasani* berries she kept somewhere in this room, and tasted the acidity of air tainted with red wine.

"Snap out of it already," Izara said. "Quit staring at nothing like a creep and fix that nipple."

I took a deep breath, my lungs expanding like they hadn't in a while, and brought the hook needle to her nipple. "Something for the pain?"

"Phf..." she huffed like expected, since Jal'zar had an impressive tolerance for pain.

One hand cupped her breast. With the other, rock-solid fingers tore the needle through thin skin, smooth and steady. Whoever said souldust was a problem had never seen me work after I took it. I just had to take it easy. Not overdo it.

What was a drug to most, was simply a medication for me.

"I was thinking about applying to surgeon training," I said, stitching that nipple together with such precise movements I could have performed brain surgery right after. "They need more of them, and I'm good at that shit."

"Adeas, they revoked your license."

"I'll get it back." I cut the thread and applied a healing salve. "Give me three solar cycles, and I'll come out of there a surgeon. Did I ever tell you that I was the healer with the highest —"

"Test results among your crop? Yeah, you might have mentioned it once or twice." She pulled on the mound of her breast, inspecting the straightest suture pattern the universe had ever seen. "They don't accept healers to the surgeon program who have a history of drug abuse."

"That's okay," I said with a shrug. "I don't even want to be a surgeon. What I really want to do is travel to different planets and learn from healers from other cultures. Don't you have shamans on Solgad?"

For some reason, she lifted a brow at me. "Vetusians aren't even allowed to step on Solgad ever since the peace treaty."

My body thrust me from the couch with such force the Jal'zar stepped away from me. Oh right, because I was so dangerous. My fingers tingled with anger. It pissed me off when they acted as if I raped pleasure workers on the regular.

She cracked open the secret door. "You should probably leave now. Thanks for stitching me up."

"Yeah, you're right."

I didn't know when I had decided to glance over my

shoulder and back at her bed, searching for that pillowcase which had the sphere hidden away.

"I already put it somewhere else, so don't waste your time ripping through my pillows when I'm not here."

"I'm not a thief," I snarled, the insult alone making me want to crawl out of my skin. "Who the fuck do you think you are?"

"Adeas, you have to leave now. If Sehrin finds you high like..."

Her voice trailed off, disappearing somewhere into the back of my mind as my head turned toward the wall across all on its own. "You hear that?"

Crying.

Determined steps carried me over to where a desk stood against the wall, my teeth clenching with each wail coming from behind it. Moments ticked by as the cries died into sobs, and I clenched my eyes shut, the sound more than I could take. It made me furious.

"Who the fuck is that?"

Izara let the gap grew wider, rolling her eyes when I refused to move. "It's *leska*. Her room is next to mine. Remember?"

Still nothing but incessant wails alternating with sobs, tormenting me, making me wonder if I should check if she was injured or push a pillow onto her face so she would shut the fuck up.

"She's doing that on purpose to piss me off."

"Okay, you're talking nonsense. That Earth woman doesn't even know you're in here. She just cries a lot."

That was true.

I'd heard her more than once.

The moment Izara walked up to me and pulled me

toward the door by my collar, I gave her a shove and she stumbled aside. "Don't touch me, Jal'zar."

"You're not allowed to be around the females when you're high."

"I'm not high."

Rule number five: no healer or guard was allowed around a female within three argos after they consumed souldust.

The reason for that ached against the constraint of my pants in the form of a painful erection, which wouldn't go away even after I jerked off a bunch of times, I knew from experience. Aside from focus, souldust also amplified the most primal urges.

But I didn't fuck Jal'zar.

Not anymore...

I made my way out the door, but not without mumbling, "I never touched any of the workers."

"And I want you to keep it that way."

The door slammed into my face, leaving me outside the maintenance hallway that buzzed with *leska's* crying. Less than twenty steps and I stood by her door, rubbing my palm over my shaft as if I wanted to get off on her misery.

Perhaps I could have.

Perhaps I wanted to.

She'd poured her drink over me as if I was nothing.

The human female was the sun of *Taigh Arosh*, rising with the night, and extinguishing herself in an ocean of tears when nobody listened — nobody but this *sgu'dal*.

THREE

Sophie

Fingertips stroked through my hair in an even rhythm, the tickle along my scalp lulling me into a state of sleepiness.

I rested in the arms of a high judge, one leg draped over his thigh, on the oversized lounger on my balcony. The purple atmosphere of Odheim glistened above us. Beyond it, cargo vessels and stargazers, nothing but tiny specks of moving light, brought in wares from Earth. Jeans, coffee, chocolate... sex slaves.

"What's on your mind, *leska*?"

How to get you to help me.

His hand trailed from hair to face, a thumb brushing my eyebrows into arched perfection. "Each time I visit, you're a bit quieter."

Because each time he paid for my company, there was less left of me. My heart petrified a bit more at the thought. How would I find a way to escape this place before all of me disappeared?

I'd been loud when they took me, tossing around and

tearing on uniforms when a Vetusian grabbed me from behind on my way to the scholar stratum.

I'd been loud when Levear *honored* me with the first fuck an hour after I arrived at Taigh Arosh, screaming and scratching until he didn't slap but punch me.

I'd been loud when my first client fucked me without mercy, begging and bargaining like I had with my crackhead mom all my life.

But then my very first client had clasped his hand around my neck and pushed me underwater in my own tub, fucking me until he climaxed, and bubbles expelled my last breath.

I came out alive.

Alive... and a lot quieter.

"Have you been to Earth lately?" I asked.

"I have." He wrapped his arm around my waist and pulled me closer to him, until my knee bunched against his green robes. "The Empire hired Kokonian workers to assist with the construction of habitats since we simply don't have enough engineers. Ardev Five returned to Cultum, finally emptied of all females."

"I was on Ardev Five," I said, stroking my fingers over his forehead in a circular motion, just like he'd told me his human mate used to. Back before she died of placental abruption. "Made me go bonkers, sitting there in my room all day."

Back then, I thought the worst thing that could happen to me was to be matched to a Vetusian. Boy was I wrong...

But they'd never found my match.

And having neither ovaries nor uterus — thanks to a stray bullet during the invasion — I would have been worthless to him anyway, unable to give him children. Wasn't that what they all wanted?

Still too pretty not to be fucked, though...

Silence lingered for a while, aside from the hum of the static barrier around the balcony. They'd installed that the night a healer caught me balancing along the stone-carved rail, when I prayed to god for an accidental misstep.

I wished I would have had the guts to jump. Smash my brains on the courtyard below and be done with this mind-fuck of a life.

"I brought you something from your home planet," he said, letting one hand fumble between us in search of his pockets. "A gift. Small, but I had to find something I could smuggle through Odheim customs without questions."

The metallic-brown wrapper crunched as he pulled it out, the red lettering putting a smile on my face. "You brought me Twix?"

"It's chocolate. Or so I was told."

From the slick feel behind the wrapper, my guess was the chocolate had already melted. So did my pride because I needed an ally. And who was better than a Vetusian with connections who actually treated me nicely?

I placed my hand where his cock rested underneath fabric. Pussy held power. Something I'd learned from my mom before I came to Odheim. Here, I was merely perfecting a skill she never exactly hid from me.

"Thank you," I forced across my lips, a jerk of surprise running through his crotch when I cradled what must have been his balls. "Now I feel like I should give you something in return."

With a groan, he thrust his junk into my waiting hand, but then he said, "That's not what I come here for."

And that exactly was the problem.

Among all the Vetusians, I hated him the least. This guy had never used my body, had never touched me other than to caress me for an hour once a week or so. Just what did it take to convince him, considering my body was the only thing I had to bargain with?

"Everyone pays the same rate to spend time with me, regardless of what they do with me... to me." I inched close enough his breath tickled against my forehead and placed a kiss onto his cheek. "Those are some very expensive hugs and cuddles."

"And I treasure each stroke through your hair, *leska*. Each moment of closeness between us. Every word spoken as friends."

Irritation clasped on my throat.

He wasn't my friend until he helped me.

What I was about to do was risky, but did I have another choice?

Hand trailing to his shoulder, I pushed him onto his back and mounted him, my dress bunching up around my thighs all on its own.

"If you're my friend," I whispered, palm stroking over his chest, "prove it and help me escape."

His lips pressed into a slash before he shook his head. "*Leska*, I —"

"Do you think your human mate would have wanted this? Wouldn't she want you to help me?"

"My mate is dead." His voice came calm, but he lifted a finger in warning. "And you will never speak of her again."

In my desperation, I pushed myself up and arched my back, grinding my pubic bone over his flaccid cock.

"All I need is someone who's willing to put me on a cargo ship to Earth," I said, rounding it up with a groan that had him reach his hands for my waist. "I'll figure out a way to get out of here. I saved up some credits. Not much, but I can make more over time if —"

"Please stop. I cannot help you, *leska*."

Oh, but he could snuggle with me.

Fury heated my veins.

Just fucking help me!

I gave another thrust. "You're the only —"

A breeze of rose-perfumed air...

The back of my head hit the tiles, sending a throbbing headache straight into the center of my brain.

He'd pushed me off him.

Blood rushed into my extremities, heating the musk of males sticking to my pores like goddamn tar.

"Fucking asshole," I shouted, pushing myself onto wobbly heels, the way he held a hand out only spiking my fury. "You come here and pet me like an animal in the zoo, telling me how much you loved your mate while you let me rot in this whorehouse."

"I..." He pulled me up but immediately let go of my hand, then fell into a pace before me. "I couldn't help you even if I wanted. And I loved Lisa more than anything."

"Well, karma's a bitch, huh? Guess she got lucky, though, considering she's dead instead of sucking dick —"

Slap.

Flames seared into my cheeks, and something crackled at the back of my neck while the balcony spun around me. Coated in pain and cold sweat, I forced all breath from my lungs as I hit the stone underneath me a second time.

"*Leska!*" Arms shoved underneath my shaken body and picked me up, only to lower me back onto the lounger a moment later. "I didn't mean to strike you. I'm so sorry. So terribly sorry."

A pillow was propped underneath my head, and another supported my calves, his voice tormented. "I am a government official. A high judge. If anybody found out that I am coming to this establishment. Just having the knowledge of it... I would be prosecuted. Lose everything." He pried my fingers open, pressed something into my palm, then closed them around it. "CAT officers are working undercover in Odheim now. You have to stay strong until they find you."

CAT? The Empire's team for preventing abductions? I didn't allow myself to hope what he said was true. But what if it was?

"Please," I begged, tears blurring the blue and green swirls of nebula above me. "Tell them where I am. Why won't they just come and get me?"

I lay on the lounger, the universe spinning above me in all its beauty, reminding me of drunk nights on top of mom's double wide. Guess the acorn didn't fall far from the tree after all. Her boyfriends hit her and apologized right after all the time.

He never answered.

I rolled onto my side and pushed myself up while half my face flared in pain. That guy might have been a scholar, but he bitchslapped like a warrior, I could tell from experience.

Blinking my surroundings back into focus, salt seasoning my lips, my chest tightened with that ugly cry I had to breathe down.

He was gone.

Instead, a heavy stillness clung to the night and kept me company.

Foolish me.

Vetusians were the ones who had abducted me. They were the ones who used me every day. How could I have been so idiotic to think that one of them would help me?

The realization of my own stupidity made the air wane

inside my lungs. Nobody would come and save me. But I couldn't save myself either...

Inside my palm, I found three Imperial Credits, the tear-shaped chips worth every bit of pain coursing through my body. I had no ally, but at least I was richer. Perhaps I could bribe my way out?

Between my legs, the fabric of my dress split and ruined, the Twix still managed to put a smile on my face. Lopsided, sparing the aching corner of my mouth.

I had no idea how much a merchant would charge to hide me between his cargo on his way to Earth. Five thousand? Ten times that? However much it was, I was three credits closer, bringing me to a grand total of forty-two credits I'd stashed away over the course of eleven months and two days.

I didn't allow my heart to sink at that math.

It sunk anyway.

FOUR

Sophie

I sat cross-legged inside my closet, damask pillows lining the walls, and blankets draping over my thighs. Metal clanked against stoneware when I dunked the spoon into the bowl, bringing another bite of cereal dinner to my mouth.

The good thing about being the only human prostitute at *Taigh Arosh*: management tried to keep me in a good mood, going so far as to allow me a synthesizer with a handful of Earth recipes.

Cold and creamy, the milk trickled down my throat. The cereal crunched between my molars. It reminded me of my childhood, the memories of how I'd fended for myself suddenly almost beautiful.

"*Leska.*" Izara stepped into my room, gazing around for a moment before she came straight to my closet.

Arms wrapped around her belly, face in frowns, she glanced inside. "I know you're done for today, but I was wondering if you could take over that client Levear just dumped on me. My stomach's acting up."

"Let the healer give you something."

"I already missed one night during the last masquerade," she said, warm eyes pleading. "He's already waiting in the bathhouse. Even if I call a healer, I couldn't possibly let him wait that long." When I dunked my spoon into the bowl again, she added, "I'll give you five credits."

My ears pricked at that.

Bowl cast aside, I pushed myself from my nest, let my nightgown slip to the ground, and grabbed my robe instead. "Who is it?"

"He only said warrior. Probably not a regular."

I made sure she saw my lifted brow because anything other than regulars were wild cards. They could expect anything from an hour of your company to choking the breath out of you as they demanded you climax with a cock up your ass.

"You owe me big time," I said, loosely tying the belt around my waist.

"I'll repay the favor."

I gave her a nod before I left my room and headed toward the bathhouse, knowing full well Izara would stand by her word. While most Jal'zar females avoided me, she often came to visit me after our shifts, telling me fascinating stories about her home planet.

The bathhouse was at the opposite side of my room on the second floor, where white stone columns marked the entrance. Salt and minerals scented the humid air, which settled onto my cheeks in billows of steam.

Lit from the bottom, the small lagoons scattered across the room cast a pinkish sheen onto the vaulted ceiling. At the far end of the room, a broad-backed figure rested with arms spread across the tiled edge, his head tilted far back.

My client, no doubt.

I hung my robe on the hook beside me, soles splashing through the occasional puddle which had formed over mosaics telling Vetusian tales. But the closer I stepped to this client, the more my feet slowed. Until they stalled altogether, curiosity quickly overpowered by concern.

That client was a warrior.

A Jal'zar warrior, his head lolling forward, purple eyes immediately locking on me with confusion. "Levear sent me a human female?"

"I... I'm sorry," I said on a step backward. "This must have been a misunderstanding."

"Indeed." Water splashed around a chest trained to bulging perfection as he slowly waded toward me. "Jal'zar were forced to share their females with Vetusians for solar cycles, but they have yet to allow us to partake in theirs. Which makes your presence all the more intriguing."

Another step back, the puddles suddenly freezing against my naked soles. "One of the Jal'zar females will be right with you."

I hadn't even fully turned around yet when his voice came rich and deep. "Fifty credits if you stay."

I would have liked to say that I stood paralyzed by fear, or at the very least discomfort, but what rooted me in place was a silent gasp at that number. If I stayed, I could make more in a night than I'd made all year.

"Is that even possible?" I asked, not fully turning back, but rather glancing over my shoulder back at him.

Water sloshed as he pulled himself out of the lagoon, pearling down his muscle-taut body. "Have a good look and decide."

He stood there for me to drink him in, unashamed, his gaze accompanying mine. It drifted lower and lower, bringing heat to my cheeks.

A thick cock stood erect, not much different from a Vetusian aside from his gray skin, and ridges lining the upper side of his shaft. That tail swiping upward behind his back I was used to. His horns twirled backward from behind his temples.

"I've never been with a Jal'zar male before."

Strong legs stalked toward me, and a gentle tug on my back invited me against his body. "That makes two of us."

I couldn't contain my giggle, which he met with a smile presenting fangs as he murmured, "You have my word I will approach this carefully, the first time a Jal'zar and a human become one."

Fifty credits. Fifty fucking credits.

"Okay."

He swooped me up with such speed my arms flailed around his neck, and he lowered himself back into the water right along with me. There, he positioned me facing the edge, the water slightly salty against my lips.

"We often mate our females from behind," he whispered with his chest pressed against my back, followed by a deep growl that sent an odd tingle into my core. "Males make that sound to arouse a female, though I doubt it would have an effect on a human. Now open for me, *kuna*. Let me in."

He did approach it carefully. Entered me slowly and with patience, scooping warm water over my shoulders in an attempt to relax me, no doubt.

This wasn't so bad.

The Jal'zar warrior claimed my pussy inch by inch, allowing me to get used to the ridges before he started pumping.

"Poor human female," he crooned, one hand holding me afloat while the other explored my body. "Mistreated and spoiled by the males who promised eternal love and devotion. You cannot expect honor from their kind, for they have no souls. Grown in bags from an artificial mother, they neither love nor care."

All I had for him was a nod because every word was true. While I'd never had any trouble with those Jal'zar I'd met, I was starting to like them a lot better at that very moment.

"Once our *urizayo* unite and our tribes grow strong, we will free Earth of their rule."

"You're planning to attack them?"

"They're growing weaker by the sun," he whispered, allowing a break as he groaned deep for a couple of thrusts. "They lost many warriors reclaiming parts of Earth from rebel control. And when they did, they executed their leaders. Weak roots grow from seeds of violence."

"I despise them," I whispered against the tile, letting him thrust me onto his cock against the force of the water.

"*Ruk*," he grunted, his cock filling me with increasing pressure. "*Kimi vi kuna wekh gam kuy*. The cunt of this female milks my cock so nicely."

The Jal'zar began rutting, flesh expanding against my walls as he groaned, "Do you want me to kill them for you, *leska?*"

"Yes," I breathed, exhilarated by my horrible answer.

"I shall present you my body marked with a tally of their deaths, *kuna*," he growled, his body jerking behind me as he came, my own body so drunk on the idea of vengeance, I barely noticed his tail flicking in the water beside me. "And then I will take you as my slave as they have done with our females, so I can fuck this *kimi* and load you up with my seed. Take a deep breath, *leska*."

A warning thrummed through my veins. "What?"

"Inhale."

Muscles stiff with confusion, my shoulders curled toward my breastbone. "W-what are you —"

Something pinched my side.

Sharp at first, the pain soon expanded across the right side of my ribcage, spreading in a deep burn that penetrated me bone deep. Like barbed wire grating through my ribs, the pain edged me near unconsciousness.

Something sleek wrapped around my waist. His tail? It hoisted me out of the water and placed me splayed on the tiles, my mind too dizzy to make out anything else but his blurred outline.

He kneeled down and wiped wet strands from my face. "Do not worry. I could not resist stinging you, but no soul-bond will be created unless I hum for you to ease your distress."

Soulbond? What?

"Why did you do this to me?" I asked, tears mixing with the puddle my face rested in.

"Because you look so much like my enemy, no matter your beauty." My side stung once more when he pressed something against it, anguish coming over me in mind-fogging waves. "I doubt any Jal'zar could resist the urge to claim a human female. Her skin so soft. Her cunt fitting my *kuy* so perfectly. Spare your healer the search for bone splinters. I aimed well."

Cheek scraping over mosaic tiles, I spotted a piece of cloth bunched against my side. With each inhale, a new gush of blood soaked it red, whatever the fabric couldn't hold soon feathering out on the wet floor.

"You are taking the pain remarkably well for a creature so vulnerable," he said, placing a small purple rock in front of me, irregular in shape but polished to a shine. "Males of my kind would pay fortunes for such misunderstandings, enjoying something Vetusians are trying to withhold. Let them perform the *zorazay*, the claiming sting, and you will be a rich whore indeed."

His words distorted right along with the heavy steps carrying him away. I didn't dare move. Didn't dare breathe the pain was so excruciating, as if he had lit a fire between my ribs which ate on my flesh.

However long I lay there, it was enough for the other half of my body to turn numb, until I finally managed to roll onto all fours.

I enclosed the stone with my palm, feeling like an idiot once more when I realized he hadn't given me the fifty credits he owed me. If not for the fuck, then at least for how he'd mutilated me.

I pushed myself up, shoulder leaning against the wall as I worked my body toward the hallway, feet stumbling underneath me. With my robe haphazardly draped around me, trembling fingers pressing the soft fabric against my front, I swayed back toward my room.

Taigh Arosh lay quiet, which was all the better since I couldn't risk anybody finding me like this. A swipe of my hand over my side confirmed the wound had already bled through the robe, tainting my fingers crimson. Injuries were bad for business. Bad business meant a pissed off boss. A pissed off boss meant a happy Sehrin, eager to put me in my place.

I pushed the door to my room open, closing it behind me with nothing but a shove of my shoulder until it fell into its lock.

Even before I managed to reach the couch at the center, I collapsed onto the ground, a dark shadow coming over my core.

I held up the rock, clasped between bloody fingers, so beautiful and so fucking useless at the same time. The only reason I stayed was because I wanted the credits. Instead, I got an oversized pebble.

I pulled the couch pillow onto the floor and let my fingers dig the hole in the cover for my hidden credits. One by one, they fell to the ground, those which hit the rock clinking.

A slight draft came and went, and I glanced over my shoulder back at the balcony. The door was closed, and yet I noticed the subtle shift of air, like a tug on an invisible string attached to my chest.

The crack of a joint sent a cold sensation down my spine. Bracing to find Sehrin standing in the door, probably with the widest grin yet, I turned back.

Instead of the guard, I found one of the healers. And although I couldn't be sure, the glare he shot me made me think it was probably the one I'd poured my wine over.

"That's a lot of credits." Chin held high, eye contact solid, it quickly became clear he loved finding me like this. "Especially for someone who isn't supposed to collect tips."

I was so fucked.

FIVE

Adeas

Posture rigid. Eyes wide.

That was how I found *leska*, cowering on the floor of her room with blood seeping from whatever kind of wound waited underneath her robe. After solar cycles of healer training, all sorts of bodily fluids included, this sight turned my stomach.

"What happened?"

She didn't answer.

Merely narrowed her eyes at me while her body began to tense, as if she wasn't sure if she was predator or prey. Pounce, or flee?

An amount of credits too much to be anything but unhealthy for her lay scattered at her naked calves, along with a polished lump of *orishi* ore.

"You're injured," I said, stating the obvious and closing her door behind me. "You left a bloody mess behind out there. Do you know that?"

I hurried toward the sideboard closest to her bed,

keeping a safe distance to this female. Her temper was unpredictable; that she would jump at me and scratch my eyes out at any moment a real possibility.

"Where is your healer pack?" I asked, never having treated her in here before since the boss didn't allow patrons to draw blood on her. Which brought me back to my question. "What the fuck happened? I'd like to know what I'm getting myself into here, because something's telling me Levear wouldn't approve."

I eventually found a healer pack in the bottom drawer and hurried over to her, ignoring her grunt as I kneeled beside her.

"Scratch me, bite me, kick me, and I swear I'll tie you down," I warned, searching her eyes before I added, "Pour something over my head, and I'll leave you bleeding right here on the floor. Understood?"

I took the way she narrowed her eyes as a *yes*, and slowly reached for her robe. "You need to take this off."

She peeled herself out of the robe with her face scrunched up in pain, exposing a beautiful body to the cool air of the night. However, she quickly covered herself with hands and arms.

A shy whore. Hilarious.

I had seen her naked before, of course, but always from afar. Never had I sensed the heat of her body seeping into my skin, and I loathed the way it pumped blood into my cock.

Leska was stunning, no questions asked, but she was also a pretentious bitch. Tame around patrons, mostly, but hostile toward every Vetusian who was of little consequence. Like me.

"Lie down on the other side," I said, supporting her head as she lowered herself onto the carpet with a groan that ached my chest. "Fucking shit... is that..." My voice trailed off, lips parted, eyes glued to the deep flesh wound glistening between her ribs. "How did a Jal'zar get to do this to you?"

"Izara wasn't feeling well, so I agreed to take over her client," she mumbled. "I didn't know he was Jal'zar until I got to the bathhouse. He offered me fifty credits if I stayed. Then he... did this to me." Trembling fingers raked the spilled credits underneath her robe as if I hadn't seen them already. "He never gave me the fifty credits. Instead, he gave me a damn rock."

"That's no rock, *leska*," I said, rinsing the wound with a solution to remove whatever germs or fungi that Jal'zar might have carried on his tail claw. "It's a metal from his home planet. Very valuable."

She glanced over her shoulder. "How valuable?"

"At that size? Around five-hundred credits, more or less."

At first, she giggled, but she soon drew the sound into a long groan. "And of course you'll snitch, which means they'll search my room. Sehrin will find the rock. The credits. They'll punish me. Badly."

"They will."

And she would deserve it.

If not for breaking the rules then for the fact that she was arrogant, treating her lessers as just that. Who was she to parade around as if she was any less of a pleasure worker?

Silence lingered and I stitched her together, all the healing salve I had to squeeze into that hole oozing over the frayed edges of her torn skin, mixing into pastel pink paste.

"I tried to bury the stitches as much as possible," I said, pushing a pillow underneath her in support before I rolled her onto her back. "It might scar. It might not."

A smooth pubic bone came into view, all hair permanently removed, her slit glistening with the leftover water from the bathhouse. Above it, a finger-width to the right of her navel, a pin-sized scar stood slightly pinkish against pale skin.

I brushed my thumb over the jagged tissue. "What happened here?"

She slapped my hand away with a snarl. "Don't touch me."

"You didn't mind my touch when I stitched you back together," I murmured. "Now you better get dressed. Sehrin loves tearing clothes off the girls before he punishes them."

I relished the way brown eyes widened with panic, the human female squirming up to sit as she groaned in pain. She was at my mercy, and my cock fucking ached at how small *leska* was now. So insignificant. So humbled.

Full lips sucked into a thin line, only to return with a smack that had pre-cum settle on my crown. How much I wanted to push my cock down her throat until she choked on her vileness. Then again on my load.

"What would I need to do to make this our secret?" she asked, spread legs inching a pink pussy toward me. "Quid pro quo. You won't tell them, and in return, I'll let you do with me whatever you'd like."

Before I could respond, she wrapped her arms around my neck, the way her tongue lapped at the side of my neck making my sack clench in warning.

"Don't you want me?" she asked, bunching up my shirt, her lips searing against my chest.

Who didn't want her?

Those pink nipples asking me to clasp them between my mouth. That perfectly rounded ass which would look even better with the imprint of my hand on it. Not to mention her hips, capable of moving in-tune with my body.

Yeah, I wanted *leska* just like any other male on this compound. Considering I'd scored a little less than three hours ago, I could fuck her all night. Shoot load after load up her cunt until my testicles were truly empty, all seed warming her belly.

But what I wanted even more than her body, was her humiliation.

I pushed her back, gently as not to ruin my perfect stitches, and swiped my finger through that mating cleft still dripping from another.

Fingers glistening with Jal'zar cum, I held them underneath her nose. "I don't take sloppy seconds."

Oh, that darkness coming over her face was priceless. The way she struggled it back down into those rotten organs of hers divine.

"You're the guy I poured the wine over, aren't you?" she asked casually, leaning back and flicking her clit like that manipulative pro she was. "I always wondered what your name was."

No, she never gave a shit about my name until now.

"Adeas."

"Pretty name."

Probably as pretty as any other she'd called that. "You'll have to try a lot harder than that."

The prettiest fake smile settled onto her mouth, lips soon parting in a moan as she fingered herself right in front of me. "I'm sure your cock would feel a lot better. How long ago did you get high?"

"I'm not high."

"Yes you are." She crawled onto her knees, hand diving into my pants where she grabbed my cock, sending a lightning strike down my shaft. "Trust me, I know high when I see it. Your pupils are dilated, though it's hard to determine considering your irises are almost entirely bleached."

"Stupid side effect and nothing else," I crooned, not oblivious to how the power exchange slowly shifted as she jerked me off. "I've got it under control."

Her lips came so close to mine I shuddered. "You could fuck me for hours on that stuff."

"For the rest of the night, *leska*," I groaned. "You'd be dripping my seed while I continue to load you up with more."

Her moan shattered my bones.

Sert, she was good.

No wonder this female was so expensive.

"Please don't tell them, Adeas," she begged. Begged! "Fuck me all night, but don't tell them about the credits or what happened with the Jal'zar."

"I could fuck you now and tell them after."

"Or you could fuck me now and every damn night from here and on, always keeping this our secret," she said, her seductive voice alone making cum climb up my shaft. "I've got some souldust in my room as well, so we can make sure you're always hard."

Fucking bitch.

I ripped her hand from my pants and got up, anger flaring my nostrils. "Why would you say something like that, huh? You think I need that stuff to get hard?"

That aggressive snarl of hers returned. "All *sgu'dals* do. Everybody knows you can't get it up when you're coming down from it."

"Don't call me that," I growled, struggling my erection back into my pants, which proved difficult. "I'm not addicted, okay? Others might be. I am not. I've got it under control."

"Yeah, right." She pushed herself up to stand, her eyes fluttering and her body swaying. "You don't have... control..."

"Shit!" I caught her body in my arms, limp and covered in cold sweat. "You're blood pressure is acting up. Time to rest, *leska*. Horizontally."

I carried her over to her bed, but she shook her head the moment she saw it, tears welling down her cheeks. "No. Not the bed. The closet."

"What are you talking about?"

Hand rising above her head, she pointed at the golden sliding door, the edge of a blanket poking from the gap. "The closet."

Confused, I carried her over, pushing the door open with a kick of my foot, and what I found made me want to crawl out of my skin all over again.

Especially now that she suddenly cried.

I hated when she cried.

"What is this?" I asked, staring at the nest of pillows and blankets, a few Earth books stacked in the corner. "Are you telling me you sleep in this closet?"

She put a crack in my heart with little more than a nod and another tear, saying, "The bed stinks like *them* no matter how often they change the sheets."

I lowered her onto the blankets, the phantom heat of her body lingering on me long after I backed away, kneeling in front of a fucking hole in a wall.

What was I supposed to do with this? And why by the heat of Heliar did it clench my chest?

"I promise I'll check in on you tomorrow," I said, elevating her legs with one of the many pillows. "We need to make sure you won't get an infection. A human stung by a Jal'zar is a first in history, so I don't really know what to expect from here. For all I know, I might as well find you dead tomorrow."

And my comment didn't even make her flinch, almost as if she would have preferred it that way. *Crk.* Another crack to my heart.

"I'm sorry for pouring the wine over you," she murmured, eyes losing themselves on dresses hanging above her.

For a moment, I might have thought she meant it.

But that would mean *leska* had a heart.

My hands tingled.

What if she did?

"Why do you hate me so much, *leska*?"

Head turning, her eyes locked with mine. "Because you're Vetusian."

I stared at her for a long while, confused as to what to make of that. The sun of *Taigh Arosh* cried almost every night, slept inside a closet, and freaked out over sheets reeking of who knew how many males.

I didn't want it to, but my heart ached for her.

This female wasn't as much a bitch as she was simply... jaded. Abducted and enslaved by my kind, sold to be raped each sun. She was desperate enough to let a Jal'zar sting her. Shit, she was even desperate enough to let me fuck her. Why hadn't I?

Eventually, I draped one of the blankets over her body. "You said I could do with you whatever I wanted if I didn't tell. What if I wanted you to do something *to me* instead?"

"If you're about to ask me to cut you, choke you, or whip you, you can forget about it. I don't do that shit."

I couldn't help but chuckle, which ebbed into silence as

I considered my options. What benefit did I receive from giving her away? None. Seeing how she slept in a closet somehow eased my urge to see her humiliated. This creature was humiliated already, I had just never gotten close enough to her to see it.

But what do you demand of someone like *leska*? She'd offered me her body, which everyone at *Taigh Arosh* considered priceless. That wasn't true, though, because every piece of her body could be bought. There was only one thing that came without a tag, except for the pride attached to it...

"Tell me where to hide your credits and the stone," I said, reaching knuckles for cheek but not daring to touch. "I'll clean up the blood outside, and nobody will hear from me what happened tonight."

"And in exchange you want..."

I crouched down beside her, bringing my face closer to hers. "A kiss."

"No." Came without hesitation, her face ungiving for exactly two breaths before it scrunched up in tears once more. "Anything. But not that. Why would you ask for a kiss?"

"Because I want something of you no other on this planet ever had," I whispered, carefully wiping her cheeks dry, hovering over her in that dim closet. "But there's an important requirement attached to it, because cleaning up blood from carpet is a lot of work."

She sniffed. "What requirement?"

"I want you to kiss me as if I'm an Earth male."

Fury flicked at the depth of her eyes, but quickly blended into defeat. "And you won't tell?"

"I promise I won't tell a soul. Though that won't change that they will eventually find the stone and the credits.

They always do. This only buys you time to figure out a better hiding spot."

And even that they would find.

At her nod, she pushed herself up onto one arm. The other rested a palm on the back of my head. Like that, she pulled my mouth onto hers, sending my muscles into a spasm.

I groaned into her mouth, her lips expert and unrushed, her tongue dipping past my teeth and teasing mine. She tasted of salt and sadness, the gesture speaking in a language my heart seemed to understand and answer with irregular beats.

I kissed her head into the pillow and broke the seal, feeling like the richest male on this planet because I had gotten something truly priceless.

Leska's kiss.

And it fucking lingered. Prickling my lips for argos after as I scrubbed blood from her stained carpet while she slept in her closet.

SIX

Sophie

Izara leaned back into her chair, feet crossed beside her meal which sat on the glass table in front of the restaurant. Above us, purple raindrops raced down along a glass cupola in rivers and creeks. This place was like its own little town, the dome it sat underneath keeping the slaves in and hope out.

Sharp and cutting, the wound from the sting drummed between my ribs, the bruise turning something as simple as breathing into pure agony.

Let them perform the claiming sting, and you will be a rich whore indeed.

Overnight, the warrior's words had taken on the sound of a prayer. No, a plan! I'd found a way to rack up credits, but even if I could pay my way out of here in pain suffered, the logistics proved... difficult.

I needed three more things for my new strategy to become viable: someone who would hide credits for me, tend to the sting wounds, and find me a way to get onto a vessel headed for Earth.

I also needed Jal'zar clients, which is where Izara came in...

I grabbed a slice of dried *tendetu* meat, almost like turkey, and leaned back in my chair so the waiter droid could remove my plate. Once he left, I slowly lifted the fabric of my shirt.

"What's your verdict? Am I dying?"

Izara fluttered her nostrils, sniffing as close to the wound as possible without drawing the attention of guards and compound workers.

"I don't notice anything that would indicate an infection, and Jal'zar have an excellent sense of smell," she said, and quickly tugged the hem back down. "Looks ugly though. Might want to have that looked at again. If you don't put a blending cream on it, the first patron will notice and demand a refund."

"Adeas promised he'd look at it today."

She shook her head and took a sip of tea, her snort blowing some of the hot brew over the rim of her mug. The aroma of herbs from Solgad, her home planet, mixed with the lingering stench of depravity the compound harbored.

"Adeas is lying unresponsive at the center of the Sweatmines," she said. "Saw him earlier. He dragged his nose over the ground all morning, sniffing for traces of souldust along the tile grout, begging them for his next sphere."

I ignored the chill coming over me. "Perhaps he'll check in on me after they fixed him up. It's not like I can go to another healer. They'll rat me out."

Or perhaps he'd forgotten about the incident altogether. A thought which Izara seemed to share, if the way she shook her head was any indication.

Her eyes flicked to her leftover lunch sitting on the table. "You shouldn't have accepted the Jal'zar as a client."

"I had no idea I suddenly have choices in my life," I said with depressing little chuckle. "Which reminds me: you still owe me five ICs."

She scoffed. "You're lucky he didn't complete the *zorazay* with his hum and force a soulbond on you."

"So you think it would have worked? Between a Jal'zar and a human?"

"What do I know?" She shrugged. "But it's not worth taking the risk considering we're talking about our souls here. It's the only thing we've got left."

"A risk that paid off for me." I placed a diplomatic pause there before I added, "A risk I wouldn't mind taking again if it means it would get me out of this place."

"You're crazy." Wide eyes proved she understood my ulterior motives. "It's bad enough that we have less Vetusian clients because they want human pussy. And now you want to take Jal'zar clients away from us as well?"

I held her gaze with the same determination I'd woken up with that day, my mind made up. Why would I beg for scraps when I could get myself a whole meal paid for with puncture wounds?

"I have to get out of here, Izara." Glancing around to make sure no guard was around to hear, I leaned over the table, letting my voice fall into a whisper. "You'll get a cut."

Her spine straightened. "How much?"

"Ten percent."

She swatted me off with a laugh. "Fifty."

"Absolutely not. I'm the one being mutilated here. Besides, how much do they pay you if *you* give them permission to sting?"

Her shrug came with a roll of her eyes. "Depends. Thirty? Forty?"

"Twenty percent." The number hung in the air for a moment while I picked a leftover *vasani* berry from her plate, and let it burst into tart sweetness between my teeth. "That's an amazing deal, considering all you have to do is offer me to your Jal'zar clients."

Izara let her tea clunk back onto the table with a groan, lifting a foot onto the chair across so she could hug her knee. "If the other Jal'zar females find out, they'll scalp you."

"I'm not taking their clients away."

"Yeah, only mine."

I took a deep breath. "And you'll see credits coming your way you otherwise wouldn't."

"And if they find them?" she asked in a whisper, and yet her voice carried enough fear for the both of us. "I have my ways of smuggling tips out and sending them to my family on Solgad. You don't. The moment they find *orishi* ore in your room, they'll know that you're fucking Jal'zar, and they'll figure out that I'm involved."

Fingers numbed inside my fists.

Yes, that was a problem.

I'd found a way to make bank, but I had no clue how to hide it all. Sehrin turned our rooms upside-down once a month, sometimes more. That guy was suspicious already; just waiting for me to get myself in trouble. It was a wonder that he hadn't found yet what I'd saved so far.

At my next exhale, an idea blurted out that hadn't even fully formed yet, mostly because it was insane. "Perhaps Adeas would stash it away for me. They don't search the healer's quarters as far as I know."

A hearty laugh pushed through polished fangs, Izara's

tail vibrating so hard beside her she wrapped it around her belly.

"That guy isn't even allowed in the atrium or our bedrooms without supervision," she huffed on an exhale. "He'd sell the trimmings of those pitiful fingernails of yours just to score."

Stomach roiling, I sunk my head to the approaching defeat. *A junkie will steal your wallet and help you search for it.*

The words of the social worker, who'd checked in on me after mom got out of rehab for the gazillionth time, rang clear at the back of my head. Nobody understood better than me that you couldn't trust a junkie. But did I have another option? No.

"He could have taken my credits last night. I counted it this morning. It's all there."

Izara slipped her foot off the chair and got up, jutting her head toward the fountain which stood at the center of the dome. "He was also high and had no reason to steal your shit. But he will. That's what they do because Levear doesn't keep them in a constant high."

We left the restaurant behind and strolled over to the fountain. A four-tiered monstrosity in front of the casino, and a hot spot for gossip since the rush of water drowned out voices.

I sat down the stone cool against my thighs. "What if I keep him high with the souldust I have?"

"That stuff's not enough to supply him," she said, tail claw flicking through the water. "It's for giving healers a quick pick-me-up before they work on us, or for the occasional client. Adeas has been a junkie for a long time, *leska.* Keeping him high is impossible. Let him see where you keep your souldust and he'll steal that too."

I sunk into myself, letting the whole weight of reality crash down on me. A junkie couldn't be trusted. Not with the credits. Not with my secret. And especially not with my life.

But then again, I had no life.

No matter how I twisted and turned all this, Adeas always popped up as the only choice. Simply because there was no other. Because staying here would kill me slowly. Without his help, Izara wouldn't agree to send her clients my way.

Aside from someone keeping my credits, I also needed a healer to stitch me up and hide my injuries. Like *he* had done it. The other two healers the compound employed were *sgu'dal's* as well and, while I didn't trust Adeas, I trusted those two even less.

What was the worst that could happen if I asked him to help me? He could steal my shit, get high, and that would be that. Credits would be gone. I would still be here. But it was a risk worth taking because the alternative was Sehrin finding the credits.

"I'll ask him," I said, the lack of Izara's reaction making it clear she'd expected it all along.

"I can't believe you're putting your trust in a sgu'dal."

That wasn't what shocked me. The fact that I placed my trust into a Vetusian? Was about to ask one for help? Yeah, that stung.

"You said you saw him in the sweatmines?"

She nodded, her eyes focused on the circles her tail sent across the surface of the water. "Just follow the groans."

I disappeared into the street between the casino and the small hotel, where Kokonian workers swept the cobblestone and trimmed hedges into uniformity. They paid me no attention, but the same couldn't be said for the occasional guard I passed, moaning *leska* as their eyes roved me over. Disgusting.

Following the ramp, I descended into what had once been an old station for public transport. Now, the massive hall served as a place where they produced souldust. A place all addicts gravitated to, some of them scratching their nails bloody on the concrete floor. Withdrawal was, from what I'd noticed, agonizing pain.

Illuminated by a special yellow light that kept the drug from losing its strength, the piles of crystals almost appeared poison green. I'd worked here once or twice between shifts whenever demand went up.

Old and rusty, the air handler hanging from the rafters rattled, sucking in the toxic fumes of production before it filtered out of the dome as clean air. The smell of ozone always hung around the sweatmines.

Jal'zar and Kokonian workers, males and females, stood naked at tables. They crunched crystals into powder, loaded heaps into spheres, and let them roll into metal crates. All of them wore masks, their eyes always fixed on the product.

"Why did you come down here, *leska*?" one of the guards asked, blue-charged weapon pressed against his chest. "Do you need a refill?"

"Actually, I'm looking for Adeas?"

He lifted his arm, index finger pointing at the small back room where workers stored their personal belongings.

I dissolved the guard's distrustful stare with an overly sweet smile and lashes fluttering from a lowered head, then worked myself around the tables.

Adeas sat crouched against the stone wall. Back and forth he rocked, sporting a black eye I could have sworn wasn't there only a few hours ago. Tousled, his brown hair stood in all directions, cheek pressed into a filthy hand.

"What the hell happened to you?"

With a start, he dropped his hands and looked up at me, head drooping back against the stone. "W-why do you taste so sad?"

Man, that guy had crashed fast and hard. "What?"

"You kissed me."

I froze to the spot, immediately regretting that kiss. None of this would remain a secret if he kept blurting it out like that. *Leska* kissing a *sgu'dal*? Yeah, all *Taigh Arosh* would lift a suspicious brow at that.

"Shut up," I said, kneeling down beside him. "Did someone punch you?"

"Yes." His lips quirked into a smile, framed by a handsome face even though it was marked by the misadventures of a drug addict. "I don't know." Wrinkles formed between his bleached eyes. "I don't remember."

"You promised you'd check on my wound today."

"Healer's on the w-way, *leska*," he groaned.

Shaky hands pushed him up, only to abandon him mid-movement. They caved in and his body collapsed back onto the ground, his head hitting the stone with a *thonk*.

Groaning, he rolled onto his side, blood seeping from a fresh cut above his temple. He lay there, his entire body trembling, chest rising and falling in quick snaps of breath.

Levear kept them like dogs. Fed them this poison whenever they needed to function. Starved them until they came begging, pledging their silence and souls in exchange for another high.

My heart hung heavy inside my chest.

Not for him. For me.

How could I have been so dumb, thinking I might find an ally down here? Apparently, ten years with a crackhead mom didn't teach me a thing. He'd sell me out the moment he needed his fix.

Though I owed him nothing, I fisted chunks of his shirt and pulled him upright. Fancy sandal shoving against his thigh, I slowly drag-pushed him back against the wall, angling him in a way so he would stay put.

He reeked of vomit, his shirt so stiff with dried bile it puffed up in a cloud of dust when I tugged the hem back down to cover his torso. A knight in shining armor looked different...

Tears burned my eyes, and the veil of childish hope lifted, leaving an untainted and chilling realization.

This was my life.

There was no way out.

"You promised." I turned away, hating myself for how I blamed my own stupidity on him. Fuck! Why did I have to be so powerless?

A tug on my ankle stopped my foot from lifting away, and I turned back toward Adeas. No matter how hard he tried to let his eyes meet mine, they continuously dropped to the ground.

"Don't believe anything I tell you, *leska*," he muttered. "It may be a lie."

SEVEN

Adeas

Time blurred, and life passed by in distorted outlines and flashes of light. Overcharged and exhausted, my mind twisted from glorious highs to excruciating comedowns and back again. Between them, a twilight zone of numb consciousness.

I hated it.

Loathed the way it posed questions I had no answers to. What day was it? Where did that bruise come from? Why the fuck did my skin crawl?

My eyes stung, and that twitch in my elbow was a sure warning that a new tremble would soon spread into my limbs. There was no escaping it, rendering those skilled fingers of mine utterly useless. When had they become so unreliable?

Dizziness hit me and I clasped to the edge of the table outside one of the restaurants, only to realize I was sitting. Who would fall off a chair while seated?

Izara pointed at a plate I just now realized stood before me. "Are you still planning to eat this?"

I poked a fork through the braised *bullhabou*, served on perfectly roasted Dunatal grains. It looked so delicious my mouth watered, and yet my stomach turned over, growling in warning.

"You can have it." I pushed the plate to her, my mind once more racing with questions. The most pressing one: how by the heat of Heliar did I get here? I spaced out like that sometimes.

"Rumor has it they got a shipment of donuts from Earth," Izara mumbled, mouth stuffed full of what must have been my early dinner. "I should snatch one and bring it to *leska*. She loves those."

At the sound of her name, two fingers wandered to my lips, stroking there while I lost myself to the bleary memory of our kiss. How long ago was that?

"You didn't check on her wound," Izara said, no, snarled. "If that wound gets infected, we're all in deep shit."

"What wound?"

An uneasy glance over her shoulder, then she leaned into me and whispered, "The sting of the Jal'zar you stitched together three suns ago? I gave her something to cover the injury. Hide it from clients."

Blood.

It was the first thing that displayed somewhere at the back of my brain, painting crimson flickers onto a crooked memory. If I remembered the kiss, how could I have forgotten the injury?

I promise I'll check in on you tomorrow.

My guts sunk low underneath the weight of flashbacks, coming together in a picture that twisted them around my neck until I choked on my dry throat. I had broken my promise!

"I'll go to her now," I said and pushed myself up, but my blood pressure refused to follow.

Everything went dark around me, and each time I blinked my surroundings back into perception, a shooting pain stabbed into my temples.

"You won't even make it up the stairs like that," Izara said. "Go ask if you can have a refill —"

"I don't need..." As if only addicts got dizzy when they got up too quickly. What did she know? "Whatever. I'm going up there now before she starts her shift."

Legs as unreliable as those damn fingers of mine, they swayed me into a stone planter, corner scratching my knee before I managed myself around it. Then I hurried over to *Taigh Arosh*, the house of flowers, taking the side entrance to avoid a lecture about how I had to remain unseen. Unnoticed.

As if anybody ever noticed me.

The twilight zone was when everyone generally ignored me, disregarding me as if I was some sort of junkie cut-off from sensory input.

They had no idea.

I saw everything. I heard everything. All their talk about shipments. Incoming cargo. Profits. Clients. Names...

Following one of the narrow hallways, I closed in on the staircase which would lead me to the west wing of the second floor. To *leska*.

"You can search her room *after* her shift." Levear's voice coming from around the corner froze my joints, and I stumbled to a halt, palms pressing against the wall paneling. "If what you say is correct and she is hiding valuables, she has to be punished. Severely. But patrons dislike finding *leska* bruised, so I suggest you do it after."

Numbness spread from my mind down my spine because I'd seen how Sehrin punished the female workers. *Leska* would be in pain for days. Bleeding where nobody saw.

Sehrin's signature chuckle vibrated through the air. "It'll be double the punishment if you let me fuck her, and then she'll go through her shift. I can go a bit easier on her."

"Like you went easy on Caroline?"

Caroline. I had almost forgotten about the first human female that had arrived here over a solar cycle ago. She didn't last long. Two weeks maybe? Suddenly, she was just... gone.

"That was an accident," Sehrin snarled.

"An expensive one."

"You owe me." The thump of a boot disabled my next inhale. "Who discovered the CAT officer that managed to get through your stringent client application process, huh? Who disposed of him for you?"

Levear sighed. "No bruising to her face, tits, or around her pelvis area. And you better supply proof that..."

I thrust myself forward, the rush of blood roaring inside my ears fading out his voice.

Leska.

It was the only thing on my mind, and for once I was happy when neither Levear nor Sehrin gave a shit when I stepped into view. They continued talking, our bald-headed boss not so much as sparing me a glance.

First trembles of my hands connected with the handrail, and I pulled myself up the steep stairs.

Two promises.

One broken.

If Sehrin searched her room now, *leska* would think I'd broken the other one as well by selling her out. Keeping promises hadn't been my strong suit lately. Why was that?

Didn't matter now.

I hurried along the corridor, my temples throbbing with liquid panic. Sehrin wouldn't press his lips to hers. Wouldn't defile that most precious thing she'd given me in exchange for this very promise.

Without a knock, without a warning, I pushed myself into her room. No concrete plan came to mind. Instead, I just acted.

Leska squealed and jumped from her couch. "You can't just come in here."

"He's coming," I murmured. "Sehrin is coming to search your room. Where are the credits?"

Hands dug through the pillowcase, grabbed the corner, shook it. Nothing fell out, which meant she'd at least been smart enough to hide it somewhere else. Because I'd seen it?

I bit down my anger, and yet a mumble slipped. "I'm not a thief."

Leska stood paralyzed in front of me, eyes wide, lips glistening. She fumbled her fingers in front of her chest, her gaze flicking about the room as if she didn't know what to do.

I grabbed her shoulders, filthy hands on soft skin. "The credits, *leska!*"

She stuttered in a breath, her chest expanding in one abrupt inhale as if my shout had acted as a defibrillator. Then she nodded and turned away.

Arms flailing by her side, she hurried over to her bed, climbed onto the mattress, and wrapped them around a poster. Her naked soles squeaked down the polished wood as she climbed up, retrieving credits and ore from the canopy.

I hurried to her side, guiding her foot back onto the mattress when she slipped down. "Give it to me."

She met my gaze with a frown. "What?"

"We don't have time for this," I said, grabbing credits and ore, which clanked when I slipped it all into my pockets. "I'll give it back later, but now I have to go before —"

Too late.

From the main hallway, boots stomped the ground so hard I could have sworn their vibration rattled my bones. What excuse did I have to be in here? None.

"Lie down." One shove, and *leska* fell back onto her mattress with a gasp, her skin drained of all color. "I'm sorry, but it's necessary."

Just as her lips parted to pose a question, I grabbed her ankle. Fingers aiming, I dug two nails into her skin with such force, I sensed her skin peeling against my fingertips.

She yelped and kicked, but I only grabbed her harder, scratching over the same spot, not satisfied until blood slowly filled between broken flakes.

"What are you doing in here?"

I searched for *leska's* eyes, brown connecting with... I actually hadn't looked in a mirror for a while. But whatever color she found in my irises was enough for her to understand what I was trying to tell her.

I am helping you.

By the Three Suns, I didn't know why, but I had no time to figure it out and turned toward Sehrin instead. "She injured herself when she slipped in one of the lagoons. Not too bad."

With my heart pounding against brittle bones, leached

of all strength, I walked to her sideboard and took the healer pack.

"Bleeding, huh?" Sehrin stepped up beside the bed, the air turning rancid with *leska's* fear. "Let me clean it for you."

He grabbed her calf and lifted her leg, smiling at the exposed mating cleft covered by thin fabric. Then he dragged his tongue over the scratches, sucking up the blood. The more *leska* tensed the more he moaned, that sick bastard ravishing her fear.

"Thanks for spreading germs all over it." I tossed the healer pack onto the bed beside *leska*, moving slowly as not to let the chips clank inside my pockets. "Now step away so I can make those disappear before her first client. They pay good credits to see her perfect. Not scratched up."

He plopped her leg back down and adjusted his hard-on, a smirk tugging on his lips. "While the *sgu'dal* takes care of you, I'll have a stroll about your room, *leska*. I hope you hid it well."

The Earth female said nothing, but her pupils tracked every one of the guard's movements. How he shook pillows, tipped the couch, ran his fingers along the underside of furniture, and ransacked *her* closet.

Sehrin checked the canopy, the balcony, the backside of paintings. He even stepped into her tub, wading and searching until his uniform clung wet and shiny to his chest.

The harder he searched the faster his lungs heaved, utter disappointment manifesting as popped veins along his neck. When red blotches on his forehead added to it, I wasn't so sure anymore what would be worse: him finding something... or finding nothing.

Leska had made herself enemies since she'd arrived, but none more than this guy.

"Where is it?" He crouched over her terrified body, balled fist coming to a stop right in front of her eye. "Where did you hide the credits? And don't tell me you don't have any because we both know it's a lie."

A thick swallow trailed down her throat as I put ointment onto her ankle. "Clients aren't allowed to tip me, remember?"

Sehrin let out a blood-curdling shout and pulled his arm back, only to let it thrust straight at her.

"If you punch her, there's no way I can make that go away in under two suns!"

He pushed himself away from her with a grunt, nostrils flared. "What about a slap?"

My stomach clenched at his question, but it dissolved into a churning liquid at my answer. "Slap's fine as long as you don't break her neck. Not even I am that good."

Slap!

He didn't hesitate a moment.

Leska's hair exploded in all directions and she rolled off the bed, hitting the ground with a *thump* that vibrated inside my chest. She groaned, eyes filling with tears, but she didn't cry. Instead, she held Sehrin's gaze, looking more beautiful than ever.

It wasn't until the guard had left that her face turned into a wet mess, makeup smudged, her left side sporting the imprint of a male's hand.

"It would have ended worse if I hadn't suggested he slap you," I whispered, the first thing I applied to her face something for the pain she breathed down so perfectly. "It won't hurt much longer, and the redness will be gone in less than an argos."

She pushed herself up and scooted back against the bed. "Thank you for warning me. For... helping me."

I only nodded, still not sure why I had done it. Something about this female spoke to my spirit beyond the fact that my body longed for hers.

"I came looking for you a few days ago." Hands still trembling slightly, they pulled her dress up until she revealed the wound. "It's not hurting anymore but started to itch instead."

"The thread is dissolving which causes the skin to itch. Doesn't appear there will be a scar." I trailed my fingertip over the tissue, already healed in most places, speaking of a job well done. "If you ever can't find me on the compound, my room is on the east wing right next to the food storage. Third door."

"I did find you."

Something pricked my chest because I remembered none of that either. At that exact moment, a lightning strike tore through my vision, so bright it burned across my brain, sending a lazy throb into my temples. Not much longer and a migraine would hit, I could tell.

"Why did you look for me? The wound?"

She tortured her lower lip, and I caught myself licking mine in response. Yet she said nothing, shaking her head as if debating with herself if I could be trusted with the explanation.

"I promise I won't tell anybody, if that's what concerns you."

One deep breath later, she leaned her head against the mattress, eyes going adrift. "Izara agreed to offer me to her Jal'zar clients. They get to sting me like the one in the bathhouse did if they tip generously. She gets a cut."

"Why would you let them injure you like this? Why go through that pain?"

Her eyes caught with mine, the fight burning behind

them sending a tingle down my spine. "Because I need to get out of here. Save up enough credits so I can convince a smuggler to take me back to Earth."

"That's a ridiculous plan," I blurted, not liking the way she pulled her gaze from mine, so I offered an explanation. "You need a small fortune for that, and that's not something you can hide in a pillowcase or on a canopy. How are you going to find a smuggler if you can't even leave the compound?"

She didn't turn back to look at me, but the way her hand settled on mine sent a flutter into my chest. "That's why I came searching for you."

I wasn't stupid.

Leska wanted something of me. A position for which other Vetusians would give up their fortunes.

Stripped of everything including her freedom, her touch and attention were the only things she had left to barter. This was manipulation at its finest, especially now that she scooted closer to me, but oddly enough, I didn't mind it one bit. Her lies tasted better than reality ever had.

"I can stitch you together and make it all disappear," I said, allowing myself to take her hand into mine, stroking small fingers I knew she wouldn't dare pull away now. "Hiding whatever they pay is tricky, *leska*, because whenever something disappears on this compound, they search the healer's rooms as well."

Her sigh went soul deep. "I had no idea."

Did she believe I was any less a slave?

Ever since the stratum stripped me of my license over some situation with souldust, a misunderstanding, really, I couldn't find work anywhere else but here. Pay was shit, but I had a roof over my head, food, along with access to medicate.

"I have a friend who teaches at the infirmary." Funny how I sounded as if I'd made up my mind, throwing myself into dangerous waters by offering help. "He's trustworthy. Honorable. I'm sure he'll agree to save the credits and ore on my behalf."

She fiddled with the gems on her neckline, her nod coming with such hesitancy it was clear she was skeptical, though had no other choice. But she clearly committed herself when she pushed herself up, dress rustling up to her waist, and straddled me between her thighs.

She ground herself against me, letting out a moan that parted my lips. "And can you find a smuggler for me, Adeas?"

Did she actually remember my name?

The sun of *Taigh Arosh*?

"I've got some connections." Hands to the slender waist of a female barely mature, I pressed her down on a cock surprisingly hard considering I sensed that migraine expanding inside my skull. "I can ask around, but it'll take time."

Fuck, I wanted her.

Every fiber of my body screamed for it.

She offered a smile, the studied qualities of it sending a violent throb against my temples. "And in exchange?"

I didn't notice my hands had started trembling again until I shoved them underneath her dress, giving a silent curse. Where I wanted to feel her breasts, a small handful matching her frame so perfectly, my fingers stuttered across her nipples.

Fucking shit.

Nothing about this would be the way I wanted if I mated her now. The moment my cock turned flaccid, a full-blown migraine grinding into my brain, I prodded her off me.

"Your compliance," I said and got up. "One of these days, I'll ask something of you, and you won't be allowed to turn me down."

She rose, arms crossed in front of her chest. "I already told you I don't do sick —"

"No blood involved. No pain. Nothing perverse. Deal?"

Leska's eyes trailed to my crotch, one brow lifted, sending a wave of embarrassment over me. It wasn't like I couldn't perform, but with a migraine and the way my skin began to crawl again, where would be the fun?

"Deal?"

She huffed but did so with a sharp nod. "Don't steal my credits."

"I won't," I said and turned away with over four-hundred IC's in my pockets. "I promise."

EIGHT

Adeas

Unlike the pleasure workers, guards, healers, and other live-in staff could leave the dome between shifts. Not that it was as simple as walking out the airlock...

The dome sat on a broken-off piece of Odheim; nothing but a lump of planet floating above the surface. Company-owned stargazers moved patrons and staff back and forth, never speaking a word about what was underneath that cupola.

Odheim was an amnesty planet, untouched by laws which governed the rest of the universe. Nobody could be arrested or prosecuted here, which had turned the planet into a melting pot of questionable morals and the most despicable crimes.

At the center grid of it sat the infirmary, a place where Vetusian healers satisfied the many suns of practical experience they had to collect before healer Corp issued their license.

Stepping up the ancient stone stairs to the building had

always been humbling, but never as much as that day. When was the last time I'd been here? Two solar cycles ago?

Other healers passed me, all dressed in the color of our stratum: white. A color I was no longer entitled to wear, so I slumped up there wearing jeans from Earth and a shirt. Everyone called it degrading. I called it casual.

Inside, the organic walls expanded at each breath. They illuminated the great hall, that whiff of astringent as prominent now as it was a decade ago when I'd first stepped in here. A surgeon. That had been my goal back then, until that nerve damage made it impossible.

I stepped up to the young healer who sat lonely behind his small reception area. "I came to see healer Titean. He's expecting me."

He stared at my eyes for an overlong moment, which only enraged that migraine that got worse by the argos.

Souldust bleached the color of irises out of your DNA. Something that wouldn't have bothered me all that much if it wasn't for how it made everyone call me a *sgu'dal*. Yes, I used souldust, but not because I couldn't control the cravings for it. It simply helped keeping the migraines at bay. Not to mention the trembles. Burnt ashes... I hated those.

"He's currently with a patient." The young healer rose and pointed toward the hallway I remembered led to the research area. "I will bring you to him. Please follow me."

We stepped through the decontamination chamber, muscle memory making me spread my limbs as if it had been yesterday. Images of my time in training put a grin on my face, and I let the psi-rays flicker around me until the holographic control panel deemed me free of germs and other nasties.

The door to the patient's room swooshed open and I

stepped inside, the monitors surrounding the recovery pod beeping in measured intervals.

"You're late," Titean growled, eyes locked on a sleeping Kokonian male with tubes coming from a flat, ridged nose. "There's a new restaurant three grids from here I wanted to show you. They serve Earth meals. Synthesized, but others told me the atmosphere is authentic."

I stepped closer and glanced over the holographic patient file, biting down that anger over how my hands trembled again.

High fever, spiking randomly with no medication capable of controlling it. Green mucus lining his tongue and gums. Claws separating from the bed, leaving a gooey substance behind on the flesh. That male was dying.

"They shut down all hover lanes because of an incoming solar storm," I said, flicking through lab results and the medication they gave him. "I'm not hungry anyway."

My cropmate turned around, disposing his white gloves into the hazard chute which burned them into dust right there. "You look as if you're starving, though."

"Stomach's acting up lately. Not sure why," I said with a shrug. "Probably just a minor virus."

His slow nod came with lips pressed into a slash as he eyed me up and down. "Probably."

At the splaying of my shaky fingers, I expanded one of the lab results. "Why didn't you check him for fungal contamination?"

"He spent the last three lunar cycles on Testam Omega. The trading station doesn't support eukaryotic life, so the disease couldn't have come from fungus."

"Cross contamination and dormant spores," I said, conjuring up a list of three different fungi capable of causing such symptoms. "All three of them are found on Solgad, and I know for a fact that Testam Omega trades with that planet. I bet you ten ICs this male has a fungal infection eating him from the inside."

Titean scanned the list before he arched a brow at me. "Fucking show off. You've always been better than me when it comes to infectious diseases."

"I've been better with pretty much everything else as well," I said with a grin. "Still am."

He grabbed my wrist and tugged, my trembles suddenly aggressive enough they took over his arm as well. "Useless fingers, though."

I pulled away from his clasp. "I've got it under control."

"With souldust."

Not that again...

"It's a medication like any other," I snapped, and yet that ass refused to wipe that look of pity from his face. "They developed it to treat nerve damage, remember?"

"That they did," he said, voice lined with accusation. "But what you have isn't nerve —"

"Don't give me that shit!" A lump of rage rolled up my throat and clogged it, refusing to let that next inhale pass. "Why do you always... fuck... shit, I can't... can't breathe."

"Alright, calm down."

Shrouded in all shades black, the room dimmed around me. Something tugged against my chest, but my lungs remained still. Coldness penetrated my pants. Gravity shifted around me.

"... Adeas, ..." Words pushed through the darkness as fragments. "... ... sick mind ... ... breathe."

"I'm okay," I mumbled, each blink adding more detail to the moulded ceiling, Titean's concerned eyes staring down at me.

"No, you're not okay, brother. You're sick. Terribly sick, and I can't figure out a way to make you see it."

A fissure, gaping with fear, formed somewhere inside my chest. What if I was sick? Titean was my friend, my brother. A healer. If he said I was sick, why wouldn't I believe him? Didn't I have symptoms? Migraines. Memory loss. Dizziness.

"You need to get into rehab." My jeans got caught on the edges of the tiles as he dragged me over the ground by my armpits, leaning me against the wall. "There's an addiction counselor from Earth coming to Odheim. Healer Melek. You need to talk to him, Adeas. Maybe he can get you into that new rehab program on Earth."

"Earth?" That word triggered a memory. "*Leska*."

"There won't ever be any *leska* for you if you don't get clean."

"No. I mean *leska*," I said with determination in my voice. "I need your help."

"And I'll do everything in my power —"

"I mean I need your help now." I straightened myself, retrieving the little bag of chips and ore from my pocket. "Can you keep this safe for me?"

Titean squatted down in front of me, eyes narrowed. "Is this stolen?"

"W-what?" My stomach churned at that first stutter. This was getting worse fast. "Why does everyone always assume I'm a thief? I've never stolen any—" As if he would get it... I raked a desperate hand through my hair, sensing the cold sweat pearling between strands. "I've got a job, okay? I don't need to steal shit."

"So those are your earnings or what? What am I looking at here? Why do you need me to keep it?"

I plopped the bag into my lap and dug my fingers into it,

letting the chips rain from my palm with clinks and clanks. "It belongs to a friend of mine who asked for my help. The company I work for searches my room regularly, so I can't h-hide it there. I need you to save it for me."

"Hide?" He sunk his face into his palm as if this wasn't the most honorable thing I'd done in like... forever. "Is this some illegal shit, Adeas? Because I can't let you drag me into anything. Not again."

"Nothing illegal." Not on Odheim anyway. "Those are just her tips."

He turned his head, one brow arched high. "*Her?* A Jal'zar female? Another girlfriend? Didn't you learn anything with the last one?"

I ignored the way that question churned my stomach. "Nothing illegal. I promise."

"Your promises aren't holding much value lately, Adeas."

I dug my fingers into the chips, smooth and uniform, letting the tear-shaped credits caress my skin before I let them pearl down my digits. There was something soothing about it.

"I'll bring you more," I said. "Every couple of suns, I'll bring more, and I need you to keep it save for me. One sun, I'll need it all to help a f-friend."

Titean grabbed the bag with a sigh. "Usually, you come here to ask me for credits. The fact alone that you're giving me credits freaks me out. Hey!" Fingers snapped around me until my eyes found his. "If I do this for you, are you going to talk to this healer Melek once he's here?"

I wasn't addicted.

Though I was clearly sick.

Perhaps this healer could point me in the right direction to investigate my nerve damage. What if it had gotten worse? What if said nerve damage had changed into something centralized, causing those fucking trembles to come more frequently? And with it, the embarrassing stutter?

"I'll speak to him."

"Good," Titean said, his nod slow and precise. "Whenever you need help, you come here and ask for me, alright? Gives me the opportunity to see more of you again."

I pushed myself up and shoved my hands into my pockets, hiding those waves of trembles before they drowned my body. "Thank you."

"How about I take you to that restaurant I mentioned?"

"No time." I struggled myself onto my feet and walked back to the door. "I still need to stop at the abandoned docks and time's running out. If I'm not back for my shift, they won't give me my medication."

His face scrunched up. "How about I walk you back to wherever you work instead? Get you off the streets? If you go to the abandoned docks now, I fear you might not make it out."

I let out a snort. Of course I'd make it out.

Back to *leska*, telling her that her credits were safe.

But first, I needed to track down the old dock master, who now made a living selling wares that should never have made it to this planet. And while he didn't trade slaves, as far as I knew, he might hook me up with someone who could return *leska* to Earth.

I had to go before my condition worsened. "Got no choice, brother."

I reminded him once more to run a fungal panel on the Kokonian before I left the room, skipping the decontamination chamber on my way out.

The abandoned docks weren't far from the infirmary, and a short walk brought me to one of the many entrances in disrepair. All the while, nerves misfired along my arms, the trembles turning annoying. Once back at the compound, I had to get my hands on souldust.

Columns stood either crooked or crumbled to the left and right. Only the crests of the Vetusian noble houses remained carved into white stone, the edges black with moss and mildew.

My skin prickled with the foreboding static of a solar storm, and the otherwise stagnant air of the dock changed into something clean, like ozone and diluted bleach. The scent followed me all the way to the lowest level, where decommissioned pleasure droids offered a mating cleft that could electrocute your cock if you weren't careful.

"Vetusian." A Toroxian tugged on the hem of my shirt, his head reaching barely to my hip and I wasn't even particularly tall for my kind. "How about an argos with this newest model, molded after a fleshborn female from Earth? Ten ICs, and I guarantee pleasure, or you will receive your payment back."

I swatted him away.

Aside from the fact that I had no credits, no pleasure from these machines could possibly compare to a kiss from *leska*. Not anymore. And I would shower her in kisses once I demanded her body. Devour her mouth until her lips no longer tasted sad.

A silver object pushed into my peripheral vision. "One sphere for eighty credits, guaranteed pure. Two for one-fifty."

Pain stabbed my brain as if someone had pushed daggers through my temples. Hands pressed to my head, I stopped and closed my eyes, which only intensified the way the metal grid swayed underneath me. My body shook so hard, strands of hair vibrated and tickled along my forehead.

This was bad.

What if I didn't make it back to the compound in time? My nerves were shot, useless, and souldust was the only thing that would kick them back into gear. If I didn't score soon, I'd end up passed-out in the street. Souldust wasn't the kind of medication you could just quit taking.

"Is the old dock master still at bay seven?" I asked. "I n-need to speak to him right away."

The Toroxian offered a sly smile. "You are in luck, Vetusian, because information is on sale today. One answer for one credit."

"I've got nothing on me," I said, tapping my pockets as if to prove it.

But his head cocked at the clanking coming from those pockets. As did mine.

Another pat.

Clank. Clank.

Shoving my hands deep into the fabric, they returned with a couple of IC's resting on a shaky palm. Irritation pinched my insides, which quickly crawled underneath my skin like insects traveling along my tendons. How did they get in there?

Those had to be some of *leska's* credits, though I didn't remember taking any. I wasn't a thief. Fuck... those migraines.

"That's certainly enough to tell you where the dock master went off to," the Torixian mumbled. "Or for a small vial. Injected."

Injected.

The word alone spiked my breathing, rapid huffs expanding and collapsing underneath a shirt that had somehow soaked with sweat. It clung to my skin, cold and heavy, fear and panic mixing inside my chest.

Rule number three: never slam souldust.

"How about one little snort for w-what I have," I stammered, because that would get me in shape to find the dock master by myself.

I knew it would.

"A sphere for eighty, or a small vial injected for what you got there. Your choice."

Shit. Fuck.

My fingers lifted to the inside of my left arm all on their own, scratching the illusion of an itch where I'd carried the occasional track mark. Slamming this stuff was bad, and more than once I'd found myself on an entirely different planet... suns later.

Everything around me spun.

No. Nothing spun.

I was rocking.

Back and forth my torso went, arms wrapped around myself, the trembles bad enough my eyeballs ached at the harsh motion. I needed to find the dock master, but how if my nerves wouldn't let me function? An injection would be potent enough to...

But those were her credits.

Don't you want to help her?

Yes.

Then you know what to do.

Right.

Whatever credit fell onto the ground as I handed them over, the Toroxian picked up. A small eternity passed as he guided me into his bay where he quickly strapped a wide cord around my biceps.

Blue liquid filling the tip, the syringe let panic freeze

over my veins. The metal tip, angled and sharp, drenched me in cold sweat. The closer the needle came, the more my cock hardened.

I closed my eyes.

A poke.

And then... a healing bliss, so intense I came straight in my pants.

NINE

Sophie

Nobody ever gave a shit when a healer suddenly didn't show up for his shift. That was the reason why we had three of them. They randomly vanished for days, weeks, always coming back to who fed them with souldust eventually, returning to work as if nothing had happened.

Five goddamn days.

That was how long ago Adeas had disappeared, nowhere to be found — with *my* credits.

Sehrin was right.

I was stupid.

So fucking stupid it hurt.

Told you so, Aunt Debby's raspy voice murmured all around me, the smoke of her cigarettes wafting into my nostrils so real at that moment, I couldn't help but cough. Mom's words followed in an instant, her breathy, *I can get you a pack of tampons from the convenient store across if you give me the money,* curling my toes. To this day, I had no idea how that woman managed to get high on ten freaking bucks.

The Toroxian maid tugged on the bedding. "I need you to get up, *leska*."

At the sound of my name, I rolled off the bed so she could strip the cum-crusted sheets. Replace them with fresh silk I would never sleep in, untouched until whoever would be the first client of my next shift sweat all over them.

I fell back into the same track I'd paced down for days, around the couch, to the bathroom, back, then around the couch counter-clockwise. Restlessness tingled my toes and my fingertips pounded with anxiety. Over five hundred credits, paid for with shattered pieces of me.

Gone.

"Would you like me to add an additional comforter?" the maid asked, her three-foot frame hanging on the corner of the sheet, feet bracing the mattress, tugging the linen back into shape. "Solar storms always bring a cold with them that creeps into the marrow of your bones."

"Not necessary," I said since my closet was always warm and cozy, no matter what. "But thanks for offering."

The moment she left, I hurried over to my desk, fumbling four ICs from the drawer track. With Adeas gone, I had no other choice but to rotate the hiding spots for what-ever patrons had tipped me, hoping it would diffuse the risk of Sehrin finding it. While he hadn't been back to search my room, I knew it was only a matter of time until he would show up again.

One credit, I hid inside a copy of Moby Dick a client had gifted me. Another, I pushed into the purple soil of my Jal'zar Drought Rose. The third, I slipped behind the headboard.

For the last one, I walked over to the fake tapestry at the back door, which was framed by carved wood, the top of it the perfect spot to hide a credit.

I rose onto my toes.

I placed the chip onto the edge.

Tok!

The entire wall vibrated.

Something collapsed behind it with a moan, and the chip brushed my shoulder before it hit the ground. Heart going ninety, clanking against my throat, I dropped to the ground, fingertips frantically shoving over the carpet. I couldn't let anyone catch me.

Suddenly too sleek for me to grasp, the chip escaped my pinch several times before I enclosed it with my palm. Then I waited, quietly crouching on the ground, listening intently for the stomp of boots or the deep voices of guards.

Nothing.

And then... *cred'sh...*

Shit. Shit. Shit.

I jumped up, toes aching underneath me, stretching my body as tall as I could. Nervous fingers, clammy with fear, *tap-tap-tapped* the credit deep into hiding, until my toes gave up, making me flail backward and away from the hidden door.

The noises couldn't have come from Izara, whose room was right next to mine, since I'd seen her leave with a client. Although there was a room on the other side adjacent to mine, I knew it was empty. Had they brought in a new worker?

Hesitant steps carried me to the door.

Palms downright sweaty now, I slowly opened the door. Cracked it only a little, until pressure built so quickly against it, I had no time to react. The door hit me on the nose, and I stumbled back, a limp body pushing the door open in roll backward.

"Ooph," Adeas breathed, face flat on the ground, all limbs sprawled out, lips shoving over the carpet. "M'so sorry..."

I immediately shut the door, praying that nobody had seen him crawling up here, and kneeled beside him. "Where were you?"

At his grunt, I rolled him onto his back, my stomach turning upside down at the sight. An angry cut stretched taut over a bruised cheekbone, grit and grass clinging to the fire-red flesh. His jawline, dusted in the first growth of a beard, sported several smaller, green bruises as if he'd hit the edge of the stairs a dozen times on his way up here. He probably had...

"Adeas!" I snapped my fingers inches from his eyes, black pupils on a backdrop of filthy-white. "Can you hear me?"

"M'so sorry *l'shka*," he mumbled, eyes pressing shut so hard his lids quivered. "Beau'ful *l'shka*. Vetushn's pay t'fuck you, but I kishd you n'paid nothin'."

The surrounding air took on the stench of my childhood: smoke, vomit, and alcohol. Booze was cheaper than drugs. A fact I was certain prevailed on Odheim as it had on Earth, finding confirmation in his sharp breath.

"What did you do with my credits?" I would have shoved his shoulder if he wasn't so filthy, the collar of his shirt torn. "Did you get high on it? Buy souldust with it?"

He shook his head, greasy hair lazily parting at the motion. "Cred'sh are at t'enfirmary."

"What?"

A deep groan rattled from his throat.

He lifted both palms to his face, oblivious to how he rubbed dirt over the wound on his cheek, tearing the skin open until red streaked his fingers.

I pulled his hands off by his wrists. "Did you use all my credits?"

"M'not feeling well."

"No shit..."

I let my ass slump to the ground, the adrenaline from minutes ago turning into a mix of anger and misplaced pity. Credits aside, what was I supposed to do with this guy?

Even if I rolled him out of my room, he'd just go blurting to the next guard that he'd kissed me. No way could I drag him all the way to his room, and Izara wasn't around to help either. I sure as hell wouldn't let him stink up my room...

"Let's get you cleaned up," I said and rose, every step after that like bad déjà vu. "Can you at least kick your legs and help me a little?"

I contemplated rolling him into my tub, but chances were he'd drown if I couldn't get him upright. Just how much did that guy weight? With his cheeks sunken in and tendons showing along his arms, it was hard to tell, because he was still a massive Vetusian.

My mind replayed that. Vetusian.

I should have rolled him into the tub to drown...

Could easily have made it look like an accident.

Instead, god help me, I hooked my arms underneath his sweaty armpits and dragged him into my bathroom. Probably some childhood trauma. Helper syndrome or something.

His kicking was of no help and only tossed his body

around uncontrollably. Forever later, I somehow managed to lean him against the wall inside my walk-in shower.

Since his clothes were ruined already, I activated the water via voice command. My pants immediately soaked at the calves, and I took the scrunchie off my wrist, twirling my hair into a messy bun.

His face wrinkled up whenever drops of water hit his face. It saturated his shirt and pants, rinsing down the drain in a brownish-green mess with streaks of yellow mixed into it. The steam turned rancid, amplifying his stench by like a million.

"I can't believe I'm doing this," I said and pulled his shoes off, tossing them out of the shower. "Next time you show up at my door like this, I swear I'll roll you into the tub and leave for a drink while you drown."

Adeas slipped into a state of conscious-enough to mumble incoherently, but too drunk to move his limbs beyond uncoordinated flails. The only words I could make out were *sorry*, and *cred'sh*, which I assumed meant credits.

Taking a deep breath against the fabric on my arm, I grabbed the hem of his shirt and struggled the soaked fabric over his head. How he managed to sustain the muscles on his stomach was beyond me, because the sides were lined with protruding ribs. Old cuts and bruises painted the picture of an addict.

With his upper body exposed and his shoes gone, the only thing left were his pants. While I'd seen hundreds of Vetusian cocks, I couldn't deny that warmth spreading into my earlobes, and it didn't come from the hot water. Never had I undressed a Vetusian that hadn't paid for me to do so.

I opened his belt buckle and undid the buttons, then struggled the heavy denim down his thighs. Adeas seemed to have taken a liking to jeans. It was what he wore most of the time, which proved a shitty choice right about now.

"Come on!" I barked, tugging and pulling on his pants until sweat prickled along my forehead, my hair soaking with water. "Can you at least lift your hips a little?"

He complied as best he could and did so with a smirk on his face. That guy had nerves, but it lent his face something handsome, bringing questions to my mind I shouldn't have cared to know the answer to. How did he slip into this because, deep down, I didn't think Adeas was a bad guy? At least aside from being a Vetusian...

Pants finally gone, I adjusted the water and made sure it sprinkled his entire body. I let the dispenser pump a blob of shampoo into my palm. With gentle fingers, I soaped his hair, tips dislodging the occasional piece of grit from his scalp.

"Close your eyes," I said when I rinsed it all, then went straight to work on his body. "If you think I'm going to wash your junk, then you're mistaken."

But I did wash everything else, letting my palms glide over a body I knew had held strength once, his shoulders broad. My fingers glided easily over his soft skin, his pectorals still muscular enough they strutted out with each inhale. I soaped armpits, chest, and calves, his smirk pulling upward into a full-blown smile when I reached his thighs.

Against all odds, he grew hard, a thick Vetusian cock jerking at each stroke of my hands along my legs. It wasn't until I lifted his arm to rinse the bodywash that I noticed the greenish bump on the inside of his underarm. A track mark.

"What by the fury of Mekara is going on here?"

I spun around at the sound of Izara's voice. "It's not what it looks like."

"You're rubbing your hands over Adeas, who's sitting

naked in your shower with an erection, but it's not what it looks like?"

I barely managed to stand up with the way fabric clung heavy to my skin. "He literally rolled into my room, definitely drunk, but most likely also still high."

"Did he say what happened to your credits?"

"He isn't very talkative right now," I groaned, stripping down before I washed all this nastiness off me. "You need to help me. We have to carry him to his room. Or at least far away from mine."

"Are you insane? I'm not going to carry him down two sets of stairs and all the way across into the other wing. Especially not naked, because his stuff is obviously wet now. There's no way nobody will see us."

I deactivated the water and dried myself, then tossed the towel onto his cock. "What am I supposed to do with him?"

With a huff, she stepped into my shower and dried him off. "Let him sleep it off. Once he can walk straight again, send him on his way."

I wrung his things out and hung them over the sink. "I don't want him in my room. That guy blew my credits."

"Don't blame him for your stupidity." She let her claw trace around the track mark and shook her head. "Shit. He hasn't slammed it in so long. Must've been desperate."

She got up and searched my bathroom for one of the tooth cleaners, then returned to him, his upper lip clasped between claws while she brushed his teeth.

"He helped you," she said. "Adeas didn't need to warn you when Sehrin came to search your room."

My spine shortened a bit.

She was right. This Vetusian had tried to help me, and I

suddenly realized how much I hated the notion of it, even though I'd been the one asking for his help.

"Yeah, well, I spent the last hour scrubbing him clean, so I'd say we're even. Why don't we drag him to your room?"

A high-pitched giggle spilled over gray lips. "This is between you and him. I want nothing to do with it. Tell me where you want him, and I'll help you carry him there."

Irritation pinched my insides while I slipped into my pj's. I didn't want this guy anywhere near me, mostly because he brought back too many painful memories. Hadn't I gone through this shit enough already? What did I do that I deserved to end up as a prostitute, and now had to babysit a junkie on top of that?

"Where, *leska*?"

I let out an annoyed huff. "What do I care? On the bed? Couch?"

"Grab his legs," she said, dragging Adeas out of the shower by his arms. "Let's put him on your bed."

We carried the naked Vetusian out the bathroom and lifted him onto my bed, where he immediately rolled onto his side and pulled a pillow against his chest.

"I'll drain your tub," Izara said. "Otherwise, he might accidentally drown himself tonight."

As if he would do me that favor...

After Izara went back to her room, I disappeared to brush my teeth, but it didn't take long until a loud *whomp* shook the tiles underneath my soles.

"What now?" I snarled and stomped back into my room, only to find Adeas on the floor.

He must have rolled off the bed, and now he lay groaning on the ground, a hand pressed to the side which must have gotten the impact. Nervous pupils tracked his surroundings, as disoriented as I was pissed, because I couldn't get him back onto the bed by myself. And what was the point if he would roll off again anyway?

I considered what to do with him next for just a breath too long, because he crawled on all fours toward the closet. *My* closet.

"Absolutely not!" I shouted, pulling naked calves and hips, but it was already too late.

That guy climbed into the only place in my room where I hadn't been fucked yet, defiling the only thing I had for myself by snuggling up inside my nest of blankets and pillows.

"Thnk's for t'kin care of me," he mumbled, head resting on his hand, unwavering eyes locked on me.

"As if you left me a choice."

I glanced over at my bed, a place where I refused to sleep. With my hair still damp, neither did it offer enough warmth since I'd turned down the additional comforter. For the same reason, the couch wasn't an option either. Naked as he was, Adeas would be too cold if I ripped the blankets from my closet from him. Which I shouldn't give two fucks about but... somehow did. He had tried to help after all.

"I'm so sorry about the cred'sh." And as if to prove guilt, he turned face to wall, presenting me his naked backside. "I swear I did'n steal'em."

"Did you blow all of them?" I asked, then kneeled beside him when I got no answer. "Adeas! Did you use up all my credits?"

A mumble.

"Huh?" I scooted closer, crouched over him so I could make out his words. "Are all my credits gone?"

"No."

He spun around so fast, the way he bumped into my

thighs made me topple, surprisingly strong arms easing the way I fell onto his chest. In the pause which followed, suspended in time, his dilated eyes shifted toward my lips.

"Maybe I used some of the cred'sh," he whispered, fingers tugging on my scrunchie until blonde strands fell over his chest. "Shit. So beau'ful 't hurts." Fist pounded against chest. "Hurts right'ere."

"Maybe? Some?" My mind screamed, overwhelmed by this life, this mess, this closeness to a Vetusian who wasn't a client. "How much did you spend? All?"

He shrugged. "Ten m'be?"

"Ten credits?" I asked, watching flickers of remorse drown in barely existing irises. "Where is the rest?"

"Friend's sav'n it for you." As I contemplated if that could possibly be true, he stroked his hand through my hair before he whispered, "Beau'ful Sophie."

My heart gave one massive thrust against my sternum until it came to a halt, the sound of my name speaking to me beyond slurs or the confused mind of a junkie. It reached deep within, to a core not yet touched by all this surrounding rot.

"What did you just say?"

"Beau'ful."

My head shook as if in trance. "After that."

He stared at me for the longest time, the bit of light filtering in from my room casting a warm hue onto his face. Scrubbed clean, with his hair sitting flat against his head, his now pleasant scent filled this tiny room.

His fingertips feathered across my cheeks. "Sophie."

"How do you know my name?" I asked, letting myself slip off his warm chest.

"I lis'n," he said turning onto his side, his hand settling against mine. "Your name 's my secret."

His eyes slowly fluttered shut as his hand closed around mine, and I suppressed the urge to curl myself against the body of someone who had spoken my name.

At that moment, I felt a little less like a whore, and a bit more like Sophie. All thanks to a Vetusian I should have hated.

Should have.

TEN

Adeas

Light reflected from a sequin-embroidered dress hanging above me cast flickers of purple and blue against the wall. Scarves, belts, and other things hung from a rod, officially making this the weirdest place I'd ever come back to consciousness.

While slamming souldust kept you high for days, the side effects were unpredictable. Dangerous, even. I'd woken with a massive headache pounding my brain, throat dry, and my entire body ached. But nothing, absolutely nothing, had prepared me for waking next to *leska*. Naked.

I carefully turned onto my side, cock hardening, and drank her in. Her face was so peaceful in her sleep, and not at all like that pretentious female who strutted around *Taigh Arosh* as if she owned it. She was young, not a single line on her face, and even more beautiful now without makeup.

She spoke to a male deep within me. One who'd had dreams once. Goals. Now my only goal was to protect her, help her escape from here though I didn't understand why any of this was my concern. Perhaps it was the exhilarating sensation of having a goal in the first place which motivated me. That hadn't happened in... well, ever since they'd stripped my license.

I trailed my hand down between us and squeezed my crown, a pulse flicking back into my palm, every fiber of my body aching to have her. Not to fuck her like everyone else did, but to mate her in a way I sensed only I could — as pretentious as that sounded even to me.

At this point, it was hard to tell if I'd been inside her already. If I had called in the debt she owed me for putting my ass on the line. Shit. I hoped not because I didn't even remember touching her. Another squeeze against my cock confirmed I wasn't particularly sensitive, the effects of soul-dust very slowly wearing off.

I scooted closer, hard flesh pressing against her clothed thighs as I took in her scent. *Leska* smelled of soap, and it didn't take long until I realized that I smelled exactly the same. What had happened between us?

Captivated by her lips, I brushed my own over them, sampling her mouth as a groan escaped me. That was when she roused ever so slightly, dragging teeth over the itch on her lips where her hands were still too heavy with sleep.

Behind me, one of her books lay upside down, open pages pressing against one of her many pillows. Beside it, a ring rested on the carpet, the socket a flaky silver, and the gemstone within a blackish purple. The moment I reached for it her fingers wrapped around my wrist.

"Don't touch it," she said. "It's the only thing I've got left of my mom. The only thing they let me keep."

I met her eyes, finding a softness in them they'd never held for someone of my kind before. "I just wanted to look."

She grabbed it and slipped it onto her finger, breathed against it, then held her hand out to me. "It's called a mood ring. The stone changes color depending on my body temperature, which is supposed to indicate what kind of mood I'm in."

It didn't take long for the gem to go from purple to blue to bright green. Earth must have been a rich planet to possess such gemstones, and I carefully let my fingertip swipe over the smooth stone.

"And what mood are you in?" I asked.

"No idea." She took the ring off with a shrug and shoved it underneath her pillow. "I forgot what the colors mean, but I guess I'm okay as long as it isn't black or brown. Your clothes are wet, by the way. We'll have to figure out how to get you back to your room without your naked ass on display."

What she said made no fucking sense, but I skipped inquiring about why my stuff was wet and went straight to the most pressing question. "Did I mate with you?"

"Mate?" she asked, her voice dripping with disgust. "Nobody will ever mate me, but if you want to know if you fucked me, then no. You didn't."

That should have relieved me, if it wasn't for her word choice and that dense pressure it caused at my core. I ignored it and pushed hard flesh against her side. She owed me and, aside from this excruciating headache, no trembles ravaged my body. I wanted her. Now.

The way her eyes flicked to my penis sent a spark into my groin. "That's what you want in exchange for helping me? What I can't turn down?"

"Yes," I groaned as I lifted myself between her legs, anxious fingers tugging her pants down.

"And my credits? Last night you said you used some of them."

Had I?

Memory wiped clean, I could neither confirm nor deny.

The last thing I remembered was giving the credits to Titean.

"A cropmate of mine is saving them for you," I whispered. "I made you a promise and I will uphold it. Now I expect you to do the same with yours, *leska*."

"*Leska...*" she whispered.

I didn't like the way she furrowed her brows, eyes turning dull, but she complied without a fuss. Lifting her pelvis, she used her legs and kicked her pants off, her pubic bone grinding against my cock.

"I won't hurt you." Because I was determined to be the first Vetusian to mate her properly, just like I had been the first one to kiss her. "Others might fuck you, *leska*, but I will be gentle with your body."

Her next inhale stuttered across a trembling lower lip. She must have been cold, so I decided not to remove her shirt. Instead, I slipped my hand underneath the fabric, cupping her warm breast.

Need seared my body and I took myself in hand, guiding my crown to part her lips. She was so stunning underneath me, her body made to receive mine, but it did so with rough pressure.

Dry. Uninviting.

That was how I found her mating cleft, this reality not lining up with how I had imagined her wet and willing, eager to let her body couple with mine.

Sophie licked the tip of her fingers, leaving a generous amount of saliva glistening there before she let it disappear between us. "Let me just... there you go. Try again."

With a thrust of my hips, I parted her, pure ecstasy engulfing me as her walls sucked me deeper. This was like nothing I'd ever experienced before. "Fuck, *leska*. You have no idea how perfect you feel around my cock."

A flinch wrecked through her body with such intensity, I sensed it rippling along my shaft. She turned her head, staring at the wall, her body entirely stiff underneath me.

Where did the human female go I'd watched from afar? The sun of *Taigh Arosh*? How she rolled her hips on the cocks of clients. How she crooned in their laps. How she moaned in pleasure.

"What is it?" I cupped her cheek so I could turn her gaze to meet mine, something sharp stabbing my innards when I found them glazed with tears. "I hate when you cry... makes me fucking angry."

A single sniff and she wiped her sleeves over her eyes, mumbling, "I'm sorry. It's just..."

"What?"

Her face distorted into nothing but wrinkles and tension, her next words pushing snot-covered from the back of her throat. "Last night you called me Sophie, and now I'm *leska* again, and... shit..."

I had called her Sophie?

Another rule broken.

She wrapped her leg around me and pulled me in deeper, blinking back tears and swallowing down the rest. "Just do it. That's what you want, right? What everybody wants." Hips lifted toward me and ground in circular movements, studied and precise, milking seed up my shaft. "Just fuck me already."

Back arched, moans resonating within the small confines of her closet, this was everything I had wanted... and nothing at all. Being inside her, ravishing a body only the richest Vetusians could afford, left me feeling... empty?

I pulled out right there.

"When we made this deal, I didn't expect you'd cry throughout my mating you," I snarled and struggled out of the closet, not sure if I was pissed at her for doing it, or myself for somehow causing it.

She climbed out behind me, hand covering her mating cleft as if I hadn't just been inside that thing. "Please, Adeas. If what you say is true and my credits are safe or... at least most of them —"

"Of course it's true. I'm not a liar."

"I need your help." A shaky hand reached for mine. "I can do better."

Yeah, I knew she could because I'd seen it.

Of course what I'd seen had been fake. Something which suddenly seemed to bother me, which pissed me off to a degree my veins ached with the rush of blood. Why couldn't I just fuck her like all the others? Why this urge to make it more than it had to be? Could be...

"Where are my things?" I asked and glanced around her room, the dim light coming through the windows indicating it was way too early to be up.

"In the bathroom."

Eager to get away from this awkward situation, I hurried over to her bathroom. But the moment I stepped in there, my entire body froze over until even the smallest tendons refused to twitch.

My shoes rested in the corner, the filthy sole imprint on the wall leaving no doubt she'd tossed them. My shirt and pants hung damp from the sink, while tracks of dirt and pure grossness stained the white shower tiles toward the drain. By the Three Suns. Was that how she'd found me?

Something akin to embarrassment swept over me, the scent of soap on me so much more intense now than it had been when I first woke. I shouldn't have slammed that stuff. Nothing good ever came from it, and it somehow bothered me that she'd seen me at my worst. That she might think I was a *sgu'dal*.

"You were so drunk you literally rolled into my room," she said from somewhere behind me, which explained the freaking headache. "I couldn't figure out a way to get you to your room, so I, like, washed you and let you crash here."

"I went to party with friends," I blurted, not even sure if that had been the case. Most likely not. Friends had made themselves rare ever since I got kicked from my stratum.

A gentle caress ran down my arm, stopping around a greenish-blue bruise with a red dot at the center. "Partied hard, huh? You were gone for five days."

Five days?

I shivered at that number.

"It's not what you think." I pulled my arm from her touch, humiliation infecting each of my heartbeats, pumping into my veins with such force it made the track mark pulsate. "I'm not a *sgu'dal*, okay, regardless of what everyone says. Addiction requires the inability to control the urge. That's not the case with me. I only use it because it helps me deal with my nerve damage."

She stepped in front of me, so fucking beautiful I wanted to take her into my arms and never let go. "You don't have to explain yourself."

Exactly! So why did I?

I had nothing to hide. Had never been secretive about the fact that I used souldust as a medication, simply because I wasn't abusing it. Many people used other things for physical ailments, and nobody called them a *sgu'dal*.

And yet that shame continued to feast on my churning insides at the sight of my clothes. How could she possibly have shared her closet with me, even after she'd scrubbed the filth off me? That place meant a lot to her. Even I understood that.

"You washed me?"

She nodded, thighs pressed tightly together, hand covering her sex. "Maybe we could ask Izara to get some fresh stuff from your room?"

The thought of this female's hands rubbing over my body filled me with equal parts of excitement and regret. Excitement because I wanted her to touch every part of me and deep within. Regret because I remembered nothing of it.

"I rarely ever touch alcohol," I said in yet another explanation as if I had to justify myself in front of her. Which I didn't. "I'm sorry if I caused trouble last night. Thanks for cleaning me up and letting me sleep here, *leska*."

The moment she sucked in her lips, new tears pushed forth, each one stealing the breath from my lungs. Why her crying affected me in such a way I couldn't explain. It was like an ache deep inside me, sitting somewhere between sternum and left lung.

"You don't want me to call you that? *Leska*?" With a jolt of panic, I shifted my weight from left to right and back again, hands reaching toward her, then dropping again, not knowing how to make that crying stop. "Do you want me to call you Sophie? Huh? I can do that. Sophie. There. Sophie."

What the fuck.

Now she cried even more.

How could I make her stop?

In my desperation, I wrapped my arms around her. She

tensed at the movement, stiff like a corpse, but I ignored how she shifted away from me and pulled her against my chest.

"You're only the second Earth female I've ever met," I said, loathing the way tears trickled down my body. "Please tell me why you're crying. But most of all, tell me how to make it stop."

She sniffed a few times, visibly trying to compose herself, this proud creature so vulnerable at that moment I wanted to coil myself around her in protection.

"Sometimes, I worry that I'll forget my name altogether." She stared up at me, brown eyes regarding me with an appreciation I immediately felt starved for. "Thank you for reminding me."

How many times had I observed this female and her spitefulness toward my kind? Her face had the ability to express disgust in dozens of ways, from snarling lips to arched brows and eyes narrowed into slits. But this look right now? As if I wasn't the species that had enslaved her? If calling her Sophie put *that* kind of look on her face, I would never call her anything else ever again.

"Sophie," I whispered, allowing myself to breathe in the scent of her hair. "Whenever you forget who you are, you ask me."

She took a step back, bringing a cold distance between us though her hand wrapped around my cock. "I promise I won't cry."

While my penis strained in her clasp, the rest of my body cooled right along with that gap between us. Each time I gravitated toward her, she worked my shaft harder, but shifted her weight away from me as well. Whatever closeness we had shared in that closet or when I'd pulled her into my embrace was gone. Sophie was gone, and in her place, I found *leska*. A stone-cold bitch, ruthless, regarding me with nothing but hatred.

I must have been insane. One-hundred-percent crazy, because I stepped away from the touch others paid a fortune for. A fortune I would never in my life possess, but it didn't matter because *leska* wasn't the treasure. Sophie was.

But Sophie wasn't for sale.

Sophie needed to be earned, and that was what I would do.

"You don't have to do this," I said. "I'm still going to help you in whichever capacity I can."

Her eyes narrowed. "Nothing's for free. Not on Earth, and certainly not on Odheim. Why would you help me without asking anything in return?"

"Our deal still stands. I simply changed my mind, and I don't feel like calling in your debt now." When she remained quiet, caution edged to her soft features, I continued. "A friend of mine will keep your credits safe. I couldn't find someone to smuggle you out yet, but I'll get to it the next time I leave here. What else do you need from me?"

Lips pressed into a thin line, she eyed me for an overlong moment before she let out a deep exhale. "We have to come up with an idea on how I can let you know that a Jal'zar stung me. I was thinking that I could maybe leave my scrunchie on the knob outside the secret door?"

"Your what?"

"This," she said, pulling a purple thing from her hair which made the strands cascade down her shoulders. "When you see this on my door, it means *wait for me*. Like, in the hallway until I tell you it's safe to come inside."

"Wait for me," I repeated with a nod. "Alright, that

works. Now let me knock on Izara's door really quick so she can at least fetch me pants."

The moment I turned to leave the bathroom, Sophie asked, "Why are you helping me?"

I turned away saying nothing.

As if I didn't wonder myself...

ELEVEN

Sophie

Chips slipped from a gray hand and onto the messy sheet of my bed, piling there in a nocturne of clinks and clanks. They shifted each time I rolled from stomach to side and back again, pain radiating from my ribs with such ferocity I couldn't breathe.

I pressed the black towel I had prepared against my side, watching an upside-down version of the Jal'zar warrior leave through the hidden door without giving me another glance.

Quieting my mind, I focused on my surroundings and counted to three. I took a shallow breath, my brain growing dizzy at the crippling pain of the sting and rolled onto all fours. Shaky legs searched for the ground until toes dug into soft carpet.

I walked over to the hidden door.

The fake tapestry opened at a push, and I quickly pulled my scrunchie from my wrist with my teeth and hung it on the doorknob. If everything worked out as planned, then Izara should have given Adeas a heads-up, telling him that she'd secretly escorted a Jal'zar to my room.

I collapsed back onto my bed, the musk of a male mixing with the iron of my blood. A disgusting combination which turned me nauseous regardless of the small treasure piled-up beside me. Body flooding with waves of pain, I didn't know where my suffering ended and I began.

Footsteps. I sensed their vibration even before my ears pricked. They approached the back door then stalled there, waiting, leaving no doubt Adeas was behind that wall.

Too exhausted to get up again, I shouted, "Come in."

Another moment of hesitance, then the hidden door opened, a frown lining Adeas' face. "I don't like this."

Neither did I, but it was still better than being raped on the daily for the rest of my life.

Breathing alone took such effort I didn't voice a response. I only lay there, staring at the canopy above, listening to how he rummaged through my furniture as he searched for the healer pack.

The mattress moved.

My body shifted.

I whimpered in pain.

"Take your hand off," Adeas said as he grabbed the bunched-up towel in my stead. "Asshole splintered one of your ribs, but it didn't separate."

"Make sure I don't bleed onto the sheets."

"That's the least of my concerns right now." He propped his knee against me so I wouldn't roll back onto my stomach, small pupils regarding me with worry. "I loathe seeing you in so much pain, Sophie. You'll need pain killers for many suns. How can you let them rip you apart like this?"

My eyes flicked to the pile of credits. "My aunt used to say pain is weakness leaving your body."

The solution he dribbled into the wound covered me in goosebumps it stung that bad. "Aunt?"

"My mom's sister," I said. "I stayed with her whenever my mom disappeared or went into court-ordered rehab."

"Is your mother still alive?"

"Died of an overdose shortly before the invasion," I said matter-of-factly.

His hand stalled at that, his gaze losing itself in my wound for the fraction of a moment before he shook his head. "I'm sorry to hear that. What about her sister?"

"The day before the invasion, I flew up to Virginia to visit one of the colleges there that I had applied to, which is why we got separated. I know she's alive, but we were assigned to different districts after I got out of Ardev Five. Haven't seen her since."

He stared at me from a lowered head. "College like a stratum? What did you want to study?"

"Human resource management," I said. "Couldn't go wrong with that one. But then you guys came, and I never even got to experience that first walk of shame."

Of course he didn't get that one, but he didn't ask further so I stopped supplying details about me that weren't any of his business anyway.

Fingers slightly shaky, they worked a blue cream into the raging flesh. He was coming down from whenever he'd scored last.

"Do you need something?" I asked. "Your hands are trembling."

Hook needle clasped between thumb and index finger, he pressed the thin metal so hard his fingertips turned white at the pressure. "It's just nerve damage. Bad enough I won't ever be a surgeon, but I can still stitch something like this even with my eyes closed."

"Nerve damage?"

He cleared his throat, thread squeaking through blood-smeared tissue. "I injured my spine during the Jal'zar invasion. That's why I get those jitters. Migraines. When it gets real bad I stammer."

"That's why you pump that poison into you?"

"Every medication is poison if not dosed correctly," he clipped before he cut the thread. "Souldust was originally developed for nerve damage. It overrides malfunctioning nerve receptors." He applied a camouflaging cream to the wound before his eyes locked with mine. "The day I slammed it was an exception. Shouldn't have done it, but that doesn't change the fact that I'm not an addict. I could stop if I wanted to, but there's no alternative medication for my condition."

Could that really be true?

That he wasn't the regular fuck-up *sgu'dal*?

I'd seen him passed out down at the sweatmines, his brain so messed up from that stuff he couldn't form a coherent sentence. Did he truly suffer from some sort of injury? Or was he in denial?

A gentle finger circled the small round scar on my stomach. "Tell me what happened."

I rolled onto my back, the pain slowly subsiding. "I got caught in crossfire during phase one. Hit my uterine artery, so they had to remove the entire thing, ovaries and all."

He placed his palm onto the scar and left it there for a moment, an unexpected warmth radiating from the touch. "That's why they supply you with hormones. I'm sorry that happened to you."

"I was never really sure if I wanted children," I said,

mostly because I feared I would suck at it like my mom had. "When they abducted me, they wanted to sell me to a Vetusian. As a mate. But nobody wanted me since I can't have children. That's how I ended up here."

"We're not all like that." He closed the healer pack and lowered himself down beside me, tugging on the sheet to cover my naked body. "I would have counted myself very blessed to have you, children or not."

My veins pulsed at his words, infused with panic and calmness alike. Adeas was the first Vetusian not making me feel worthless simply because I had nothing to contribute to their agenda of saving their race.

Seemingly all on their own, my eyes slipped to those lips I'd kissed, because surely I wouldn't do so intentionally. What was this guy to me other than a Vetusian I bargained with? Someone I used so I could get out of here? And yet those lips...

"What about you?" I asked, not sure which one of us needed more distraction from this sudden intimacy palpable in the air. "You don't have a match?"

"I wouldn't know since I never went in for the DNA profiling. When they started collecting samples, I wasn't mature yet. Once I was, I knew they wouldn't allow me to go to Earth anyway, so what was the point?"

The moment he stroked his hand over my cheek, I turned my head, so full of self-loathing it burned my eyes. "I don't want you to touch me when I'm like this."

Nor in any other state, I reminded myself.

"Injured?"

"Filthy," I whispered. Used and discarded, seed sticky between my thighs.

Why it bothered me so much I couldn't even have said. It wasn't like he didn't know that I was a whore. Not by choice, but that had no effect on what those males did to me. What I had to let them do to me.

A long, drawn-out exhale later, he climbed off the bed. He pulled his shirt over his head, pausing for a moment when he gazed down at himself as if ashamed for a body consumed by abuse. Adeas slipped out of his shoes, pants, and socks, his cock slightly erect.

Would he call in my debt now?

Fuck me ten minutes after my last client?

"Hold on to me." That was all he said as he peeled back the blanket and scooped me up, a pain-ridden body draping over arms which shook underneath the strain of my weight. "Nothing about you is filthy, but I'll gladly return the favor and wash you if it makes you feel better."

He carried me over to my tub and descended the stone stairs in the corner. There, he lowered himself into the heated water, and me right along with him.

"The cream on your wound is waterproof," he said, sitting down on one of the tiled benches as he lowered me onto his lap, water rising to just above my sternum. "Try to relax your muscles. It'll help to keep the bruising away but tell me if you get dizzy."

Cradling me, he took his hand and scooped water over my head, already glancing back at the many soaps lining the edge of the tub. "What do I use for your hair? All this stuff seems imported from Earth and I can't make out a single label."

A gulp went down my throat, voice thin with something I wouldn't name. "The purple one."

"Tell me about Earth," he said, circular motions lathering my hair with shampoo. "I know your waters move. A friend told me you have animals with noses so long they reach the ground. And precipitation that settles as a white blanket onto the landscape?"

"Snow," I said with a smile. "It's like rain that gets so cold it freezes into flakes."

"Snow," he repeated, carefully lowering my head into the water.

Fingers tousled through my hair and rinsed out the soap. All the while, he stared at me with a longing that sent an unexpected pulse between my legs, his cock hardening underneath me. I ripped my eyes from his, torn between enjoying his touch and reminding myself that I shouldn't.

His hand ran down my hair with a squeak as he forced the water from it, twirling it around his hand before he draped it across my breast. Colorless eyes connecting with mine, he held my gaze once more, and I sensed his fingers venturing down along my waist. They climbed between my legs where they swiped through my folds, his breathing turning heavy, labored.

"Sophie..." he moaned low, touching every inch of my body, rubbing me clean from the gap between my toes to the tip of my fingers.

I melted against a chest that shouldn't have held any comfort. But as much as Adeas was part of this hell, at that moment, he was just someone holding me, washing away the evil.

Soft and pliable underneath him, I sensed his next exhale on my mouth before his lips feathered over it in a gentle kiss. He did so slowly, each stroke of his tongue tasting like a question.

Can I? Shall I? May I?

I answered by letting my tongue search for his, an overwhelming sense of control rushing over me. Nothing of this was bought, the fact that I kissed him because I fucking *chose* to making this cage fall away from around me.

Eyes still closed, with his lips still pressed to mine, I only noticed that he carried me out of the tub when the chilly air let my nipples grow taut.

"Towel?" he asked.

When I pointed behind me to the sideboard, he grabbed the big fluffy towel, shook it, and supported my buttocks with his lifted thigh as he draped it across my body.

Alarm spiked my senses when he walked toward the bed, but he only shook his head, saying, "Don't insult me." Then he carried me to my closet and lowered me onto the blankets, drops of water landing here and there. He climbed in with me, wiping a wet strand from my face before he stroked the towel over my hair.

We sat in silence like that for a while as he dried my strands, my arms, my torso, and everything else down to my heels. Whatever corner of the towel wasn't damp after that, he used to dry himself before he tossed it into my room.

"Lie down," he said and tapped a pillow, draping a blanket over me as I eased into my little nest.

He climbed behind me, a hard shaft nestling between my thighs, pulsating and swelling against my pussy, his deep groan rocking through me.

I wouldn't cry if he took me now.

Chances were I might enjoy it, my body cleaner than it had ever been on the outside and humming with my name at the core. I wanted to despise him for that. For making me enjoy the touch of a Vetusian. Long for it, even.

"Sophie," he whispered, entrancing me with how he kissed my shoulder. "I finally know what I want in exchange for my help, and you won't like it."

A heat I'd never experienced before engulfed my

crotch, and yet he remained stiff and still between my legs. Not moving. Not taking. There was something innocent in his restraint, which made me want his possession all the more.

"Give me your soul, Sophie," he murmured as if he was the devil himself. "Your body might belong to everyone, but I will be the male who washes you clean from them. The one to hold you in my arms after they've used you, watching you fall to sleep. The only Vetusian tasting your kisses and whispering your name so you won't forget."

I forgot more than my name at that moment.

I forgot *myself*, sick with remorse over my dissolving pride as I strained my neck to kiss his smooth jawline. How bad was selling my soul to the Vetusian devil if it helped me escape his hell?

"Deal," I said. "You've got my soul."

Adeas wrapped his arm around my chest and pulled me closer against him, his heat penetrating my spine. He pulled the blanket higher, covering both of us, his finger painstakingly tugging here and there until it covered all but my face.

"Sleep," he whispered as he nuzzled the back of my neck. "Once the weather settles, I will go to Odheim again and find a vessel that can take you home."

TWELVE

Sophie

Round and silver, spheres of souldust clattered against each other. I grabbed one of the palathium crates down at the sweatmines, the air stagnant now that the remains of the solar storm stopped lingering. Every now and then, I caught myself glancing over my shoulder, but the Vetusian I tried to catch a glimpse of wasn't here.

Time seemed to pass faster on those days I spent with Adeas. Sometimes, we would meet at one of the restaurants together with Izara, though he usually just pushed the food around his plate.

In the evenings, he often waited until my shift ended before he stole himself into my room, the sequence always the same. He washed me. He held me. He watched me fall asleep before he slipped away at daybreak, since we couldn't risk anybody catching us like that.

Rule number two: don't get involved with pleasure workers.

While Adeas never tried to fuck me, regardless of how

hard his cock pressed against me, there was no denying I gave him something other Vetusians would have sold their organs for: closeness.

Not so much to my body as to that soul I'd traded.

Our closeness came in the form of words whispered inside a closet, sometimes until one of us passed out from sleep mid-sentence. I told him about how I chipped a tooth when I was a kid because I'd slipped off a chair. When he was high, he told me about his plans to develop a procedure to regenerate nerves. When he wasn't, he told me about how one healer friend after another had somehow abandoned him. It was a strange feeling, this confiding in someone I should have despised. The truth was that I liked him. Liked him a lot.

"We shouldn't have to do this," Izara snarled, taking the crate off my hands before she lifted it onto a large hover container. "How am I supposed to entertain an entire Jal'zar fleet tonight if I have to slog all day down here?"

Behind me, a Kokonian male handed me another crate, which I carried to the container underneath the relentless stare of guards. They stood gathered in little groups, weapons charged across their chest, making sure nobody slipped a sphere. The main reason why everyone worked naked down here. Luckily, *leska* was allowed to remain dressed, the view of my naked body something Levear wouldn't hand out for free.

Not allowing us a break, one of the guards immediately pointed at the next table, stacked high with more crates. Beside it, a Kokonian female continued to hold empty spheres underneath a dispenser. A deep sparkling cobalt blue, the powder spilled into the small container. Snapping the sphere shut, she placed it into the crate beside her. Then she repeated the entire procedure.

Everything about her movements was monotone, and yet something caught my attention; a flicker whenever she tilted her wrist to close the spheres shut.

I stepped up closer, my hands blindly scouting for the crate handles while my gaze flicked to her fingers. That was when I saw it, and my stomach began to knot up, guts tying around my organs until my entire core convulsed.

My fingers snapped around her wrist and turned her hand, souldust spilling from sphere to table while an emerald stone rose into view. "Where did you get this ring?"

"Don't touch me, human," she hissed, ripping her scaled hand from my clasp.

"That's my ring!"

With my shout, I darted for her hand once more, the empty sphere falling from her fingers. It fell onto the table with an echoing clank, and my thighs crashed into the table with such force crates swayed beside me.

I didn't care.

One strong tug pulled the female halfway across the table, my eyes fixed on my mother's ring. In no way, shape, or form valuable, the socket made of freaking plastic, cracked in one place, but it was a remnant of a time when she hadn't succumbed to drugs yet.

"*Leska!*"

The bark of the guard got lost in several *whomp-whomp-whomps* as crates hit the ground, followed by the crunch of metal spheres rolling over dirt and grit.

"Give me my ring back!" I snarled, fingertips frantically shoving over scaled skin in a desperate attempt to slip it off her finger. "You fucking stole it!"

A punch against my sternum and I stumbled backward, my hip all but shattering when I hit the stone ground underneath me. Searing pain drove into my elbow, and wisps of hair whipped around my face.

"I didn't steal anything you stupid whore!" the Kokonian shouted.

An unforgiving hand pulled me onto my feet by the collar of my shirt. "That'll be a spanking, *leska*. Boss won't be happy with the delay your little drama caused."

"Fuck you," I snarled as I slapped his hand away, stomping straight toward the tunnel connecting this place to *Taigh Arosh*. "If boss wants to punish me, then boss knows where to find me."

I ignored Izara's pleading to slow down as she hurried naked behind me.

Sweatmine workers weren't allowed to step into *Taigh Arosh*. And even if this Kokonian had, she couldn't have known where I'd hid the ring. Adeas fucking stole it. Stole it and probably bartered it for her to slip him an extra sphere. Perhaps more, considering they had no clue it wasn't even a real stone.

"Slow down," Izara's shout shattered from the tunnel walls. "They will punish us for walking away like this."

"Then turn around and go back."

"What happened?"

I glanced over my shoulder, pure rage stiffening the tendons along my neck. "Adeas stole my mom's ring. Where is his room?"

Long, slender legs eventually caught up to me, falling into a jog beside me. "What did you expect?"

She was right. What had I expected?

That I could trust a junkie not to steal my shit?

That he'd told me the truth about having it under control? That all this falling to sleep in his arms meant anything?

Apparently I had, because I found myself slowing my pace, asking, "Did he ever tell you that he has some sort of nerve damage? From when the Empire sent him to fight off the Jal'zar invasion and got injured?"

"*Leska*," she said, the way her hesitance turned my innards to liquid hatred second only to the frown on her face. "Adeas is barely older than you. He was still in the middle of his training when the Vetusians fought us off. That healer has never seen a war, let alone gotten injured in one."

Foolish *leska*.

Stupid *leska*.

It wasn't like I'd believed him when he told me that story, but somehow, *somehow* I might have hoped, might have —

"I'll kill him," I grunted and picked up speed again, following what turned into the back hallways of *Taigh Arosh*.

Third door next to the food storage.

That was what he'd told me, and the floor vibrated underneath me when I stepped up to it. And yet, angry as I was, I hesitated at the door, something dense coming over me.

Fuck it.

I turned the knob.

I stepped in.

I froze to the spot right there.

My stomach spiraled lower and lower, and the strangest thought crossed my mind. *For a junkie, his room is pretty tidy*. But I wasn't shocked by how dozens of books sat neatly in a bookshelf next to his desk. I wasn't taken aback by several sets of white uniforms neatly folded away on a chair in the corner. Neither was I surprised by pictures of Earth pinned on the wall above his bed, arranged in a perfect square.

No. What threw me off were the two Jal'zar prostitutes staring back at me with raised brows. Actually, only the one slumping in his desk chair with one leg propped up irked me. Mostly because her naked pussy spread so wide I could see up her egg pouch. It ached me somewhere, though I didn't understand why.

"Oh shit," Izara mumbled behind me.

"Adeas," the other Jal'zar, the dressed one, said, her head resting on his chest as she gave a shove against his stomach. "The mating cleft wants something from you."

That comment hurt, but not nearly as much as the fact that she rested where my head had been every night for over a week. An insane thought for which I had no excuse.

"Huh?" Adeas grunted, one arm draped over his forehead.

"The human whore."

He pouted. "*Leska*?"

Never had that name stung as it did right then, though I refused to acknowledge it. Fuck him and all of his kind. Yeah, I was *leska* the whore, but at least I wasn't a fucking thief, liar, and good-for-nothing junkie.

I straightened my spine and stepped up to his bed. "Did you steal my mom's ring?"

A lazy arm slipped off his forehead and he pushed himself up to sit, the Jal'zar's head slipping off his chest with a giggle that rattled my bones.

"What do you want?" he asked, cold eyes barely acknowledging me before he gazed about his room.

"My mom's ring," I repeated slowly, hands curling into fists by my sides. "You stole it from my closet."

"What's your problem?" Adeas shoved the Jal'zar off his

bed with such force she rolled across the floor. Within seconds, he jumped up and towered over me, pure spite in his expression. "Are you calling me a thief?"

Yes.

The answer settled on my tongue but wouldn't come out, and when I only blinked at him for the longest time, teeth flashed as he grunted, "What the fuck are you looking at?"

My rage was tempered by a sudden onslaught of fear, the predatory snarl sitting on his upper lip making me gasp.

This male standing in front of me with his chest thrust out, staring me down with supreme confidence, was nothing like whatever version of Adeas I had met before. Not the lost one. Not the kind one. And certainly not the one who could possibly help me escape this hell.

"You," Izara barked and pointed at the Jal'zar. "Get out of here right now before I call Sehrin to check your rooms for souldust."

Both females immediately scrambled to their feet and left, taking nothing of the throat-cutting tension with them. I seethed with anger, loathing, and perhaps disappointment as well, each emotion darkening and distorting the other. Adeas *looked* like the male who'd held me in his arms so many nights, but his aggressive posture was all wrong.

"What did you do with those last couple of credits I gave you?" I asked, hating how fear tensed my vocal cords.

"I didn't do anything with them."

"Liar."

"Fuck you!" He bumped into my shoulder as he pushed me aside with his entire body, gripping one book after another from the shelf which he tossed to the ground underneath curses. "I didn't steal your stupid ring."

And I was the idiot who, for just a moment, wanted to

believe him. A part of me might have trusted that he was sincere. Apparently, that never went away, no matter how often someone chose drugs over me. But a bigger part in me knew it was wishful thinking.

A hand settled on my shoulder, claws pressing against my collarbone. "We should go, *leska*. He just got high, and that's not the time you want to be around him."

No, clearly not. Nor any other time.

"Here." Without warning, he tossed the bag with ICs and a few bits of ore, which crashed against my sternum before it hit the ground. "Take your credits and get out of here. I don't have to listen to your accusations. I don't have to help you either."

I picked up the bag, knowing I should turn around and leave, but somehow, I tortured myself by taking him in. By letting that hostility in his eyes brand itself into my memory. Perhaps I'd learn something. At the very least, it might serve as a reminder that I would never get out of this shithole.

Turning away from him, my brain throbbing in-tune with my heart, I shoved the bag between my breasts. It did a poor job at hiding it but was still better than carrying it dangling from my hand.

"That's right," Adeas yelled behind me, and I imagined his eyes rimmed with animosity, finger stabbing in my direction. "How about you take better care of your stuff instead of just... blasting in here uninvited and... fucking shit."

Bam.

His door slammed shut, sending a tremble through my body strong enough that I touched the wall in support. "What if he really didn't steal it?"

Something in my stomach pulsed as if I'd grown a second heartbeat there, so jarring and uncomfortable I couldn't will my foot into another step. Had I falsely accused him?

"Did he see where you kept it?" Izara asked, and at my nod, she added, "Then it's safe to assume he took it."

But he hadn't taken my credits from what I could tell. Perhaps not everything was in the bag, but there was no doubt in my mind most of it was. *Trying to find excuses and explanations for a junkie again, huh?*

Izara pressed her lips into a thin line, observing me. "I've known Adeas for long enough I can tell you for a fact that he didn't touch them."

"The credits?"

"The Jal'zar females." She leaned her back against the wall, naked as she was, her eyes searching for mine. "He might have gotten high with them, but he doesn't mate with them." A deep inhale which rolled out through parted lips, and then, "At least not anymore."

What did that even mean? Not anymore?

Not anymore ever since he started washing sweat and seed of other males from my body only to stroke through my hair until I drifted off to sleep? There was nothing between us but a quid pro quo. My soul in exchange for his help.

Soul, Sophie. Not heart.

"Why are you telling me this?" Why I even asked I couldn't say, because it wasn't a question I wanted an answer to.

"I smelled your heartache," she said with a tap against her nose. "Do you really believe I didn't notice how he sneaks into your room almost every night? Your closet is right next to my desk, *leska*."

"We're not fucking."

"If you'd jump his bones for a good time, I wouldn't be half as concerned as I am." She glanced about the hallway, first left then right, and eventually leaned in closer. "You talk almost all night. Sometimes I wake from your laughs. That's far worse than riding his cock for fun."

With a tap of her tail, she pushed herself off the wall, two hands gently stroking my shoulders as she let her eyes lock with mine. "Forget whatever you want, *leska*. All that stuff I taught you ever since you got here? Forget about it. Just do yourself a favor and *always* remember the rules."

THIRTEEN

Adeas

I balled my hand and reached it toward Sophie's door, dropped it, picked it up, then dropped it again. All the while, I shifted my weight from one leg to the other as if I was about to wet my pants, which made sense, given the way my stomach hung heavy.

Every medication came with a list of side effects, but none was as long as the one for souldust. The worst of them all? It turned me into a real ass right after I took it.

My stomach convulsed with hunger and yet I had no appetite, the acid eating away on my insides not nearly as biting as I'd been to Sophie yesterday.

All morning, I'd replayed the scene over and over again, the bits I remembered anyway, shame choking me with such force I'd thrown my hands to my throat more than once. My conscience burned with the memory of the awful things I'd said. How I'd intimidated her, because I remembered the fear in her eyes when she'd shrunk away from me.

Half a lunar cycle ago, I thought she'd seen me at my

worst when I showed up drunk at her door, covered in filth and injuries. Now I knew I'd been wrong, because what could be worse than me scaring the very female I wanted to protect? To help?

I took a deep breath, each knock on the door a reminder of what I'd promised myself when I sneaked up here.

One for the apology I'd give her.

Two for the credits I'd bring to Titean.

Three for the dock master I would find today.

She neither opened the door nor could I detect any noises coming from her room, and my stomach slipped yet a bit lower, almost as if my organs wanted to fall right through me. What if she refused to see me? Who would hold her at night? Tell her that she was Sophie, the female who would make it out of this place?

"She's not here," Izara said, head poking out from her room beside. "*Leska* got an early client. Punishment for walking away at the sweatmines."

My chest tightened, ribs clawing to my heart, and I wasn't sure which part triggered it: that she wasn't here for my apology, or that she was with another Vetusian.

The thought of another male touching her pulsed my veins with greed. But hadn't that been our deal? Everyone fucked her, and I held her after? Cleaned her body each night so the ugliness of this place wouldn't reach that vulnerable female underneath a tough shell?

"In any case, she doesn't want to see you," Izara stated what I'd already feared. "You should probably stay away from her for a while, otherwise, you might join Sehrin's club and find yourself with a bionic eye."

"She's that pissed at me?" I raked a hand through my hair, desperate to make this right. "The way I acted was terrible. They'd just dispensed my medication and... I didn't steal her ring."

The Jal'zar female stepped into the hallway with pity etched to her features, tugging her yellow robe where it had slipped from her shoulder. "Except that you did, Adeas."

"Why would say that? Just because I had access to her room —"

"I went to the Kokonian who has her ring and explained the situation," she said, her pause riding shivers up my spine. "When I asked her where she got it from, she said it came from you."

A surreal laugh wormed from my throat, my body turning hot, cold, and numb all at once. "Well, she lied, because I can tell you for a fact that I did not take that ring."

"Perhaps you didn't notice?"

"Didn't notice stealing something?" How was that possibly something someone wouldn't be aware of? "Are you kidding me?"

"So you never took stuff without realizing it? Or you suddenly found something on you with no fucking clue how you got it?"

The memory of Sophie's credits came back with such force I swung my hand onto my head to contain the excruciating pain it caused within my skull. What if I did steal her ring? Just like I'd stolen a handful of her credits at the infirmary? One moment, I'd handed over the bag, and the next, bam, I found credits in my pocket.

But that was an exception...

Right. I wasn't a thieving addict.

"The Kokonian is lying," I said, my voice as solid as my resolve on the subject. "I didn't take her ring."

I didn't!

This was all bullshit, and I let my palms run down my face, wiping off this nightmare.

Izara arched her back and stretched her arms over her head, waiting out a yawn before she spoke again. "And why would the Kokonian lie? What are her motives? How would she have gotten the ring when she isn't even allowed to step foot into *Taigh Arosh*?"

I had a million explanations for that, but somehow, I couldn't voice a single one, my throat tying up all over again. My ribs squeezed my heart a bit tighter, ends piercing the muscle. What if I had lost control, slipping into an addiction without even realizing it?

Izara lifted a brow when I reached my hands out before me, fingers splayed, not a single tremble wrecking my body. Steady, reliable fingers, capable of performing little miracles.

Your dosage is just fine.

Exactly. And neither did I steal that ring.

"Did you tell her what the Kokonian said?" I asked.

She crossed her arms in front of her chest. "Not yet."

"I'd appreciate if you didn't."

Izara shook her head in disbelief. "Why? So I won't confirm what she already knows anyway? By the spirit of Mekara, Adeas, her mom was an addict."

Anger flooded my veins.

"I am not —" I swallowed that roar in my voice right there, took a deep breath, and said, "I'm not an addict, so please don't put that idea in her head. She needs my help, and I will find out who stole her ring."

Izara turned away, halfway disappearing between door and frame as she said, "You should fuck her."

"There are things more precious about her than her body."

"I know," she breathed, her parting words trailing faint from the closing gap. "Don't steal yet another treasure from her."

———

In the end, I did steal something.

With Sophie gone from her room, I'd sneaked inside and turned everything upside down in search of the bag with the credits and ore. A shitty thing to do, yes, but I'd rather have her pissed at me than find her beaten and bruised after Sehrin got to them before me.

After I handed them over to Titean — triple-checking my pockets to make sure everything was indeed inside that bag — I made my way to the old dock once more. No excuses this time. No slamming, no snorting, no nothing.

I'd medicated the morning before, generously, making absolutely sure I wouldn't mess this up. This time when I returned to Sophie, I wouldn't literally *roll into her room*, as she'd called it, but walk in there with an apology and good news. At least once in my life I wanted to be a hero, and what better way than to help this Earth female to escape to her home?

I caught myself grinding my molars at that thought.

Once Sophie made it off-planet, the female would be gone from my life. Just thinking about it ached my chest, because I enjoyed caressing her beautiful curves when I washed her. Loved the way she rested her head on my chest when she got sleepy. Relished when she ran her manicured nails up and down my chest in something between a stroke and a scratch.

When I reached the old dock, I climbed through one of the abandoned maintenance entrances, starting my search from the bottom. I walked swiftly along the bays, each of them bustling now that the solar storm had passed. Crooked merchants sold stun wave rifles, most likely stolen from the Imperial armory. Pleasure bots got Vetusians off, that thing called privacy coming with an additional price tag nobody cared to afford.

My steps quickened after I went up the palathium ramp, one misstep away from falling into the abyss underneath since the metal rail was missing in most places. Slowly but surely, the old dock was falling apart, bursting from its seams as crime expanded at its core.

Where my bleached irises brought me judging looks wherever I went, here, they kept thieves away since addicts were usually broke. And while I wasn't an addict, I was just as broke — courtesy of healer Corps for kicking me out.

I passed each sphere and vial reached out to me, reminding myself that I should be good for the rest of the day, perhaps even into the next morning. That slight tremble jerking my knuckles? That crawling underneath my skin? I was just anxious.

The old dock master sat on a cargo crate with his hands bracing against the metal, his white wisps crowned with a bald spot and yet he had the lips of a pleasure bot wrapped around his cock. Silicone lips slipped down his length, the corner so torn with age the material flapped around with each thrust.

"What can I do for you?" he asked, his gaze meeting mine as if my looks might help him get it over with faster. "Rubik's cubes won't come in until the next lunar cycle."

"Rubik's what?"

"Rubik's cubes." He turned left toward the desk standing behind the crate, age-speckled ass peeking from a half-lowered pants as he stretched for a cube and tossed it.

"The goal is to move it around until each side unifies in color."

I caught the oddity and stared at it, each side a chaotic mix of red, blue, and others.

"You have to twist it," the dock master said, gesturing with his hands before fingers dug back into fake hair that had lost its luster.

"This thing came here from Earth?" I twisted the layers, resonating the bay with *clack-clack-clacks* as I lined up squares with the same color. "What else do you smuggle in?"

The moment his face scrunched up, I turned around and ignored his grunts, not turning back until a belt buckle clanked. After working at *Taigh Arosh* for two solar cycles, not much shocked me anymore when it came to sexual pleasure. Vetusians soiled their pants pretending to nurse from Jal'zar breasts. They whipped females bloody with one hand and jerked themselves off with the other. And I was no better, because I got hard before each snort, and spilled seed if I ever slammed.

The dock master huffed. "Chocolate, rare stones, cannabis, —"

"Cannabis?"

"An Earth drug." He slipped off the crate and, at a voice command, sent the bot to clean herself up. "Haven't tried it myself, but customers say it helps them relax for the most part."

Turn after turn, the sides of the cube lined up with promise. "What about human females?"

His snort came with such force it triggered a cough, and he bumped a fist against his chest until he dislodged the phlegm. "I won't dirty my hands on something so despicable. Apparently, decades without females have taught us nothing."

My body eased at that statement. "What about the other way around? I know Levear supplies you with soul-dust for Earth. Anything else you ship back there?"

"You have an awful lot of questions for someone who doesn't seem too intent on buying any of my wares." He observed me, shaking his head like everyone else each time his gaze reached my eyes. "Don't look like someone selling anything either, unless it's a tight fuck up your ass."

I glanced over my shoulder, making sure nobody else had stepped into this bay, then lowered my voice into little more than a whisper. "Assuming there's an Earth female trying to get back to Earth, which merchant might be willing to hide her in his or her vessel?"

Long fingers rubbed down his chin, the male himself giving me another once-over before he sighed. "What's her name?"

"That's none of your business."

"If it isn't any of my business, then I'm afraid I wouldn't know how to help. Do you think me a fool? Helping one of the female slaves escape will bring the wrath of the cartel down on my head if they find out."

This wasn't going well at all, so I quickly charged the subject back to something that might tug on the old male's heartstrings.

"I've never seen a Vetusian female in my lifetime," I said on an exhale. "I assume you had a mate at some point?"

He nodded as he stared out of his bay, his palm stroking over the bald spot at the top of his head. "We only spent a very short time with each other. She was captain of a large vessel traveling between Cultum and Dunatal. Kokonian pirates captured her ship. Killed everyone and stole the grains."

I said nothing. Only stood there, letting the memory of his mate do the work for me before I said, "I can offer pay of course."

He started at that. "What do you offer?"

"You know someone then," I said. "Someone who would be willing to hide her and take her back?"

The dock master walked around to his desk and crammed small packages into the drawers with such force the desk vibrated, as if he hated himself for caving in. "Captain R'kesh. A Jal'zar warrior whose mate was captured and sold into slavery back then, where she died as she tried to escape. He will be... open to the idea if I approach him."

Odd how, sometimes, the enemies of the Empire could turn out to be your strongest allies.

I strolled over to him and placed the finished cube onto his desk. "How much?"

FOURTEEN

Sophie

I let the nightgown slip down my waist, my ribs hurting where two pink, puckered scars itched underneath a layer of camouflaging cream. I'd only been stung twice, and already the injuries were taking a toll. How many more of those could I take until my body revolted?

Glass of white wine in hand, I lowered myself onto the layers of blankets I'd prepared on my balcony. I propped my elbow against one of the many pillows and took a sip, losing myself to the beauty of the purple-specked universe above. Life had been shitty ever since they'd abducted me, but things had turned downright unbearable the moment Adeas walked in on me when I'd bled all over the place.

He wasn't just part of this hell.

He was possessed by a devil.

"Sophie..." And now the devil whispered my name.

I didn't bother turning around. "Get out of my room or I'll scream so loud the guards will come."

With each of his steps, my heartbeat amplified as it

pounded against my injuries from the inside, until a silver, round, covered tray came into view. "I brought you this from the central district."

"I don't want anything from you."

Neither his help nor his embrace, no matter how something deep inside me longed for it right then. What had this guy done to me? Why did I feel as if something kept tugging me toward him?

"A friend told me about this place that serves Earth meals." Another hand pushed into my vision and removed the cover, the puff of steam rising into the night full of traces of garlic and parsley. "They call it chicken and shrimp carbonara on fettu-something."

I despised how saliva ran down my gums and pooled on my tongue. While Levear had been kind enough to allow me a synthesizer, that thing made nothing compared to this, my eyes dipping down to the pink shrimp. I licked my lips at the sight of the sauce, creamy and rich, with pieces of mushroom.

Fine. I'd take the damn food, but I wouldn't forgive him for the way he'd treated me.

"Thank you." I made sure I snarled that and took the container after I put the wine on the ground, dipping my finger into the sauce and licking it off with a moan. So delicious! "When I came back from a client, I found my entire room turned upside down and my credits gone. You don't happen to know who could have done that, do you?"

Adeas finally stepped around me and into view, lowering himself onto the blanket in front of me. A half-convinced smile tugged on the corner of his mouth, and the plea in his eyes wasn't lost on me.

"You hid them well," he said on a sigh, his gaze steady, somehow rooting my pupils into place where they should have ignored him. "Took me almost an argos to find that bag."

"At least this time you're not denying it."

"I know I fucked up, and I'm sorry." His fingertips stroked over my knee so fast I had no opportunity to evade his searing touch. "I didn't steal your ring, Sophie. I did, however, steal your credits and ore. Brought it all to my friend at the infirmary for safekeeping."

This guy was just something else.

He stood there, looking all innocent like Dr. Jekyll when Mr. Hyde waited just underneath the smooth surface. How could he go from condescending asshole to this sweet guy, who not only apologized, but did so with freaking delicious pasta while following through with our plan?

A weird hum fluttered behind my sternum.

I grabbed the black fork this meal had come with, and Adeas watched with awe how I spiraled the pasta into a nest before it disappeared into my mouth. My gums ached and clenched at the explosion of spices inside, and my eyes fluttered shut to enhance the experience. So thick. So creamy.

"Oh my friggin' god this is sooo goood." I twirled another nest around the fork, poked a shrimp to hold it all in place, then handed it to him. "Try some."

Instead of taking the fork, he gently grabbed my wrist and let me guide it to his mouth. Lips I remembered kissed with passion clasped the food, and he kept my gaze throughout the chewing and swallowing before he smiled.

"I could get used to this," he said. "The sauce is delicious."

I should have hated his guts, but at that moment, my chest filled with pure relief because I'd never seen this Vetusian eat before. He was handsome — that was a fact, not a fancy — and I was certain he would keep those prominent cheekbones even if he gained some weight.

With his eyes nothing but black pupils on grayish-white irises, he looked more alien than any other Vetusian. And yet, his eyes somehow no longer made me uncomfortable.

"Sophie, listen..." Tugging his knees against his chest, he released a sigh toward the universe first before his eyes locked with mine once more. "The way I acted when you came to my room and the things I said? I was awful, and I want to apologize. And while I'm not trying to make excuses for my behavior, I want you to understand that I'm not in a good place right after I take my... medication."

He pronounced that last word differently than usual, as if something had altered the taste of it, and his tongue twisted at the odd sensation. One might almost believe he had doubts, questioning for the first time if, perhaps, he did have a problem.

"Medication," I repeated, taking a bite of the fettuccine and a piece of breaded chicken.

He lifted his hand toward the underside of his arm, thumb rubbing over the faded track mark. "When I'm like this, I need you to stay away from me. That guy you met in that room? That's not me, Sophie."

Yeah, there were many versions of Adeas living in that body. He could go from the kindest, gentlest, most respectful guy I've ever met, to slicing my heart into pieces my saying nothing more than *leska* with such disgust it shredded my soul.

The best thing I could do was stay away from him. And then who would spend time with me? Talk to me for hours? Adeas wasn't just *that healer junkie* anymore. He was my healer junkie friend.

When I offered him the fork, he took it and tried

twirling the pasta himself like he'd watched me do it, losing the nest only twice before he took a generous bite. He even moaned at the taste.

"Perhaps you should bring us food from there more often," I said. "We could eat it together."

"I'd love to, but it's pricey. As much as I'd like to afford it for you, I can't."

I tensed at that. "Then how did you pay for this?

"Not the way you think I did," he said with a boyish grin and loaded up on another shrimp. "I sold some of my old textbooks so I could bring you something. And I also got you this..."

He reached behind his back, retrieving one of those colored cubes for smart people. "The dock master gave me this as a gift. Said it's imported from Earth, so I thought you might like it."

I turned it in my hand with a chuckle. "Goodness, you sure have faith in my intellect, huh?"

"It's easy. Just requires focus and patience."

"Yeah, well..." I began twisting the layers, messing up the perfectly lined-up colors since I knew that was about all I could do with this thing. "I'm more of a Slinky kinda girl."

"Slinky?"

"A spring you watch going down the stairs." When he lifted a brow at me, I added, "Don't judge until you've seen it for yourself. It's fascinating."

As much as I liked the carbonara, I loved watching Adeas eat it even more. So I busied myself with pretending I was trying to solve my messed-up cube while he ate the rest of my meal.

Eventually, he pushed the empty bowl aside, his face stern. "I found someone to smuggle you off-planet and back to Earth."

My heart shouldn't have jumped at that the way it did. Didn't I know better than to put my faith in a junkie? Mom had promised me once that we would get out of that mold-infested trailer. And we did... when the owner of the trailer park came and kicked us out since she hadn't paid rent in four months.

"You don't trust me anymore," he said and scooted up next to me, running his hands through my hair until my scalp tingled. "I mean to uphold every promise I make you, Sophie. The vessel leaves in a little less than two lunar cycles, and you will be on it."

Instead of pulling away from his touch, my head somehow plopped onto his shoulder, taking in that body which had grown so familiar to me. "And how do I make it to that vessel, huh?"

"There's a hidden way out through the sweatmines. A friend of mine, Yorim, will wait with his personal stargazer at the end of the tunnel and bring you straight to the cargo dock. I was thinking during the next masquerade since most guards will be at the casino then."

An overwhelming, grinding mix of hope and doubt stirred the recent meal until my stomach ached. How much I wanted to believe him. Before Adeas, my life had been agony, but at least my misery was constant and reliable. With him in it, it was a rollercoaster with peaks of intimacy and valleys of betrayal. How did I know when I could trust him? And when I couldn't?

His arm wrapped around me, not forceful and yet somehow prodding me against him. "Let me take you to your tub. I can tell you the story of how our second sun took the Joseon mountain as mate while I wash you."

That did sound amazing, but I shook my head. "I showered right after my shift."

"Hmm." Lips brushed a kiss against my temple as he got up. "Be right back."

He returned less than a minute later and sat down behind me, legs wide. Arm wrapped around my middle, he gave one tug and pulled my ass flush with his crotch. Before I managed to voice a complaint, something tingled my scalp so nicely my head all but lolled back into my neck.

Adeas brushed my hair, the monotone *phft...phft... phft* of the rounded teeth gliding through strands comforting. With a deep exhale, I closed my eyes and allowed myself to lean back against his chest.

"I could do this all night," he said. "It's a soothing experience somehow. Probably because I don't even own a hairbrush. I just rake my fingers through and that's it."

"That gets tough once your hair reaches a certain length."

"Please forgive me," he whispered, his breath caressing the side of my neck. "I'm not usually like that, and I want nothing more than to save you."

"Why?"

"Because you have two sides as well," he said, what followed taking my breath away. "*Leska* is cold and bitter, and I worry that she'll make the sweet Sophie fade away if you stay here much longer."

The brushing slowed while his other hand stroked down along my neck, fingertips feathering over my breast before he cupped it. "I like Sophie way too much to let her disappear."

I arched my back with a moan, once more enjoying his touch to a degree I could neither explain nor justify. Adeas had a way of making me want to give him everything although he had asked for nothing. Nothing but my soul...

Lower and lower his fingers trailed, circling my navel

while his kisses became demanding. My head turned to search for his mouth all on its own. His lips immediately claimed mine, his tongue swiping over them before he pushed through.

The brush hit the blanket with a muffled *tok*, and his other hand cupped my cheek, making a retreat from this kiss impossible. Adeas tasted as if we'd returned from a date at Olive Garden, moaning into my mouth while his chest expanded furiously against my back.

Eager fingers dropped from my knee to the inside of my thigh, the fabric of my nightgown caressing my skin as they shoved it upward. It gathered around my hips, exposing me to the slight chill of the late, quiet night.

The moment he pushed my panties aside, I gasped as if nobody had ever touched me there before, my heart drumming so hard he had to hear it. This was different than anything else I'd ever experienced, but Adeas didn't allow my legs to clench shut.

"Sweet Sophie," he whispered against my ear, hand cupping my pussy and rubbing in circular motions too delicious to be anything but wrong. "When was the last time a male has tended to *your* needs."

Never.

The answer was never.

And while I didn't voice it, Adeas seemed to have understood just fine, his hand still holding my sex in his palm while one finger slowly dipped inside of me.

"Ahh," I gasped, riding up against him as I braced my feet for the blanket, toes curling underneath.

"Do you hear this?" He wiggled his hand, sending a throbbing into my clit while everything down there smacked. "My finger is drenched in your need for release, but I will stop if you ask me to."

"I — I shouldn't," I stammered, and yes, that was a fact. He was an addict, unpredictable, and I was a whore who couldn't afford to feel, to long. To *be*long.

He scooted closer, hard shaft throbbing against my ass, finger curling inside a pussy dripping wet with need. "Ask me to stop and I will."

No, he couldn't stop.

I frantically shook my head, gasping at my own reaction, but was it so wrong to get something in return after a year of giving?

A second finger joined the other, making my slick hunger pool where the rest of his hand still cupped a place defiled by so many. So many. And yet he treated it with such care, thumb putting gentle pressure onto my clit while delicious heat engulfed me.

My thighs spread wider and my breasts moved above the heave of my chest, sweet little moans mixing with the ones coming low from his throat. I lifted my pelvis ever so slightly to meet each thrust of his fingers, angled so nicely inside me my walls convulsed in warning. Or promise?

His cock swelled against me, twitched, pulsed, but he only did so much as grind against me with a groan now and then. Otherwise, his attention lay purely on how I arched my back. From the corners of my eyes, I watched him observe me, his brows furrowing as he studied my reactions. He tried to please me. Me, the prostitute whose entire existence had been reduced to pleasing others.

"I can hear you thinking," came as a warning rumble from his throat. "Stop thinking and just give in to how good I make you feel. Take something for yourself, Sophie. I'm providing it gladly."

He fused his lips with mine once more, fingers fucking me with more intensity while he pulsed the pressure on my clit. My body clenched up tight and my eyes pressed shut, a whole-body shiver encapsulating me, *oh hell*.

Something alarmingly close to a scream lodged from my throat.

Adeas swung his palm onto my mouth and pressed down to muffle it, slamming his fingers hard, again and again, as everything inside me convulsed and the cage fell away from me a second time. Everything spun, waves of pleasure coursing through me before they ebbed into the muffled silence of the night.

"What about you?" I asked, panting.

Without a word spoken, he lay us down and pulled me against him, my head resting on his chest. Slightly trembling fingers stroked down my back, and I lifted my head to meet his face. "Your hands are starting to shake."

"It's wearing off," he said with a strained smile.

"Do you need to leave to... take care of it?"

He hesitated for a long while, an internal battle playing out all over his features. When he arched his back and shoved on the blankets, I lifted my weight off him so he could get up and leave. Feed that demon inside him with poison. But he never got up.

Adeas merely pushed one arm underneath his head to get comfortable, then pulled me back against his chest. "I'll manage. For now, all I need is you in my arms."

A picture of the Jal'zar resting on his chest played before me, that anger it stirred in me... nasty and vile. "When I came into your room, you held a Jal'zar in your arms just like you're holding me now." When he frowned, almost as if recalling if what I said was true, I added, "I didn't like it."

A long exhale blew from his nostrils. "That surprises me, considering how much you hate my kind."

I soaked in the heat of my trembling healer, something deep within in me resonating with this very moment. The Empire had let me down, yes, but they had let him down as well. Suddenly, I wasn't so sure anymore which one of us needed saving.

"I don't remember holding a Jal'zar female," he whispered. "But I recall every single night I've held you in my arms like this. Those memories burn so deep I won't ever be able to forget."

His words smoothed over my heart.

"I hate your kind for making me feel worthless," I said with a kiss against his jaws. "But I don't hate you." *Don't hate you at all...*

FIFTEEN

Adeas

The next evening, my body burned on the inside, the sweat it pushed from my pores turning me itchy, turning me so fucking furious I wanted to scrape the skin off my body. Rip my shirt off and drag myself over the stone wall inside the tunnel until everything came off in layers.

I shouldn't have stayed with Sophie...

Should have left and medicated before it got this bad.

"P-please," I already stammered where I still should have managed okay. Assholes must have spiked the product. Why else would it suddenly not last long enough anymore? "Just a l-little so I can... you know... p-pull through until later."

"You get it when you get it," the Kokonian female said, glancing over at the guards before she whispered, "If you pay, I can slip you some."

Right, right, right.

Fingers nervously dug into my pockets, scavenging, searching for credits. Over and over again, they came out empty, and rage stiffened my knuckles to a degree I couldn't punch my hands into my pockets a fifth time.

I sunk down onto the ground and pulled my knees deep into my chest, rocking back and forth, back and forth, back and forth, fucking shit. Was I running a fever? Because why else would I be sweating like this?

"W-what if I get you something o-other than credits?" The moment I grabbed the edge of her table and pulled myself up, an earthquake seemed to shake the surface. "I c-can maybe look for —"

"Credits only." My stomach convulsed at her words, but it fell right through me when she added, "I'm not taking any of your stolen shit again. That ring you gave me? *Leska* caused a massive scene over it and I'm not having any of that drama."

A noisy retch pushed from my throat. "I didn't steal her ring."

Her scoff licked the marrow from my bones.

Vision blurry, my very existence distorted, my eyes searched her fingers. She better not be wearing that ring. Seeing it on her finger would kill me!

Bam.

There it was.

A bright green gemstone on a scaled digit, with specks of dark blue around the socket as if it wanted to change color. Turn black, like that gaping hole opening at my core, threatening to suck me in, swallow me whole.

I stole Sophie's ring.

And while I didn't remember it, it had to be true.

My head hit the ground, hard, and I stared up at the arched ceiling, my brain spinning inside my skull without mercy. I wanted to score so bad but even more so I wanted to die.

I let my mind sink into empty oblivion, a sort of limbo containing nothing but the fact that I was a thief, a liar. An addict?

Organs smoldered. Blood boiled.

I swung my palms onto my face as if to hide from the sickening truth, but the way I clenched my eyes shut only gave room to memories. Nothing but snippets floating there without sense or rhyme, and yet powerful enough they drove shame into my core. How I'd reached for the ring while Sophie slept in my arms. How I'd placed a kiss onto her forehead before I'd slipped it into my jeans.

How could I have done that to her?

My head turned toward a stomp right beside my ear, black boots so close they gave off the scent of polish. "Just give him his cut before he vomits all over the place."

One hard tug yanked me to my feet.

The guard tossed me against the table where I almost doubled over, knees threatening to buckle underneath me. My entire world shifted around me, but that searing heat I carried inside me wouldn't go away. Neither did the itch, prickling underneath my skin like parasites, crawling, creeping, coursing along my veins.

"Take it and get out of here."

A silver sphere pushed into view.

One tremble chased the next, my body quivering underneath floods of heat and tides of freezing cold.

I wouldn't take it.

Wouldn't touch it.

I didn't need to.

I could stop. Right now. And I would.

How had that sphere ended up in my palm?

Why did my thumb reach toward the button?

Click.

Just a little.

Fuck no.

I had to speak to Sophie. Admit to what I'd done and tell her that something was terribly, terribly wrong with me. Something had to be, right?

It took an eternity to will my fingers into closing that damn sphere. Body and mind growing equally exhausted at something that required less than four muscles, telling my hand to drop it was impossible. It formed into a tight fist around it.

Fine. If my hands wouldn't listen, then I'd command my legs instead. They carried me back into the tunnel, traces of mildew whipping my face when I sprinted back toward *Taigh Arosh*.

Just a little.

Fuck you.

I had to get better. For Sophie.

What for? She'll leave for Earth.

Shut up. Shut up. Shut up.

Rivulets of sweat ran down my spine, each of them burning into my skin like acid. My shirt clung to it, rubbing the layers off until it grated over my exposed vertebrae. I must have left a trail of blood behind, but a glance down the stairs revealed nothing. Just empty space trying to pull me down. I wouldn't let it.

After I spoke to Sophie, I would find Titean at the infirmary. Hadn't he mentioned a healer and a new program? I could talk to him. Yeah, I could do that. They'd fix me up in no time and I could be better for Sophie, because she deserved only the best male by her side.

I would go to Earth with her.

She's only using you to get out.

I ignored that voice right along with those clambering

legs hushing across my skin. Her soul was mine. She'd bargained it away, and I refused to return it.

I opened her secret door.

I sneaked inside.

No matter how quiet I tried to be, I must have tumbled in there given the way moans and grunts resonated from every-fucking-where. Wait a moment. My lips were pressed shut, not a single sound vibrating from my chest.

My body stiffened, eyes fixed on the bed.

The most beautiful, innocent creature I'd ever seen tossed her shiny blonde hair, her back arching as she sat astride a Vetusian. And unless this was some fucked up out-of-body experience, then that Vetusian wasn't me. The guy underneath her wrapped his filthy hands around her waist, pushing her down onto a cock that wasn't mine.

She glanced toward the door.

Sophie stared right at me, her pace first slowing, until she startled and picked it up again, her eyes filling with pain, but it didn't hold nearly enough to match that agony inside my chest.

It was more than I could take.

I stepped back out of her room and closed the door, sinking to the ground between the frame. Those parasites must have gobbled me down to bone, and yet my hands shook in front of me, entirely intact, skin still attached.

What did you expect? She's leska.

No. She's Sophie.

Sophie for you, but leska for everyone else.

True.

And while I'd never given it much thought, it now filled me with a rage that seeped out of my mangled body and left me in a pool of self-pity right there in the hallway. Everyone fucked her. Everyone but me.

Knowing it was one thing.

Seeing her writhe her body...

Smelling the moisture they created...

Hearing her fake moans...

Just a little.

Yeah. Just a little.

Or maybe a lot?

By the time the sphere rolled out of my palm and across the hallway, it seemed to spill very little souldust onto the carpet. My nostrils burned with dry dust and even dryer air, pushing its way into my sinus cavity, my nerves, my brain. Everything turned bleak around me, the only proof that I was still alive my watering eyes and that rage gushing in my arteries.

"Why did you come here in the middle of my shift?" The moment I lifted my head toward the sun of *Taigh Arosh*, she threw a palm to her cheek. "Did you just use out here?"

I pushed myself up and floated into her room. "Fuck you, Sophie."

Seriously. Fuck her.

Fuck all of this.

This was too damn painful.

Why did this hurt so bad?

"You asked me to stay away from you when you're like this, and then you get high right in front of my room?" She pushed a towel against my chest. "Wipe your damn face because you've got blue smeared all over, and then leave."

I shoved the towel back against her, making myself stumble back at the motion. "Did you kiss him?"

"What?" She stared at me from furrowed brows, then shoved the towel across my face with such force one might have thought she wanted to drown me in fabric. "You know very well that I don't kiss."

"You kiss me."

"That's different."

"Why?" Angry hands gripped the towel and tossed it away, only to wrap around her arms and hold her in place. "I want you to... to —" I sidestepped at a wave of dizziness, and she flinched when I ripped her right with me, refusing to let her go. I would never let her go. "Tell me why you kiss me."

Tell me that I'm more than just a means to an end.

A punch against my chest too strong for such a small creature shuffled me back. "Because I like you more than I should, and this moment is just more proof. You need to leave this room."

"So another Vetusian can come and fuck you?"

"You're so damn high you can't even stand straight anymore," she snarled, throwing her palm at something that appeared to be rock-solid legs underneath me. "I regret the day I let you in my life, Adeas. This isn't fair... isn't fair... You need to get help, or you'll end up dead."

Dead?

Rage pumped from arteries into veins and all the way into the tiniest vessels. Proof enough that I was very much alive. I gave myself a quick scan.

Trembles. Gone.

Stutter. Gone.

What the fuck was her problem?

"I don't want you to help me anymore," Sophie mumbled. "I want you to help yourself because I can't watch you fall apart. I've done that once, and I won't do it again with you."

"You need me," I said with a snort. "Do they ever make you come like you did against my fingers last night?"

"Stop this." Angry stomps loosened the belt around her robe, exposing a body I'd never enjoyed, occupied by a soul I'd enjoyed too much. "Get out. I don't want you around me while you're high."

"I'm not high."

"Yes, Adeas, you're fucking high because you're an addict. A *sgu'dal*."

My fingers dug deep into her upper arms, rage-spiked blood pumping into my cock. I pushed her against the wall with a *thump* and ground against her, watching those disobedient hands of mine clasp her way too tightly, and yet I couldn't stop.

"Maybe I am high," I growled, something inside me dying when she flinched, eyes wide in fear. I had to stop this, I knew, but my mouth kept on running... "At least then I don't give a shit about who touches you. Won't picture you fucking every damn Vetusian clanking credits."

"I know you don't mean that." A thick swallow wandered down her throat. "You need to get yourself into rehab."

"I don't. I can stop."

Now her fingers trembled, gently stroking over my chest as her red-rimmed eyes begged me to ease the strain. I sunk my forehead against hers, then tasted her lips, forcing my knuckles to open up.

"I could stop if I wanted to," I whispered, my heart drumming harder and faster than it ever had. That was how much I wanted her. How something deep inside me said she was mine.

Small hands pushed against my shoulder, bringing

distance between us. "You don't even acknowledge that you're an addict."

"Because I'm not!" I shouted, slamming a fist against the wall before I pushed myself away from her. "You know nothing about me."

I paced around her tub, something dark expanding at my core, squeezing the air from my lungs. Who did she think she was, telling me those things? What did she know? *Leska* all high and mighty again...

"How did you get that nerve damage, Adeas?"

I kept my gaze glued to the ground, watching my ankles cave at every other step because they fucking melted. "During the Jal'zar invasion."

"You were still in training then. Probably didn't even have your license yet."

Both ankles popped out of their sockets and I stumbled back, arms flailing until they caught one of the bed posters. "I got shot in the back."

A blurry outline of Sophie appeared in front of me, face distorted but voice carrying enough accusation for me to picture her eyes cold. "You never participated in that war."

"You think you know me?" I snarled, sinking into something soft underneath me. "I got shot in the back. Why else would I have the trembles? The migraines?"

"Where exactly in your back?"

"I don't know." But shouldn't I? *Of course you do.* "Third lumbar."

My vision turned into nothing but flickers of light and dark, with specks of colors floating here and there. All the while, my heart seemed to slow right along with time, something soft caressing my vertebrae.

"There's nothing. No scar. No injury," a voice said,

sweet, but with a slight tremble on the undertone. "Do you remember the first time you got your medication?"

"*Choke on it, Vetusian,*" a menacing voice whispered, and I pushed myself onto legs that felt brittle underneath me in all this panic.

"Stay away from me!" I shouted, feet stumbling, body swaying. "Don't touch me!"

"Adeas... Adeas..." So much panic in that voice.

I caught a glimpse of Sophie reaching her arms toward me. Like a holographic image, unmoving, so fucking beautiful it tore my chest apart from the inside.

Then everything went dark.

Cold speckled my cheeks, my forehead.

Something wrapped around me.

Pulled me under.

Suffocated me.

SIXTEEN

Adeas

I woke to something astringent burning my nasal cavity, but it had nothing on that bite blazing down my throat. *Where am I?*

A blink.

Another, slower blink.

White sheets wrapped cool around my body, reflecting the bright light from above. Someone fumbled with my wrist. A freezing sensation tickled the top of my hand and deep into my vein. I flinched and turned my head, my pupils catching on the drip-drip-drip of the saline solution hanging from a hook next to me. I was at the infirmary?

A swallow.

It got stuck around my esophagus, immediate panic tensing my muscles. Something constricted my throat, and I swung my hands onto my face.

"Don't pull the feeding tube." I'd heard that voice before. "Relax your entire throat, Adeas."

Seemingly endless, the tube dislodged and retreated. It

tickled along my esophagus and seared my nostril, tears running down my face. I suppressed the urge to sneeze, which only increased the pain stabbing behind my temples.

Another swallow, this one tainted with iron.

"What... wha —" My voice broke off, entirely hoarse.

"What happened?" Bright light shone into my eyes. Left. Right. A sip of water was offered. "An engineer found you inside a maintenance bay at the cargo dock, drenched and unresponsive. Good thing he did because you were close to respiratory arrest."

Fog permeated my thoughts.

The last thing I remembered was... a sphere of souldust rolling from my hand. And then, nothing. *No wait!* A picture pushed through the fog: furious fingers wrapped around Sophie's arms. My stomach convulsed, the retch it triggered scraping along my already inflamed throat.

"Bowl's right there," Titean said, helping me clasp my fingers around the cool metal.

Nothing came out but grunts.

"Ask him about her." *That* voice, I'd never heard before.

Titean sat down beside me on my recovery pod, the regenerative lights warming me from underneath. "Adeas... who is Sophie?"

I let out a groan. "Sophie."

"That's right, brother. Can you tell us who she is?" A pause, and then, "*Where* she is?"

Who was *us*?

"We should just have taken his DNA sample," a second, unfamiliar voice grumbled deep.

Three people in this room. Only one familiar. What was going on here?

"I couldn't allow you to overstep his rights, Captain Balgiz," Titean said. "Law states he needs to give his consent for us to extract his DNA and run it through the databank. And even then, it might not come back with the result you're hoping for."

"Bullshit," the Captain snarled, swinging two massive arms in front of his chest, back leaning against the wall of a recovery room. "Sophie's clearly a human name. She's the only one we haven't tracked down yet. The only reason why we're holding back. By the heat of Heliar, I'm going to arrest his sorry ass if this *sgu'dal* passes out again. "

"Don't call him that." A healer, who wasn't Titean, stepped up to my bed, his eyes leeched into specks of green and blue. "Now that he's finally awake, how about you show him her hologram?"

With a grunt, the warrior pushed himself off the wall, gaze pinning me down as he stepped over. "Is this Sophie?"

He swiped over his com, one hologram after another coming together in nothing but mesmerizing smiles. Sophie, during a time before the invasion, sitting in the sand with moving waters in the background. Another showed her hanging upside down on a rod with her tongue poking out. She looked so... happy. So young. Unjaded.

"By the three Suns, healer," the warrior said, lip tugging into an aggressive snarl. "Have you seen this Earth female or not?"

Whatever puree they'd been feeding me, I groaned into the metal bowl. Easy-to-digest protein from the rancid taste of it...

"Step away from him," Titean said, pushing the Captain aside. "This is too much for him."

"Too much for him? For *him*?" The Captain kicked against a hover cart until it hit the wall across, all sorts of healer supplies clanking to the ground, grinding my brain. "And what about this eighteen-year-old girl, huh? Warden

Torin ordered me to extract her, and that's the only thing CAT cares about. I will make sure the High Court classifies him as informant, and I'll lock him up in this room until Sophie is found."

CAT. Fucking shit.

They would beat me up. They would arrest me against intergalactic treaty. Try me for... I didn't know... surely something. Conspiracy.

My heart didn't pump nearly as fast as I needed it to, heavy legs kicking the blanket off me. I rolled off the pod and landed on the hard ground with an *oomph*, soles slipping out underneath me.

"Whoa... where do you think you're going?" A thick arm wrapped around my chest, my limbs flailing as the CAT officer hoisted my naked body back onto the pod. "If you think I'll let you leave this building, then you clearly fried you brain with that shit."

"I didn't do anything illegal!" I frantically slapped at their hands, until all six of them held me in place. "You can't arrest me, and I didn't do anything. I know nothing."

The pod hummed low, like an electric current, sucking all strength from my limbs until I could no longer move. Quick bursts of breath rushed through dry, brittle lips, my mind going dizzy.

"Way to protect whoever you're working for, Adeas," Titean snarled. "They ditched you in a damn maintenance bay. Left you there to die on an overdose."

Overdose.

That word stung.

Stung deep and bled me out.

Of course Levear had kicked me to the streets. No business wanted a *sgu'dal* healer to die of an overdose right there at the establishment. Memories swamped me, reminding me of the ring, the argument with Sophie, the fact that I was a *sgu'dal*, an addict, a junkie. I'd realized it that night, the fact that I almost died only putting a ribbon on it.

"Leave me alone with him," the other healer said.

Reluctantly, the warrior left the room, and Titean followed behind after he turned down the electromagnetic restraints, offering me more comfort.

The remaining healer pulled himself a stool and sat down beside me, color-drained eyes meeting their equal. "How are you feeling?"

I had nothing to say to that guy.

But his question sparked an odd observation, none-theless. My body neither trembled nor shook. Aside from the brain fog, I felt... different.

He grabbed behind him and lifted a small box, letting it rattle. "Human healers call it Paraprofin. It's a drug containing an antidepressant, along with a slight stimulant and nerve inhibitors. Two maintenance injections a day. It suppresses withdrawal symptoms and significantly reduces the cravings for souldust. It's still in trial but, between us, it's a miracle coming straight from Earth."

When I only stared at him, wondering why he told me all this, he continued. "We've been treating you with this for close to eight suns now. You were out for most of it, always mumbling that name. Sophie."

Eight suns? Did Sophie know they'd kicked me onto the streets to die? Was she okay? Scared? Alone?

"Who are you?"

"My name is Melek," the healer said, crossing his legs in front of him. "I was once where you are now, barely alive. Until I dragged my sorry ass to rehab, went to Earth, found my *anam ghail*."

"Liar. You're not allowed on Earth."

"And what a drama that caused," he said on a chuckle. "You don't believe me? Check this out." He conjured up holograms, showing him with two Earth females. "That's my mate Katie. She's carrying my son, still very small in her stomach. Beside her is Grace, her daughter. She joined the healer stratum, so we don't see her very often right now."

"No *sgu'dal* has a human mate. The Empire doesn't even allow *recovered* addicts on Earth."

"Ah, but things are changing. Our sort has gained a very powerful voice, and she's speaking up for us before the Empire. It was Eden da taigh L'naghal who established the new rehab program on Earth. I work as head counselor there."

That was too good to believe. "Why are you showing me all this? That CAT officer wants to arrest me, doesn't he?"

"He does. And he probably will," Melek said. "Warden Torin sanctioned a mission trying to extract all abducted Earth females from Odheim. Quietly. No fuss. Out of sight of the intergalactic community, though he parked his entire brigade just outside the belt, willing to fight the cosmos for those women if it comes down to that."

I struggled against the remains of the electromagnetic forcefield until I pressed a palm to my sternum, as if it would help with this confusion. Someone other than me was coming to save Sophie? But I would save her.

"Are you aware of the fact that you're an addict, Adeas?"

Where I expected rage, I found paralyzing shame, agonizing guilt, as if whatever he'd given me had lifted a veil of lies. Lies I'd told my friends. Sophie. Myself...

I clenched my eyes shut. "Yes, I'm addicted."

There. The truth was out.

My next inhale expanded my chest wider, against the pod's restraints, filling me with a serenity I hadn't experienced in so long. I saw everything so clearly now, lies no longer constructing the world around me the way I wanted it to look. Instead, they all fell away, painting an ugly picture of what was my life.

Melek patted my arm. "Good. Now that we're being truthful here and all, tell me about Sophie. Somehow, you know that human female. Perhaps you're her... healer? Titean told me he's saving up credits for you, so I assume you're trying to help her? Get her out?"

I said nothing, and yet confessed to it all with one single nod, my heart shattering into millions of pieces. What made me think that I could actually help her, if I couldn't even help myself?

"Captain Balgiz wanted to run your DNA through the databank while you were out, so he could see if she might pop up as your match. Prove that you are, indeed, in contact with her."

"My match?" My chest constricted.

Regardless of how drawn I felt to Sophie, it had never really occurred to me that she might be my *anam ghail*. Surely fate couldn't have such a twisted humor, forcing an abducted female to rely on a fucking junkie? Was that why I'd felt so compelled to ask for her soul? Because I'd sensed it belonged to me all along?

"It would make sense, wouldn't it?" the healer asked. "Fate has a way of throwing people together in the unlikeliest of scenarios. Trust me because I speak from experience." He shook his head and glanced at the floor for a moment. "Do you want to find out?"

I stared at the DNA tester he pulled from one of his

pockets, the looming weight of responsibility scaring the crap out of me. "I'm not sure."

He gave a nod of understanding, as if he could read the concerns from my face. "For cooperating, the Empire will allow you to join the new rehab program. There's no reason why you wouldn't make a good mate to her. Once you're clean."

"And then?"

"And then, the hard work begins." Tester clasped in his hand, he leaned over, his eyes narrowing. "Paraprofin for six lunar cycles to help you with the physical withdrawal. We'll slowly wean you off it after that. We can start treating you here until CAT extracts Sophie, and you head to Earth, where you can then complete the program."

Six lunar cycles.

My heart gave one massive wham at the thought. Almost half a solar cycle separated from Sophie. But wasn't that worth it if it meant I could be the mate she deserved? But what if she didn't want me? We'd talked a lot about *her* going to Earth — never about *me* going with her.

I slipped my arm off my sternum and reached toward him. "Take my DNA."

"You don't have a lot of old track marks, that's good," he said, the poke of the machine barely noticeable. "Can you tell me where exactly they keep her?"

"I'm not telling you anything until this is a DNA-coded deal."

He chuckled. "Braincells are still working fine, it seems. That increases your chance of success drastically. I will leave for Earth in two suns, but Captain Balgiz and his team remain here on Odheim," Melek said as we waited. "They're put up here at the infirmary, where their mission can go unnoticed."

"I never liked working for them," I mumbled, more to myself than him. "Hate the way they treat the females."

"Nobody gets it more than me. Addiction messes with your moral code. And yet you chose to help her. It's honorable."

A scoff wormed from my chest. The way I remembered it, I hadn't been quite so honorable the last time I saw Sophie.

He placed the little computer on a stool beside him. "It's a priority extraction kit, but it'll still take a while until we have the result. Assuming she's your fated mate, may I ask if you bonded yourself to her?"

I shook my head. "No. We never mated."

Didn't we, though? Because, technically, we had mated, even if we'd never completed the act. Assuming Sophie was indeed my fated one, had we unknowingly bonded ourselves to each other?

"They keep that close of a watch on her?" Melek asked, turning the electromagnetic restraints off.

"No. I just... chose not to. She's more precious than that, and I didn't want to be like... like..."

"All the others." A painful silence expanded there for a moment before he added, "How long have you been using? Do you remember the first time you decided to snort it? Slam it?"

Weak arms pushed me up to sit. "Someone decided that for me."

"What do you mean?"

I raked a hand through my hair and pointed at my clothes sitting in the cubicle across. Not every truth could be faced at once. "Mind if I get dressed?"

"Not at all. The credits your friend saved up for you are over there as well," he said, reaching a hand out to help me onto surprisingly steady legs. "You gained some weight already. Don't forget to eat, because your body needs to be strong to go through rehab. Nausea is very common, so we serve most foods in puree form, which is easier to digest."

I climbed into my jeans, torn around the knee but they'd washed them. As they had with my shirt, which I slipped into before I put my shoes back on. "How quickly can CAT get her out?"

Melek shrugged. "Captain Balgiz can answer that better, but I know they're planning to extract all females at once to avoid a prolonged presence."

"I can smuggle her out," I said. "Everything's set up. Instead of putting her on a cargo vessel, I could bring her here."

He gave me a pitiful smile. "You're an addict, Adeas. I know you mean well, but chances of you succeeding are slim."

I leaned back against the pod, my thoughts spinning. Sophie most likely had no idea what had happened to me. She was alone, scared, and maybe, just maybe, she was concerned for me although, burnt ashes, I didn't deserve it.

She'd asked me to save myself, and that was exactly what I would do. But not returning to *Taigh Arosh*? I couldn't just leave her there for however long it would take CAT to get her out. And that massive officer? He hated my guts already. Who said I could trust him? He might just as well lock me up, and Sophie would never find out what happened.

But Melek had a point.

The moment I would step out of here, I would fall back into old habits without the Paraprofin.

"This medication won't do the entire work for you," Melek said. "You need to focus. Keep your mind occupied.

If the urge returns, distract yourself. Work out. Read. Jump on the bed or do whatever the fuck it takes to keep your mind off it."

"I will get better," I said.

For myself. For Sophie.

Melek gave a nod of approval. "After the six lunar cycles of initial withdrawal, you will join cognitive and behavioral therapy in our inpatient program for one or two solar cycles."

Wait... what?

My stomach clenched, convulsed.

"You're going to lock me up?"

"Of course we'll lock you up," he said. "It's a nice place, though. You've got your own room. Food's excellent. The park is stunning, especially in fall when the colors change. We offer so much to get your mind in the right place. Wood-working, pottery, something called yoga..."

His voice faded into a rushing sound at the back of my mind, talking about all those things with such pride as if it didn't mean it would separate me from Sophie for several solar cycles. He could just as well have made it an eternity. Fuck, where was that metal bowl?

I wanted to throw up all over again, my stomach already irritated from the feeding tube, but this made it worse. Sophie would flat-out forget about me.

I couldn't just *not* return to her now, letting her rot in that awful place, alone, and then show up in three solar cycles like, 'Hey, it's me, that junkie who disappeared almost three Earth years ago. Want to be my mate?' No fucking way.

They wanted to save her? Fine by me, but I would be there, drying her tears until this was over. That was the least I owed her.

"Adeas?"

I stood up straight. "What?"

"I just asked you if it's okay if I go look for the Captain now?" he asked, head cocked. "He can draw up a DNA-coded deal, and then you can go straight to work. Sounds good?"

"Yeah. Sure. I'll wait here."

I watched him leave.

From the hover cart, I grabbed a holo-pad and wrote down the location of *Taigh Arosh*, along with Sophie's room and other helpful information. Then I grabbed the credits, box of Paraprofin, and fucking ran.

SEVENTEEN

Sophie

Thick and gooey, the mascara clumped my lashes together, the deep black only accentuating my puffy, red eyes. I pinched the lump between my fingers, then took the brush and went over it a second time.

Even after several layers of concealer, the girl staring back at me from the mirror carried a sadness plastered to her face not even the winged eyeliner could hide. There was only so much make up could do when you'd cried all night. Every night. For a week.

I regret the day I let you in my life.

An easy thing to say during a moment of fury.

Now Adeas was missing again, and I regretted my words. When he was bad, he was the worst; but when he was good, he was absolutely amazing.

I closed the mascara and placed it back onto my vanity, that invisible thing hooked behind my sternum aching like a never-ending cramp. Not sure what I hated Adeas more for:

the terrible things he'd said, or how he had me sitting here, praying for his safe return.

Ripping the scrunchie from my wrist, I tied my hair into a messy bun, my thoughts drifting to the night he'd almost drowned.

I'd pulled him from the tub, screaming bloody murder until guards came, and dragged him out of the water with blue and red foam bubbling from his nostrils. Mom and her boyfriends had put me through enough close-calls I recognized an overdose when I saw one.

The guards had carried him off, and that was that.

Nobody saw him. Nobody talked about him.

Adeas was just one *sgu'dal* healer of many: here one day, gone another. Maybe to return. Most likely not. Nobody really gave a shit, and I'd heard Levear talk about finding a replacement. What else could that mean other than that Adeas was dead?

Another cramp behind my sternum, almost as if that Vetusian had planted something there. A seed of some sort. Growing daily, threatening to crack through my ribcage. This wasn't normal. Who would develop feelings for the Vetusian addict she used solely for the purpose of getting out of here? That was just sick.

Another cramp.

Ouch.

I threw my head into my neck and blinked back tears, fanning my hands over my eyes because I couldn't risk smudging everything a second time. Why did I feel as if someone had ripped a part of my soul from my chest? When he'd demanded it, I had no issues giving away. A soul wasn't real, was it?

Until half of it was missing, the pain of it so agonizing I cursed that healer. And while I cursed him, I wished him back because... dammit... I missed falling to sleep in his arms. I missed *him*. Not all versions of Adeas, but the one which made me feel like a normal young woman. Just dating a broke healer who'd scrambled his credits together to bring me pasta.

Why did he have to walk in on me while I was busy with a client? He was fine then, and there was no doubt in my mind it was what had triggered him to snort himself into nirvana. Even now, I couldn't forget the hurt he'd carried in his eyes, or the shame I'd experienced at that moment, no matter how little say I had over my body.

I was a whore.

He was an addict.

Together, we were nothing.

Except for, maybe, unhealthy.

Numb fingers grabbed the red lipstick and started on the outside of my upper lip. A steady hand glided toward the center with one smooth move. I switched sides. Slow. Easy.

The moment it set into motion, my door flung open with a screech. "He's back!"

I startled so hard the lipstick went off track until it came to a stop at the tip of my nose. "What are you talking about?"

Izara swung her hand toward the door, her eyes ripped wide open, her tail flicking so fast it was dizzying. "Adeas is back."

My heart faltered to a halt. "No." *Please be true...*

"Yes! He's in Levear's office." She kicked my door shut, hurried over to where I sat at my vanity, and kneeled down. "I walked by and heard them talking. Apparently, Levear ordered the guards to ditch Adeas somewhere at the docks after he overdosed."

My lips pressed tightly together, slathered so thickly I sensed the lipstick squeeze away underneath the force. "I figured they'd just kick him out to die." It wasn't like Levear would put him up in the infirmary or something and pay to treat a case of overdose his drugs had caused.

I placed my elbow onto the vanity and sunk my head into my palm. What was I supposed to do? See him? Not see him?

A tingle started in my toes and wandered up my calves, turning my legs restless. Why did I feel like I wanted to run down there and hug him? I was setting myself up for disappointment.

He would use again.

He would overdose again.

One day, he wouldn't return.

"Adeas is asking for his job back," Izara said. "I couldn't hear anything else because Sehrin turned the corner, and I had to hurry back upstairs. But I'm sure Levear will take him back in since there's no alternative."

Better stay away from him, Sophie.

I rose and tossed the lipstick onto my vanity. "I have to see him."

"*Leska*, you really shouldn't —"

Dodging that clawed hand trying to hold me back, I rushed out the back door and along the corridors, down down down the stairs, then left. I had to see him. That was all. One look.

Carpets worn and ceiling stained yellow in some spots, the back hallways showed the true value of the otherwise opulent *Taigh Arosh*. Back here, traces of mold swept in from the tunnel, which connected to the sweatmines, but I turned the other way instead.

I headed toward the opposite wing, which housed most

staff as well as Levear's office. A direction I usually avoided, but I had to make sure Adeas was truly back.

Just one look.

Only one.

All I needed was to see him alive, and I would turn around and go back upstairs. Ignore him from now on and avoid him at all costs because this male stirred feelings in me I couldn't allow.

And yet, while my entire body hummed with dread, the undertones of hopeful excitement turned me nervous. He was nothing to me, I reminded myself. Just a junkie I used to get out of this hell. I would find him alive, nod, then turn around and go back upstairs.

No, fuck that.

I would tell him how much I hated him. How much he'd scared me, and that I never ever wanted to see him again. Demand he stay away from me and shove him for good measure. One punch for each time he'd insulted me.

Turning the next corner, I took a deep breath.

I would tell him all those things, I would —

Thud!

I hit a wall of warmth and familiarity.

Adeas bumped into me full force, and I flailed my arms for balance. Where his feet stumbled back, his eyes immediately found mine. They locked, and not even the sway of our bodies broke them apart. His hands darted for my waist, strong and sure, saving me from tumbling to the ground.

An eternity passed.

Or maybe just a second?

However long or short, it erased all those things I had to do, all those things I had to say. I lifted my hand for that punch, but it cupped his cheek instead, his skin too warm for a corpse.

That thing behind my sternum crooned.

Only one look.

And that one look fucking tore me apart from the inside, turning my body into a shivering mess of relief. "I thought you were dead."

Adeas glanced around the empty hallway. Without a word in reply, he grabbed my wrist and turned on his heels. He pulled me a few steps back to where I'd come from and turned left, pushed down the handle to his room, kicking the door shut behind us with his heel as he wrapped his arms around me.

And I couldn't resist.

My lips pressed against his with such demand my teeth ached, feeling his heat, his breath, the expansion of his lungs. I kissed him so furiously, hunger rising, heating my chest and, shit, I wanted him to touch me so badly.

"Fuck, Sophie..." He rumbled low, sucked my lower lip between his before he let it go and followed it up with a lick of his tongue. "The way you kiss me makes me wonder if I turned into an Earth man overnight."

Adeas smelled like cotton, fresh and clean, his mouth passionate against mine. Dead healers didn't kiss like that, and the realization made heat course through my body.

But he retreated on a long exhale, red-smudged lips parting and pressing back together as if unsure what to say. And I just stared at those cheeks, more rounded than only a week ago, or was that a trick of the light filtering in from the tiny window?

Not only was Adeas not dead, but he looked more alive than ever before. Not exactly healthy, but the veins didn't show as much around his neck. The tendons on his under-arms had all but disappeared. What had happened?

"This isn't the welcome I'd expected," he said on an

insecure chuckle. "I was more thinking along the lines of you smacking me, or throwing stuff, but I won't complain."

"Don't ever do this to me again." I cupped his cheek with one hand and cleaned lipstick off him with the other. A wasted effort because he pulled me in for another kiss.

"I'm so sorry," he whispered, chasing after his own words with hot and succulent kisses. "It won't ever happen again."

Yes it would, but I didn't care nearly as much as I should have and let my hands roam down his chest. A chest my fingers had mapped countless times when I'd rested against it. I sensed his chest expanding against my touch, faster, faster, and let my fingertip trail down along those abs which had his torso curl slightly at the sensation.

I took in the shift of muscle, rasped in a deep breath for courage, and let my hand drop to the bulge straining against his jeans. A hard shaft pulsed against thick denim, and I traced along the outline of a cock I wanted inside me.

Adeas moaned against the corner of my mouth, fingers digging into my ass as uncoordinated steps swayed us over to his bed. He lowered me down with something between a groan and a grunt, which lasted the whole agonizing grind of his cock against my crotch.

Pressed into his sheets, his scent was undeniable and wafted all around me. I turned my head, let his kisses burn across the sensitive skin on my neck, counting less books in his bookshelf than the last time I'd been here. This could just as well have been a dorm room at some college, and I wanted it to be. Wanted us to be two young people, getting it on before they would head to the movies.

I let my hand slip into his jeans, small fingers wrapping around his hard shaft. Each time I ran them down his cock, his crown bobbed against the inside of my wrist, pre-cum settling warm and wet against my skin.

"It's too much risk," he said gently, and of course he was right, no matter how much I ached for his touch. "I'll mate you properly if that's what you want, Sophie. But not here. Not now."

Adeas pulled his lips away from mine as he stared down at me, squinted eyes taking their sweet time to drink in every detail of my face. His fingers dug into my hair, fumbling, gripping my scrunchie before he pulled it from the strands.

He could have said many things.

Made a promise he wouldn't keep. Explained where he'd been for an entire week. Apologized for the things he'd said as he always did. But what followed made my heart skip a beat.

"I stole your ring."

That wasn't news, but his confession came as a surprise. He had been so adamant that he hadn't taken it, and while I'd known it was a lie, I'd also understood it had been a truth to him. Whatever had happened in the last eight days had changed something about Adeas, and that wasn't just wishful thinking. I sensed it like a string hooked between us, no longer playing off-tune when his words tugged.

"It was just a cheap plastic thing from a gumball machine."

But he shook his head. "I stole your ring and traded it for a sphere of souldust." An inhale stuttered over trembling lips. "I stole your ring because I... I'm an addict."

Shock crept through me like a living thing, starting as a twitch around my eyes from where it spread, cascading down my body in little quakes. His eyes betrayed no lie or deception, leeched irises sparkling with tears and something else. Awareness? Determination? Hope?

"You asked me to save myself, and that's what I'm going to do," he said as he pressed his forehead against mine. "Because I realized that I won't be able to help you, unless I help myself as well."

My teeth chattered, not because I was cold but Adeas wrapped me tighter anyway. "You're going into rehab?"

He let out a little sigh. "Eventually, yes. But not until I got you out of here."

Heavy on its threads, my heart plummeted. "Adeas, my mom had the idea of detoxing —"

"Shh." Fingers stroked over my lips to silence me, and he glanced over his shoulder, where footsteps came and went from the hallway. He didn't speak again until everything was quiet once more. "It will work out, because now I have this."

He rolled off me, leaned over the edge of his bed, and pulled a box out from underneath it. "An addiction counselor, um, gave me this at the infirmary. It'll help me overcome the withdrawal."

The box popped open, and he pulled the leaflet from it, which crinkled as he unfolded it. "I get it's not easy for you to put trust in me, especially with your mother and all. I'm determined to get better, but I might need your help."

I took the paper from his clasp and held it against the window. "Paraprofin. Does this come from Earth?"

"Yes, and he called it a miracle. They treated me for eight suns with it, and look at me, I mean..." He tossed the box onto his bed with a rattle, holding his splayed fingers out in front of him, only trembling at each of his chuckles. "Look at those hands, Sophie. Those are surgeon hands right there. One bottle is half empty, but it should be enough to get me through this."

His soft laugh filled me with such concentrated joy, it radiated into every single of my cells, warming me from within. "Can you find it in your heart to help this Vetusian *sgu'dal*?"

His choice of words hit home, and from the way he pressed his lips together, I could tell there had been purpose in it. Weeks ago, he'd asked me why I hated him so much.

Because you're Vetusian.

My heart contracted at those words because I didn't see a Vetusian when I looked at Adeas. Not anymore. I saw a young guy with tousled light brown hair, whose kisses reached deeper than I'd admitted to myself. I saw my healer. My Ally. A guy I had a crush on?

Letting myself fall in love with him would have been so easy. And if I could love a Vetusian, why wouldn't I be capable of forgiving? Perhaps not all of his kind, and if so, perhaps not all of them at once. But him? Yeah, I could start with him.

I leaned my forehead against his. "What do you need me to do?"

"Take the paper with you and read through it for me," he said, reaching my scrunchie toward me. "See this little thing?" He turned the scrunchie in his hand. "I'll return it to you tonight, and we'll talk because there's going to be a change of plans."

He took my hand into his and placed a kiss onto the back of it, whispering, "I meant every single promise I made you, Sophie, and I swear to you, on my life, I'll keep them all."

EIGHTEEN

Sophie

Steam settled hot and wet inside my nostrils, and billows of it fogged my bathroom. I closed my eyes and leaned my palms against the tile, trying to let the pounding of drops relax that tingling excitement inside my chest. Ever since I'd been sold to *Taigh Arosh*, I'd waited for many Vetusians — always with dread.

But this was different.

I wasn't waiting for a client, but for a male that had my clit throbbing to the beat of water hitting the ground. All those kisses, all those touches... it should never have given me anything, but now I was starved for more.

With my heart pounding in my throat, throwing my head back to rinse the conditioner from my hair brought me close to choking. Making love. Just once in my life I wanted to experience it.

"There's so much steam in here I can't even make out your outline." Adeas' voice brought a smile to my lips.

I turned around and wiped the water from my face,

slowly blinking him into perception. He stood there, arms folded in front of his chest. Was he truly alive?

"Do guards ever come into your bathroom?" he asked.

It was silly how I placed one hand in front of my pussy and draped one arm over my breasts. Something I never bothered with when around a client. And although Adeas had seen me naked — many times — had fingered me to orgasm, his presence triggered a modesty in me I thought I'd lost forever.

"Levear is adamant about the guards not seeing me naked," I said. "Unless I call or somehow fuck up, they never come in here."

Adeas stepped out of his shoes and pulled his shirt over his head, but hesitated when his fingers reached the buttons on his jeans. "Can I join you?"

He would ask that? Seriously?

"Yes." How could such a word come out as a needy whimper?

He hid his smirk underneath a lowered head and stripped down. Adeas knew. I'd made myself plenty clear how far I wanted to take this earlier, and every touch, every whisper, would lead to it.

Half-erect cock dangling between his thighs, he stepped into my shower. Splashes of water reflected from his head and sprinkled my face, and yet my eyes refused to blink, taking him all in. He was handsome, his eyes intriguing, both our bodies ransacked though we still carried beauty on the inside.

Closing my eyes from the water, I blindly searched for the wall-mounted shampoo dispenser, rubbing a blob of it between my palms, scenting the steam with traces of mint.

The moment he wiped the water from his face, I gestured him to step out from underneath the sprinkle, rose onto my toes, and rubbed the shampoo into his strands.

"I spoke to CAT," he said, palms clasping my waist the moment I sunk back onto my heels at that. "They're here on Odheim, and instead of smuggling you onto a cargo vessel, I will help you flee the dome and bring you straight to them."

My heart stumbled over that next beat.

So it was true!

"When?"

"The night of the masquerade." He nuzzled my head with his nose, his voice falling into something deep. "Though there is a chance they might come and get you before that, since I told them where you are. But it might just as well take them some time. We either wait, or I'll break you out."

My stomach tensed. I wouldn't spend any longer in this place than necessary, but was Adeas capable of going through with it?

"I hate being so useless in all this. Planning to escape will be stressful for you."

"I can do it." He cupped my face between his hands. "No more stings from Jal'zar. You'll have to turn down all your tips from now on, because we can't afford anyone growing suspicious. Sound good?"

Shocked into silence, my fingers stilled in his hair and I nodded. Only a week ago, everything had seemed so lost, and now... would I really finally escape this place?

I pressed myself closer against him. "Thank you."

Gentle hands wrapped around my wrists, guiding my arms down until foam-covered palms soaped his chest. "I'm so sorry for the things I said."

I covered his mouth with my fingers and shook my head, saying nothing though he understood just fine. We could have gone through hours of apologies, explanations, and planning. Not tonight.

With a nod, Adeas lifted his chin and kissed my fingers. His tongue trailed up and down between them, sending a shiver down my back and straight between my legs.

He brought his hand to his mouth and let his fingers intertwine with mine, guiding them down along his body. The moment long nails brushed through pubic hair, my hand first jerked, then froze.

Hundreds of clients, and yet my breastbone curled as if I'd never touched a male before. "I'm sorry."

"Don't be," he whispered. "You decide what happens tonight, and what doesn't. I can mate you now, later, or not at all."

His other hand coaxed my mouth onto his, each kiss taking the tension out of my stiff fingers. Slow and patient, he guided my hand to his penis. Not because I needed any guidance.

It was a gesture, returning some of my innocence, and my heart swelled with affection over it. Adeas was giving me a choice no other Vetusian had ever offered. And I chose to wrap my hand around his shaft.

His fingers first tensed then eased against mine, cock twitching and swelling underneath my touch. Together, we stroked the head of his cock, and a shiver wrecked his entire body. He gave several small moans which almost turned into whimpers, his lips stiff and tense against mine.

"Easy, or I'll spill my seed right here," he choked out before he gave a suckle on his lower lip. Long fingers wrapped tighter around mine, the rim of his head sliding across my fingers in quick movements. "That's how I like it best. If I want to release quickly, I usually just stroke the head, only going down the entire shaft if I want to last a bit longer."

"And do you want to release quickly?"

"I want to make this last," he groaned, leading fingers over hard flesh all the way down to its base. "And when I release, it will be deep inside of you, Sophie."

He left me to my own devices, trailing his hand down between my legs, swiping a finger through my drenched slit.

"You long for my touch, Sophie," he said, his voice nothing but a dark rasp. "Ask me for it, and I will give it to you. Take care of all your needs until you're thoroughly mated and satisfied."

I didn't tremble at the words but the certainty in his voice, along with that freedom to choose over my own damn body.

Releasing his cock from my clasp, I stepped up to him until his bobbing crown pressed against my stomach, eyes fluttering shut. Then I said the unthinkable. "Mate me."

His breath feathered over my clit. "Spread for me."

When had he dropped to his knees?

I cried out, sensing his chuckle against my wet pubic bone, which sent my entire body into a spasm of pure pleasure. He shoved his head from side to side, prodding me to spread wider for him.

Tongue flat and powerful, he stroked it over my labia. He lifted up one of my legs, draped it over his arm, exposing me so fully he made a meal of my pussy.

He licked me again and again, sweet friction either making me choke or moan. Sometimes both, which had me tousling his hair, digging into his wet strands as if to keep myself from collapsing.

"I could do this all night." He glanced up at me with his head tilted, a self-satisfied smirk sitting on his lips. "Finger you to orgasm or let you do it while you rub yourself over my shaft. You tell me how you want it, and I'll make it feel good."

Yes, he would!

And as if to make a point, he clasped my labia between his lips and tugged. He sucked and licked and slurped, the tiles almost making it echo. I was wet with need and the occasional rivulet of water, which ran down my body and collected between my legs, but he didn't seem to care and drank it all in.

His tongue dipped into my center, twirling there, and I craved it more than anything ever before. So much so, I rotated my hips in desperate need of more, spreading my juices and drops of water over his face.

"Oh my god," I screamed, my limbs tingling and my head spinning. "Don't stop." And while he promised me that he wouldn't, tongue swiping through my folds, my entire body convulsed. "I'm coming."

"Come against my mouth," he mumbled, his voice husky with lust. "Let me taste your pleasure, Sophie. I want to suck it, swallow it."

A powerful force rippled through my entire body in waves, so intense I couldn't make a single sound. If Adeas wouldn't have dug his hands into my waist, I would have crashed into the wall behind me.

And yet he kept on licking, the sensation soon becoming too much... and not enough. "Please, Adeas..."

With a tug on his shoulders, I brought him back up, the way my hand wrapped around his cock once more teasing a groan from him before his lips turned into a snarl. "Are you sure?"

Yeah, I was fucking sure.

If I hadn't been certain about this before, then I was

now, because each time this male refused to take my body, I wanted to give it to him even more. Freely, with nothing exchanged but whatever feelings grew between us.

He pulled me aside, wrapped me in a towel, and draped my body over his arms. "You better be certain about this, Sophie, because I won't let you forget me after this."

That made no sense unless he was awfully convinced of his skills, but I didn't care. I just tightened my arms around his neck and took in his heat, closing my eyes because I knew I'd open them again inside my closet.

And I did.

Adeas lowered me onto the blankets and climbed in beside me, pushing the door shut on its rails until nothing but a small gap remained.

For a long while, nothing else happened.

I pulled the towel out from underneath me and cramped it into the corner, my legs spread wide and inviting. And while Adeas climbed between them, cock jutting between his thighs, he did nothing else but letting his eyes worship me as if my body was still something precious.

Shaky hands trailed up and down his chest, his skin still damp. I tugged on his midriff. Pulled until he lowered himself down on me, his cock nudging on my entrance.

"Beautiful, innocent female," he whispered, supporting himself with one arm while his other hand brushed clingy, wet hair from my face.

"I used to be." I hated how my voice frayed when I carefully added, "I'd never done this before when I first came here. Not really."

He clenched his eyes shut. Did I scare him off with that confession? But when those pale eyes of his finally opened again, settling steady on mine, time and space faded away for a moment. As if nothing else mattered but the way we held each other's gaze.

His hips moved ever so slightly as he dipped into me. "Close your eyes."

I pressed my eyes shut, sensing his lips lingering against my earlobe as he whispered, "This is what you would have felt had we met on Earth a solar cycle ago. I would have been so, so careful with you."

He parted my wet folds and dipped into me, his groan so deep I sensed it rattle against my breastbone. Inch by inch, his crown asked my walls to stretch for him. When I tensed, he stopped, waiting patiently, unmoving, until I pulled him back into motion.

I clung to his broad, warm shoulders, feeling the joints shifting as he kept his weight off me and worked himself deeper, a moan accompanying each exploring thrust. His hard shaft rubbed so deliciously along my clit I cried out in pleasure.

"You feel wonderful around my cock."

Weak legs swung around his waist, tugging, prodding, but he braced against it and trailed his tongue over the side of my neck.

"Do you want more of me?" he asked, and his devilish tone wasn't lost on me because my nipples grew taut at the question.

"Yes!" I moaned, wiggling my hips, sucking him in deeper. "I want all of you."

His mouth claimed mine, and he dipped his tongue past my teeth, almost, almost, distracting from that single deep thrust he gave, seating himself fully inside me.

"Fuck, Sophie." Adeas exhaled on a groan and locked his hips in place, pinning me so hard between the depth of his invasion and the floor underneath me, I gasped for air.

He remained like that, unmoving, as if he had to soak up the experience of having himself fully sheathed with my body, his crown pulsing at the very end of me.

A whimper escaped me, not of pain but longing for friction, but he immediately picked up on it and pulled back.

"Fuck, you feel so good," he rasped.

I wrapped my legs tighter. Needed him deeper. "More, Adeas."

"More?"

"Yes!"

"Shit," he cursed low and fell into a rhythm of punishing retreats and hard thrusts back inside, unrushed but hard, my walls clenching around his thick shaft. "Feel how I mate you, beautiful thing. Sophie."

My pulse drove up, not at the sound of my name, but the way he said it. As if it had something reverent, powerful, like a pure and divine oath that would make certain he'd never let me forget who I was.

I was Sophie. If only for one night.

My eyes fluttered shut at the sensation of his cock rocking in and out of me, my belly igniting with a lust I'd never known before. Perhaps there was a difference between fucking and mating, my passion for this male burning so hot it was as if he branded himself onto that soul he'd demanded.

My stomach tightened at the way he picked up his pace, one arm pushing underneath the small of my back, lifting me into an arch so he could penetrate deeper.

He could have worked himself up, hooked my legs and pulled me onto his rock-hard shaft. Could have draped my calf over his shoulder to ram home. Instead, he remained pressed close against my body, simple, ordinary, and yet it shook the very foundation of my being.

Adeas sealed our lips together once more, slamming into me as he whispered, "You're mine. I have your body and soul."

"I'm yours," I said mindlessly, my pussy clenching at the idea of belonging to one instead of many.

He tipped his head back at that and growled, the tendons along his neck showing with the way he clenched his jaw. Adeas held back his climax, rolling his hips whenever he needed to slow, and hammering into me whenever he regained control.

I tugged on his shoulders and pulled his chest against mine, skin against skin, heat against heat, and met his every stroke with a roll of my hips.

My body trembled in need of release, and my pussy clenched around him so hard Adeas let out a grunt which turned to a hiss and ended on a curse.

A warm rush of heated blood exploded inside my veins and pooled in my belly, and my entire body stiffened as my second orgasm wrecked through me with such paralyzing force, I wasn't sure if it hurt or healed.

Pale eyes grew wide when Adeas watched me come undone underneath him. His movements slowed for a moment as if he'd forgotten all about himself, watching me with a devotion that sucked the air from the tight space between us.

Only slowly, he began rocking again, his lips brushing mine yet not kissing, his eyes locked on mine with such force there was no escaping.

"Feel my release," he said on an exhale.

His entire body turned as still and unmoving as his gaze, but I sensed every throb, twitch, and pulse of his cock as he filled me with his seed. For a moment, everything stilled around us, our chests breathing as one, while I reveled in a strange sense of belonging.

Adeas remained inside me as he rolled over and pulled me on top of him, my head against his chest, positioning it in that crook we'd long established as my resting spot. I fit perfectly there, listening to the wild pounding of his heart which only slowly calmed.

I glanced up at him. "You're so handsome."

"Am I? When did you come to that conclusion?"

"The night I washed you," I said, then hesitated for a moment before I stated a fact he couldn't deny. "You've done this before."

I've had my fair share of Vetusian virgins, and there was no doubt Adeas wasn't one of them.

He stroked a hand through my hair, his voice strangely detached. "I have."

"A pleasure worker?"

"No," he said muffled against my hair as he placed a kiss at the top of my head. "I'll tell you about her another time. Tonight, I just want to mate you over and over again and hold you in-between."

NINETEEN

Adeas

That vibration between lung and heart seemed to have grown into its own entity overnight, almost as if I now carried a second heartbeat.

I'd noticed it more than once ever since Sophie came into my life but had always shrugged it off as a weird physical reaction. Was that what the Gaia link felt like?

Never before had it been this strong, this... all-consuming, which had me lean toward yes. And as much as I wanted it to be true, longed for Sophie to be my fated mate, I wasn't certain. I needed to find out the meaning behind that flutter inside my chest.

Restlessness turned my limbs itchy, but I remained unmoving, with Sophie only slowly rousing in my arms. It was the first time I'd stayed all night. Watching her fall asleep was wonderful, witnessing her wake was breathtaking.

She rubbed her nose against my chest, took a very long inhale, only to release it with a faint moan. Blonde wisps caught on the stubbles around my chin, and the way she smacked her lips was nothing short of adorable.

At some point during the night, she'd slipped off my cock, leaving a trail of seed where she'd slid down along my hip. I'd mated her thoroughly, with gentle strokes, all night long and into the morning, until she'd collapsed into slumber.

I rubbed my eyes with my free hand.

I'd woken argos ago, unable to fall back to sleep, my ears ever so vigilant to the noises outside Sophie's room. Staying here all night had carried a certain risk.

Another wave of anxiety.

I had to figure out this medication.

What dosage? How often?

I clenched my eyes shut and breathed through it, trying desperately to funnel the energy into coming up with a solid escape plan. If CAT rescued her sooner, fine, but I wouldn't waste my time waiting on them. The masquerade was in a few suns — failure not an option.

At that next wave of panic, I stroked my fingertips over my female's rosy cheeks. "Sophie."

She mumbled something incoherent but didn't wake, so I wiggled my shoulder a bit. "I need you to wake up."

A deep inhale sucked through her nostrils, the way she slowly blinked her eyes open bringing my heart to a standstill. "What's wrong?"

"I'm sorry for waking you," I said, gently lowering her onto the pillow so I could sit up. "It's probably time for me to inject myself because I'm getting rather restless, and I need to hear what the leaflet said."

She rubbed her eye and frowned as if my mating had caused her to forget where she even was. Perfect. Once this was behind her, I would mate her until she forgot the cruelties she had to endure. But those would continue until I got her out...

My teeth clenched at that.

"Do you need to leave?" she asked, peeking through the gap in her closet before she pushed the door open and stepped outside.

Fuck, she was beautiful. Not because of her slim waist, her taut skin, or the luster of her hair. At that moment, the most gorgeous thing was that red imprint on the right side of her face from how she'd slept pressed against me all night.

"Actually..." I rolled out of the closet and rose, regretting it immediately when everything turned black around me.

"Adeas?"

"Dizzy," I said, swaying a bit, waiting until her room reappeared. "Levear prefers his staff addicted since they're easier to control that way. When I came to your room last night, I put one of the Paraprofin bottles inside the healer pack in your sideboard. Just in case I'm with you and need it. Nobody will notice that it doesn't belong to the standard medications in there. Also, it'll make it less suspicious than me having all three of them."

She grabbed the robe from her bed and slipped into it. "Unless another healer checks on me."

"I'm the best of them," I said with a wink and walked over to retrieve the medication. "No need to call another."

"You're my personal healer," she said, and I liked the sound of it. Though I had the desire to be much more than that, and no time to tiptoe around the subject.

Sophie strolled to her synthesizer and grabbed a bowl, hesitated, then reached for another. "Do you want me to make you breakfast?"

"I'm starving," I said, loving that smile on her face as I

took the brown bottle containing the drug. "Did you read over the leaflet yesterday?"

After she pushed a bunch of buttons, the synthesizer rattled and hissed. Probably one of the older models, barely keeping up as it coughed out whatever she'd requested.

"It's mostly warnings and a summary of side effects."

I took the injector gun from the healer pack and loaded the drug into it, hoping, praying, healer Melek had meant what healer Corp considered a maintenance dose for a mature Vetusian of average height. "What side effects?"

"Dizziness, insomnia, impaired vision, vomiting, constipation —"

"Lovely," I chuckled, bringing the injector gun to my upper arm, which must have been where Titean had injected me since that muscle ached already. "You had my attention at constipation, though the insomnia part sure explains why I couldn't sleep."

With the barrel too long, injecting myself was out of question, choosing another muscle an unnecessary risk.

"Remember yesterday, when you agreed to help?" I tapped the perfect injection site with the tip of the gun, then reached it out to her. "Press the barrel flat against it and pull the trigger."

All color drained from her face. "You're not serious, right?"

It only took a few moments of silence before she took the injector with a huff. "Is it going to hurt?"

"Nothing I can't handle."

I helped her lining everything up, cold metal barrel clasped between my fingers to battle the shake in her hands.

She pulled the trigger.

Click. Hiss.

The gun dispensed the medication, which immediately

burned along my muscle before it spread cold up my arm. "Let's hope you didn't just kill me."

Her raised brow reminded me of the fact that I was technically on the run from CAT, returning to Odheim mainland potentially getting me arrested. "The healer who gave you this didn't give you instructions?"

"Full disclosure." After everything that had happened, we needed honesty. "The healer at the infirmary didn't exactly *give* me this stuff."

"You stole it..."

"Yeah, I stole it, but I had a very good reason."

She raised a brow at me. "And what would that be?"

I took the injector from her and placed it back into the healer pack, then took her hand into mine. "You. I couldn't just leave you alone here, especially with the way we parted. Not knowing what happened to me? How sorry I am?"

She lifted my hand and stroked her cheek over the back of it. "I cried all week, Adeas."

"Spilled tears over a Vetusian, hmm? Bet you didn't see that one coming." When she rolled her eyes, but did so with a smile, I pointed at the brown bottle sitting on the side-board. "Any other side effects I should know of?"

Now her smile turned sly. "Loss of interest in sex, and erectile dysfunction."

I wrapped my arm around her middle and pulled her against me. "Yeah, I don't have that one."

"Clearly," she said, glancing down at my hardening penis before she kissed me.

"Which reminds me... I should probably get dressed."

I headed to her bathroom and jumped into my jeans and shirt. When I returned, I found Sophie on the couch, two bowls filled with white liquid waiting on the low table, brown pebbles floating at the surface.

"What is this?" I used the spoon from the bowl to poke at the floaters as I sat down beside her.

"Cereal with milk. It's the only thing I eat for breakfast. Not that the synthesizer offers many options…"

"Can I ask you something?" Spoon abandoned, I leaned over to her and put my palm to her sternum. "When you think of me, do you ever sense something in here? Like an ache when we're apart? Or a soft vibration when we spend time together?"

A glint caught her rounded eyes, her lips first parting and then hesitating to form words. She stiffened, her body answering me before her mouth did.

My breath hitched at that.

She'd sensed it as well.

Sophie reluctantly placed her hand onto mine, slightly adjusting its position. "When I thought you were dead, it hurt so bad in here I feared my ribcage was about to crack open." The remnants of agony in her voice clenched my stomach. "But when you're close, it's like… I don't know. It hums? It, um…"

"Vibrates," I mumbled, a shiver rippling along my spine, leaving behind a paralyzing numbness.

Captain Balgiz might have been right in his assumption, because if this wasn't what the Gaia link felt like in action, then I wouldn't know how else to explain it. It had been there before tonight. We'd been bonded for many suns — I was just too high to make sense of it.

The full, crashing weight of its potential responsibilities squished me. I was a bonded Vetusian with a mate to take care of, provide for. Protect even if it meant protecting her from that sickness harboring at my core.

Sophie frowned, her young age shining through for the first time. "What does it mean?"

A deep, settling inhale.

"It means that I have to get better, yes or yes." I leaned my forehead against hers. "Sophie, I believe there's a chance they never found your fated mate because he didn't show up for testing."

She pulled away and stared into her room, clearly processing. What was on her mind? Did she curse fate for chaining her to someone like me? Could she love me anyway? Help me find the male I used to be?

I wasn't unfamiliar with romantic love and still understood full well that I was falling for her. Falling so fast and hard I'd given up the notion of catching myself. But what about her?

"Because he knew they wouldn't let him go to Earth anyway," she eventually mumbled. Aside from how her hand briefly flinched above mine, she took it surprisingly well. "Because he's a *sgu'dal*."

"But a very handsome one," I joked, her mouth twitching into a grin before reality made her lips press back into a thin line. "The CAT officer at the infirmary was the one who brought it up. They checked my DNA, but I took off before I got the result."

She took a spoonful of cereal, stared at it for an overlong moment, then let the brown stuff crunch between her molars in slow-motion. A hard swallow followed. "How are we going to find out if it's true?"

"No idea." I shrugged. "DNA testing has only been around for like... a century or so. I guess we'll have to figure it out on our own until CAT breaks into the dome, or I break you out."

"And if we're fated?" Her next exhale stuttered. "What

then?"

What then...

A Vetusian who had his shit together might escape to Earth with her. Get an assignment. A habitat. Make himself a nice little family with his human mate much to the satisfaction of the Empire.

I wasn't *that* Vetusian.

Even now, after I'd injected myself, jitters raced up and down my veins, urging me for something the inhibitors couldn't quite decipher anymore. This was hardly going to be easy, and I'd dragged her right into it.

I grabbed her bowl and placed it next to mine on the table. One tug on her waist, and I pulled her onto my lap, placing her hand back to that spot where I sensed love growing for this female.

"If we're fated, then you own my soul," I rasped, threading my fingers in her hair, determination coursing through me. "As soon as you're heading back home, I'll sign myself into a new rehab program they've established on Earth."

"Earth?" She gulped as if she'd just realized I would follow her to her home planet.

"You don't want me to go with you?"

Did she notice my muscles tensing? Because she immediately reached her hand for my cheek. "Odheim. Earth. I don't care, Adeas. I just want you to get help because you're an amazing guy."

An amazing guy.

Would that be enough to sustain this connection between us until I would return from rehab? I wanted to show her the real Adeas before we parted, but how many suns did I have left? CAT could raid this place at any moment.

Sophie leveled her gaze at me. "There's something you're not telling me."

My chest grew painfully tight.

I stared at her tendril wrapped around my finger, my chest squeezing a bit harder until I could barely breathe. The moment Sophie would be free, I would be the locked-up in rehab. All I had were these stolen moments, showing her the male I had once been. The male I wanted to be again. For her.

"The program's withdrawal period is around six lunar cycles." Wow, I hadn't even choked on the words.

"That's not so bad." And her sweet smile crushed my heart. "Six lunar cycles is nothing, Adeas."

I must have mumbled something, because she clasped my face between her hands, bringing my gaze to hers. "What?"

"One to two Earth years," I said, swallowing. "That's how long I'll be in their inpatient program after the withdrawal period."

If I'd thought her pale earlier, then now her skin turned translucent. Her fingers cooled against my cheeks, her eyes dulled. Yes, this female had feelings for me. A bittersweet revelation.

Sophie's lips squeezed together and parted several times, and she shook her head in disbelief. "One to two years on top of the withdrawal period?"

I only nodded.

What else was there to say?

"My mom was usually gone for thirty days," she said. "Sometimes up to ninety. But those were all state-funded programs. My aunt paid for a private one, but only once, and that one was nine months. Even after that she relapsed, so I guess one to two years isn't unreasonable... considering."

I leaned back into the couch and pulled her closer. "You never told me about your mother."

"There's nothing to say," she mumbled. "My dad skipped town when I was four. She worked three jobs, changed her boyfriends weekly, and one of them probably got her hooked at some point."

"How old were you when she started using drugs?"

With a lazy shrug, she snuggled her head into the crook between my shoulder and neck. "Too young to remember. I think I was twelve or thirteen when I first went to live with Aunt Debby."

Another wave of anxiety swept over me, but the Para-profin quickly calmed it into a mere ripple of discomfort. "I hate myself for doing this to you, Sophie."

Another shrug. A creature so young shouldn't have such a lack of reaction to something so terrible. This female had collected a lifetime of bad memories. I would not add to them. I would succeed. Gift her with another lifetime of good ones.

"On Earth, we say that addicts won't be able to get better until they truly hit rock bottom." Her eyes searched for mine, they locked. "Did you hit rock bottom that night? The lowest point of all this? Can't fall any deeper?"

"Yes." And I tasted the truth of my words. "I thought I was going to die. Lose you before I ever had you."

"Then you'll get better," she said, leaned over to grab my bowl, and handed it to me. "And now eat."

I took the bowl and started eating.

Not everything had been said between us, but it was a promising beginning after everything had seemed so lost. But it would all mean nothing if I couldn't get her out of this shithole.

TWENTY

Adeas

Being a *sgu'da*l had its benefits.

All morning, I'd staked out our escape route without so much as a sidelong glance from anybody. As long as I occasionally thrashed myself against a wall, I was nothing but a junkie coming down from a trip.

Four times a solar cycle, Levear invited his entire clientele to a masquerade. A pompous event. High-ranking Vetusians everywhere, pretending to be the very best of my kind with their credits, estates, and trade deals. Fucking farce.

It would be loud and packed, but most of all, it would have most guards patrolling the casino instead of the sweatmines. There wouldn't be a better chance to escape.

I stumbled along the table where the Kokonian female filled spheres with souldust, three sets of hands working perfectly synchronized. The skin along my arms flared up with a new wave of parasites.

Healer Melek had been right. Paraprofin might suppress my physical cravings, but my mind turned restless at the sight of the blue powder. I had to ignore it. Stick to the plan.

For the sake of authenticity, I lowered myself onto the ground, putting it on real thick with a groan. I stared at the overhead filtration pipes, which came from the casino and connected to the air handler. Good thing I'd lost so much weight during the last two solar cycles. I would fit in there, and so would Sophie.

"How much longer?" My spine cracked with the way I rolled my vertebrae over the cold stone underneath.

My eyes tracked each of the female's scaled digits until they locked on the target: Sophie's ring. I had to make amends. Show Sophie the male behind the mess. That trinket was step one out of an entire journey I'd walk to the end.

"Sehrin," she called out without sparing me a glance, only looking up when the massive guard stomped up next to me. "The *sgu'dal* is asking for his cut."

"Useless piece of shit." He narrowed his eyes at me. "Next time, I'll toss you into the streets head-first. Bunch of work getting rid of your body, only for to you come crawling back here."

Breathe! Don't argue.

I was a junkie coming down from a trip. Anything else, and I'd blow this entire plan. The last thing we needed was anybody growing wary, so I played my part with shocking ease, arching my back, groaning.

"Give it to him," Sehrin snarled with a dismissive wave, then walked off.

The Kokonian tossed it onto the ground, turned, and walked away toward one of the back rooms.

The sphere clanked against my head.

I rolled onto all fours and grabbed it, almost like a reflex, and pushed myself up. My palm seared against the cool metal, the sphere so heavy inside my clasp it pulled my arm toward the ground.

Just a little.

That voice hollowed my core, bringing a violent urge, a corrupted need. I wouldn't listen.

Fingers shaky, they struggled the sphere inside my pocket. Showing up here to get what Levear promised was risky, but not doing it would blow our cover right there. As far as the staff was concerned, I showed up here every day, claiming my cut. So I did.

A glance over my shoulder revealed Sehrin checking on the cargo crates in the back, making sure nothing had gone amiss. I took the opportunity and stumbled behind the Kokonian into the back room.

"What do you want, Adeas?" she asked. "I already gave you your cut, so leave me alone."

I leaned beside her against the wall, tapping the ring before she managed to pull her hand from her locker. "I need that ring back."

She pushed the hand underneath her armpit as if she expected me to rip it right off her. "I happen to like it. It's not for sale. If it suddenly disappears, I'll have Sehrin search your room."

"Not even for one of these?" I gave a tap against my pocket, where the fabric sat tight against the sphere. "You can easily get a hundred credits for it on the outside."

Now she crossed both arms in front of naked breasts. "Do I look stupid? They pat me down before I leave here. What do you think the boss is going to do to if the guards find a sphere on me?"

"I'll meet you at the airlock before you leave. That ring for this sphere."

Slitted nostrils flared, and elongated, black pupils widened. While she eyed me warily, the Kokonian also tilted her head carefully back toward the sweatmines, listening for footsteps, guards. I almost had her there...

"Two spheres," she hissed.

"One. After your shift."

She slammed her locker shut. "Go fuck yourself."

Shit. That itch came back full force.

While I still had Sophie's credits, I needed them elsewhere. Using them to buy back her ring wouldn't be fair either. I'd stolen it, and I would get it back, waves of anxiety, crawling skin, and all.

"Alright, two spheres," I said. "Tomorrow after your shift, I'll wait for you at the airlock with two spheres, and you'll give me the ring back."

She splayed her fingers out in front of her, ogling the ring for long enough my shoulders tensed. Saying I didn't consider ripping it off would have been a lie.

Luckily, she nodded. "I'll check the spheres for content, *sgu'dal*, so don't even think about fucking me over."

"I won't."

When she left the room, I let out a sigh of relief. No matter how chaotically this rescue plan might have started, everything finally had come together.

Transport vessel waiting at sweatmine exit. Check.

Escape plan through air handler. Check.

Distraction at the casino... coming right up.

Like most Jal'zar females working at *Taigh Arosh*, Izara used her tips to support her family back home on Solgad. She wouldn't turn down a bunch of credits in exchange for a diversion the night of the masquerade.

With a bounce in my step, I turned and made my way

back to *Taigh Arosh* to find her. But the moment I pulled back into the tunnel, a broad chest blocked the way.

Sehrin leaned with one hand against the mildew-covered stone, aggression coming off him in waves. His finger tapped the trigger on the gun holstered to his chest, his jawline as stiff as that snarl which refused to go away.

"I keep wondering..." His voice carried a sharp edge. "Why did my guards fish you out of *leska's* tub? She had no injuries. Levear didn't send you up there either."

Something cold crawled its way up my spine, freezing my veins solid. Sehrin had always been unpredictable, but he'd turned into a ticking bomb the moment Sophie cut through his eyeball. How much longer until he exploded?

"I don't remember," I said and let myself stumble back, gaze dropping to the ground.

That warrior better let it go.

But he didn't...

Stiff and unyielding, his fingers wrapped around my throat. My inhale squeezed to a halt. With one thrust, he slammed me against the wall, shoulder blades crashing against hard stone.

"You're a fucking liar," he snarled, his bionic eye locked on me. "Do you talk to her?"

I punched his wrist until his clasp eased, my voice a rasp. "I'm her healer, of course I talk to her."

A healer. Not *her* healer.

Fuck. Fuck. Fuck.

Did he notice?

His eyes narrowed tighter, the sudden darkness sitting behind them sending a rush of blood into my fists. Yeah, he'd caught on to it alright.

His black boots stepped up to my sneakers, shrinking the distance between my chest and his gun. "*Her* healer?"

A deep laugh shattered from the walls, menacing and cutting. "A fucking *sgu'dal* healer, having a crush on *leska*?"

"She's a business asset." Fuck, I hated myself for saying that. "I'm just making sure she can perform as such."

He leaned in closer once more, trying to intimidate me but I refused to back down. "Be careful, *sgu'dal*."

"Are you threatening me?"

"No, I'm warning you." His nail clinked against his golden iris. "Whatever attention that cunt is giving you, don't assume it means anything. *Leska* is using you."

My next swallow turned rancid at the back of my throat. *She's just using you*, that little voice at the back of my head whispered, *she'll never be yours*.

I wanted to drop to the ground and rock myself through this sudden onslaught of misery and despair. What if she used me? What if she wanted nothing to do with me after the escape? She faked orgasms like there was nothing to it, so what if she could fake affection?

Bile pooled at the back of my throat. This wasn't a good time for my mind to go into complete meltdown. Whatever. She could use me all she wanted as long as she made it out of here.

"Get out of my way, Sehrin," I said. "Go harass someone else because I've got shit to do."

Wrong thing to say.

One good eye flared up.

"You've got some nerve talking to me like that." His fist crashed against my jaw with such force, my skull thumped against the stone behind me, sending a stabbing pain deep into my brain.

"Fuck off!" I shouted and rammed shoulder-first against him.

He stumbled back and, with my fists balled, I sent a

punch right after. Knuckles met nose and cartilage crackled, not enough to break the bone but a blood vessel burst anyway.

Where I hoped Sehrin would press a hand onto his face, the red droplets grew dark against the filthy stone underneath. Blood poured out of his nostril, ran down his scarred lip, and dribbled from his chin.

Underneath it, he fucking smiled. "You sure are packing a punch for someone who's supposed to be a stammering mess by now."

Rage and anxiety poured out of my pores as sweat, thickening the already saturated air inside the tunnel, but I breathed it all down. Fighting him would only make this worse.

"I just want to be left in peace," I said, sidestepping as I held my hands up. "Just let me get back to my room. That's all I want."

Slow, carefully placed steps backed me away from him, my stomach hardening with tension. That warrior was one step away from boiling over. Something I had to avoid at all costs, at least until I got rid of Sophie's credits still hiding in my room. I needed those to pay Izara to help us create a diversion.

Sehrin thrust out his chest, his disfigured mouth turning into an ugly sneer, but he remained still, watching as I turned around.

My blood rushed so fast it pounded behind my eyeballs, but I kept my steps unhurried. I couldn't rack up more trouble. Dread and the onset of a panic flooded my system, the solution for it sitting tightly inside my pocket.

All I needed was a little pinch to take the edge off. The thought alone had my fingers tug on my pockets, so fucking tempted.

"Keep walking." I wrapped my hand around my finger and, one after another, pulled until they cracked to distract myself.

Keep walking. *Crack.*

You made a promise. *Crack.*

She's using you. Crack.

Argh!

Did this disease ever shut up?

I rushed into my room and slammed the door shut behind me, leaning against it as if to barricade that voice on the other side. Everything around me spun. Bed. Shelf. Desk. Bed. Shelf. Desk. I had to inject myself. Had to —

A thrust catapulted me away from the door, followed by a menacing voice. "It's been a while since I searched the healer rooms."

Just as I caught myself on the shelf and steadied my legs, the desk beside me moaned. Sehrin pulled it from the wall, his hands trailing along the back edge.

The credits.

My first clear thought.

I stood there, frozen with terror, my legs refusing to move.

Sehrin pulled desk drawers from their tracks and tossed them across the room, papers of research studies raining to the ground. My shelf went next, collapsing to the ground with cracks and shatters. He took my entire room apart. Not once did the idiot check a book, one of them carved out on the inside to hold the credits.

"What by the heat of Heliar is going on here?" Levear poked his bald head into my room. "Captain Inuzet is waiting at the sweatmines for the load going to Earth, and you're busy turning a room upside down?"

Sehrin stabbed his finger toward me, his chest heaving. "That *sgu'dal* is hiding something."

"Of course he's hiding something. He's a fucking junkie. Your time is better invested elsewhere."

"You shouldn't have hired him back," Sehrin huffed. "He's sneaking around *leska*."

Levear stepped into my room, hands parked on his hips. "Everyone's sneaking around *leska*, including you. Now get your ass to the sweatmines. I want you to accompany that load until it's securely stored on the smuggler's vessel at the trading post."

The moment Levear left, I had Sehrin's hand wrapped around my throat once more. "If I ever find you sneaking around —" he swallowed, "Sophie... looking at her, if you as much as sniff the hallway where she walked, I'll personally drown you in your own vomit."

It wasn't the way his lips trembled that announced we had a bigger problem here. It was the fact that, for the first time in a solar cycle, he'd spoken her name. And he'd done so gently, a breathed caress almost. This warrior didn't hate her nearly as much as he'd always pretended. That didn't make him any less of a sick mind — just more dangerous.

He released his grip and stormed out of my room, leaving me behind a shivering, trembling, itchy, I-want-to-scratch-my-skin-off mess. The sphere inside my pocket burned a hole into the fabric, shouted, and bounced against my thigh all at once. Paraprofin. I needed it. Now.

And as I lifted up my shelf, clear liquid and shards of brown glass splattered across books, I realized just how fucked I was.

TWENTY-ONE

Sophie

It was like bad déjà vu.

For the second time in a month, Adeas rolled into my room, but immediately scrambled onto shaky legs. Frantic fingers shoved over my sideboard, nails scratching drawers open.

He better not be high.

I fought gravity and dread, both turning my legs brittle underneath me. He looked like a man possessed, as if he had the devil himself sitting on his shoulder, whipping him to raid my stuff.

"H-help me," he stammered, blue veins popped along the side of his strained neck.

He grabbed the healer pack.

A wave of shame crashed down on me because I'd expected the worst. He was neither high nor looking to get there. Adeas was searching for the Paraprofin!

I immediately ran over to him and took the white bag from his trembling hands. "How much do you need?"

Because there was no way he'd manage dosing the gun himself.

"Maintenance dose."

"How much is that?" I grabbed gun and bottle, my hands shaking almost as hard as his now, hating myself for every drop I spilled while loading it. "Like this?"

"M-more," he whimpered, dragging his nails over an already bloodied underarm.

I lined the barrel up with his arm just like he'd showed me the last time, fear tugging on my tendons. This could go terribly wrong with his jerky movements.

I pulled the trigger, holding my breath until the click of the injector ended on a hiss. "What happened?"

Tossing the gun onto my bed, I replaced its metal with Adeas' cold cheeks clasped between my hands. "Please tell me what happened!"

Why hadn't he injected himself sooner?

He stumbled back and crashed against my sideboard, which thudded against the wall as his body pressed against it. Like that, he collapsed into a pile of misery by my feet. I followed right behind him, never letting go of his face, kneeling down beside him.

If Adeas closed his eyes willingly or if they fluttered shut, I couldn't say. His head tilted toward his shoulder, but the tension in his posture soon eased.

"Tell me what to do," I whimpered. Hell, why did I have to be so powerless all the time? "I want to help you, but I don't know how."

He struggled his hand toward his face, letting our fingers intertwine before they dropped in a knot onto his lap. "Stay with me."

I nodded, though he couldn't see it, using my free hand to pull one of those pre-packaged wipes from the bag.

Tearing it open with my teeth, I took it out and began wiping the blood from his arm. Several scratches came into view, the pattern erratic.

"Why didn't you inject yourself earlier?" I asked, the wipe soaking red inside my clasp.

"I had a run-in with Sehrin," he said, his eyes slowly opening, though this gaze remained unfocused. "He tipped my shelf and the bottles shattered."

A chill crawled up my spine. "Are you saying this is the only bottle we've got left?"

He sighed in response.

That thing had already been three-quarters empty when he brought it. "How long is this going to last?"

"Perhaps another three suns or so. We can stretch it," he said, squeezing my hand. "Don't worry about me. I'll be fine."

He didn't look fine, but I said nothing, and instead waited until some color returned to his face. I'd promised I would help him, so I just sat there and held his hand.

I stroked damp wisps from a forehead misted in cold sweat. He was so handsome, his features masculine though he had a boyish look about him that would probably stay with him all his life.

After five minutes or so, he wrapped his arm around my shoulder and pulled me against his chest.

"Is it working?" I asked. "Are you feeling better?"

"That stuff enters the bloodstream quickly." Quivering lips pressed a kiss to my temple. "Sehrin didn't find the credits. I have them with me and, as soon as Izara returns to her room, I'll make sure we get ourselves a distraction for the night of the masquerade."

I pressed my ear against his chest, the rhythm of his heart as inconsistent as the scratch pattern on his arm. He was in agony, mind and body fighting an invisible enemy, and he did it all for me. My heart bloomed at that. Where others had failed me, given up, he refused to and kept trying.

"Tell me what you feel inside your body," I said, and the moment he shook his head against mine, I added, "It's a technique from Earth."

He tensed underneath me, and a grunt vibrated from his chest before he spoke. "My heart is beating fast. I have a... um... a fire burning underneath my skin. And I..." He swallowed. "I don't like confessing this to you. It's shameful. You shouldn't have to be subjected to my failings."

"Shame feeds addiction." I glanced up, finding stunning eyes immediately locking with mine. "Back on Earth, they invited family members of addicts to attend classes, so we could better understand and learn how to help them. My aunt only took me twice. Said I shouldn't be exposed to such heavy subject matter at sixteen."

"She was right."

"Was she? Someone at sixteen wants to help just as much as someone at twenty. Forty." I gave a tug on his chin. "Please don't exclude me, because if you think you're protecting me with it, let me tell you you're wrong. You asked for my help. Let me help."

His brows furrowed as if he'd only just now realized that we were in this together. "I feel like I want to rip my hair out, though the urge is slowly going away."

"Do you want to get high?"

A moment of uncomfortable silence, and then...

"Yes. I've got a sphere right here in my pocket." His arms squeezed around me, and he dug his nails into my sides until I let out a faint giggle. "But for that, I would have to let go of you, and I just can't bring myself to it."

It took many more minutes for his heart to return to that soothing *ba-boom* I'd grown so familiar with. After a while, he stroked his fingertips through my hair, placing kisses onto my scalp.

"Sophie..." he eventually said, his voice wavering. "Do you have feelings for me?"

How could he doubt it?

His question stalled my breathing until my chest burned for air. Not because I lacked an answer, but because the answer terrified me. At that moment, I rested in his arms. Hours later, I would rest in the arms of another, and the thought alone distorted that hum inside my chest into an ugly screech.

Rule number one: never fall in love.

When Levear had first taught me that rule, it seemed like a bad joke. How could I possibly fall in love with a Vetusian? Then again when Izara urged me to remember it.

Now, I realized just why some rules weren't meant to be broken. Because if you did, you yourself might break underneath the weight of the consequences.

His lips tugged on my earlobe, his voice deep and raspy. "I love you, Sophie."

Words spoken hundreds of times by dozens of Vetusians, all deflected by that numbness which encapsulated me. But not his. His reached deep and caressed a soul I knew existed, half in my chest, the other half in his.

And yet, I couldn't say it back, because love was just another name, like Sophie, and names didn't fare well in this place. Underneath our filthy layers of drugs and depravity, there was something pure, innocent, and I would rather keep it hidden than expose it to corruption.

Turning around, I climbed onto his lap instead, straddling his thighs between mine. I raked my fingers through his hair and kissed him. Slow and consuming, sending tremors of lust over me. And with it came proof of this link between us. It felt right. It felt... fated.

And while he moaned into my mouth, I told him that I loved him in the only way I had the courage to do.

"You have my soul," I whispered against his soft lips, placing his hand onto my chest, and mine onto his. "And I have yours."

He nodded as if he understood, that string between us humming a melody that carried everything unsaid. I was the rhythm and he was the resonance, and together we sounded fucking beautiful.

"See this?" I tapped against the scrunchie sitting on my wrist, pulled it off, and slipped it onto his instead. "I don't care how long that rehab program takes, Adeas. One year. Two. Three. I will wait for you. And once you've completed it, I'll show you elephants with long noses. We'll make a snowman together."

"I have no fucking clue what either one of those are, but it sounds amazing."

"I'm pretty sure they did away with Olive Garden," I said, letting my thumb glide over his bottom lip. "We'll find an Italian restaurant and eat fettu-something together."

"I love fettu-something," he laughed, and the strain on his lips made his eyes glisten. "I won't let you down, Sophie, I swear. If you think I'll come out of there better, then you're mistaken, because I'll come out of there the best damn mate my kind has ever seen."

Yes, he would.

Legs still weak underneath him, Adeas struggled himself up, his arms wrapped around my ass. He walked us over to the closet, heat taking root in my belly.

"What if Sehrin walks in?"

"Ready for me again so soon?" he asked as he lowered me onto my blankets. "Levear sent him to guard a shipment, but that's not what I had in mind."

He positioned himself beside me, one hand propped underneath his head, the other wrapped around the back of my head. With a long exhale, he gave a tug and pulled my lips onto his. He kissed me once, twice. The third kiss lingered far too long, dragging seconds to infinity while my entire body sizzled with arousal.

Until his features darkened.

"There's something I want you to know," he rasped. "It's only fair, and I've been wanting to get this off my chest ever since you asked me."

I stilled beside him. "Asked you what?"

He lowered his head onto one of the many pillows, a deep inhale expanding his chest as if the air contained courage. "I used to have a girlfriend once, which is why our mating hadn't been the first time for me."

Did he think that bothered me? Me? The whore?

I felt a brow quirk up and a smile tugging on my lips. "A girlfriend?"

But Adeas didn't smile. If anything, the air inside the closet turned stagnant, rigid, right along with his jawline.

"She was a Jal'zar."

He placed a long pause there. Good thing he did. A Jal'zar in a romantic relationship with A Vetusian? I'd never heard of anything like it.

"And no, she wasn't a pleasure worker," he eventually added. "She was what Jal'zar call *uiri*, like a servant who tends to a warlord's mate."

"Does that happen often?" I asked. "From what I know, Jal'zar and Vetusians can't conceive together."

"It's rare enough people pointed fingers at us whenever

we went out together. They stared when we walked through Odheim, held hands, went to the opera, a restaurant."

That came with a pang of my heart. Those were all things I wanted to do with him… but couldn't. The fact that another female had enjoyed him in such a way, likely before addiction, brought on a wave of uncomfortable heat.

"That's why you don't care that I can't have children," I said, something that had been a distant thought at the back of my mind. "Because, obviously, you didn't expect it with her either."

"Well, I had just gotten my basic license then, and a child wasn't on my mind."

And now? In three years? Five? Why did this subject make me feel inadequate all over again? He'd known from the start that I couldn't carry a child.

"Your thoughts are straying to places they shouldn't." His fingers curled into a fist and he pounded against his sternum. "Whatever it is you're thinking, it hurts me in here."

I froze. Was that what this link did? Made it impossible to hide anything from him? I'd always reminded myself to watch my mouth. Seemed like now I had to watch my thoughts as well.

"You know, it wasn't a Vetusian who shot me." His gaze followed to where I revealed my scar. "When I decided to surrender because we were fucking starving, one of the guys called me a traitor and pointed his gun at me."

There was a strain around his mouth, and he lifted my shirt higher, his thumb finding the scar and circling it without even looking. "You told me you didn't want children. That wasn't true?"

"I don't know." And it didn't matter anymore. "The

Vetusians were the ones who saved my life. At first, I was grateful. Until they abducted me. I waited for someone to come and rescue me. And I waited. And waited."

"That's when you started hating us..."

"No," I said, old pain cracking through a still aching core. "I started hating you when the guy who took me called me a poor investment, called me useless, worthless." Refusing to let more tears fall over this, I quickly wiped my eyes. "I'm not worthless."

"No you're not," Adeas said. "You're very precious to me, and nothing could change that. If there's no child, then there's no child. We can travel instead. Visit other planets."

I lowered my head onto his chest, but not without placing a kiss there first. "Did you love her? Your girlfriend?"

"I did." His next inhale lifted my head high and shook it when he stuttered out his exhale. "Most Vetusians fall into addiction because their lives are so empty. Not me, Sophie. My life was full, and I was happy. I had it all going for me."

He stroked his fingers over my back. "I was good at my job and on my way to surgeon training. I had friends. I had a girlfriend to share my life with."

"What happened?"

"The night I almost died, you asked me about the first time I used." His breath hitched underneath me. Was that the sound of an old scar cracking on his heart? "One night, my girlfriend and I watched a movie together at my place. She kneeled down before me. She opened up a sphere of souldust and... she blew the entire load straight into my face. Just like that."

His arm clasped me tighter as we both shivered at the same time. "Choke on it, Vetusian." Adeas cupped my chin and lifted my gaze to meet his. "That's what she said when she did it. Whatever I accidentally inhaled was enough to get me hooked."

"Adeas..." My voice drowned in tears and I pushed myself up so I could stroke his face. Yes, life had let us both down. "Why did she do it?"

"Revenge on my kind," he said. "But that realization didn't hurt me nearly as much as the fact that she never truly loved me back because, apparently, I wasn't her only boyfriend. She'd done the same to two other guys." He scoffed. "I guess the signs were there but we were love-struck fools who let their guards down. They eventually caught her on a different planet and executed her."

My core hollowed. It was as if that last lump of hatred had lodged, leaving behind an emptiness waiting to be filled. And as if Adeas knew, he scooted down and kissed my stomach, filling it with love.

"I'm very sorry she did that to you."

"Fate is never wrong, Sophie. Cruel perhaps, but never wrong." His kisses trailed lower, once more flaring heat. "My kind enslaved hers, and I suffered from it. My kind enslaved you, and now I'm holding you in my arms. My first love ruined my life, and my true love will help me put it back together."

TWENTY-TWO

Adeas

Blue and polished to a sparkle, Sophie's ring sat clasped between my fingers. Steady legs volleyed up the stairs into one of the back hallways, which bustled with prostitutes getting ready for the masquerade in a few suns. They giggled and laughed, exchanged dresses and pressed feathered masks to their faces.

"Hey Adeas," one of them called out, a Kokonian famous for all those things her six hands could do at once. "How about you join us later for some fun? We're playing dress up."

Fun meaning getting high together, and the Jal'zar beside her was quick to shake a sphere as she winked at me.

"Yeah, he should be the judge," she crooned, blown pupils telling me she was high already. What had been me ten suns ago, now disgusted me. "I'll look like a warmaiden at this masquerade. Maybe I'll find myself a nice mate."

Except that most Jal'zar males shunned their females if they'd been touched by one of my kind, regardless of how little choice they'd had. Most Jal'zar females were free — unless they had skills like the ones slaving at *Taigh Arosh*.

"I'll pass," I said with a dip of my head.

I turned into another hallway, this one so narrow only Toroxians usually used it, feeling fucking great. With my body strong, mind clear, and escape imminent, that fat grin on my face refused to go away. Sophie and I would be free, and the thought alone expanded my lungs wider, and my spine grew straighter.

Then I stepped around the corner, spine curling.

A broad back patrolled the hallway, most likely Sehrin, though it could have been one of his guards. Either way, I took a step back and disappeared behind the corner again.

This complicated things.

Taking the back door to Sophie's room was out of the question. Front wasn't an option either since her door was visible from the atrium, currently packed with staff decorating for the masquerade.

One option remained, which curled my toes: I had to climb.

I turned around and squeezed myself through the tiny hallway once more. Barreling down the stairs, I left *Taigh Arosh* through the glass double doors which led outside.

The courtyard stood dark and, to my relief, empty from the looks of it. Around it, hedges stood trimmed in shapes of ellipsoids and spheres, the occasional Cultum ice berry bush illuminating the walkway in a shimmer of blue.

A glance upward along the exterior of *Taigh Arosh* for orientation, and I made my way to Sophie's balcony. It was the one in the middle, to the left of Izara's.

Granted, I hadn't climbed ever since basic combat training, but that didn't keep me from grabbing that protruding stone.

Foot scouting the edges for grip, I pulled myself up and started climbing. The higher I got, the faster my heart beat. *Don't look down.*

I reached the edge of the balcony.

Everything went great.

Until I touched the damn edge...

I reached my hand for the worn stone.

Zzk!

A zap of electricity sizzled through my fingertips and I let out a whimper. My foot lost grip and slipped off the edge, dangling, kicking. Shit!

Every single muscle inside my body contracted. Joints locked up. Panic flooded my veins. I couldn't break a bone. Not suns away from escape.

I clenched my teeth.

Throwing my burning hand against a stone, I steadied myself. The sole of my sneaker dragged over the wall, searching, searching. There! I found grip on another protruding stone.

So far so good. I wouldn't fall to my death, but neither would I get to Sophie. Those motherfuckers had installed a force barrier.

I had two options. Without another thought wasted, I went for the dangerous one.

Arms heavy, tendons burning up underneath the strain, they pulled me sideways, all the way until I reached Izara's balcony. If I would make it through another zap without falling and cracking my skull on the stone underneath I couldn't say, but I had to try.

I reached my hand for the rail.

I stretched my entire body.

Damp fingers touched coarse stone.

Drenched in sweat and fueled by adrenaline, I pulled

myself up with whatever strength this abused body still had left in its muscles. I swung my leg up and, after some struggling, rolled myself over the railing and tumbled onto the tiles of Izara's balcony.

I allowed myself a breath.

And another. And a third one.

A glance through the window revealed the room empty, aside from the Jal'zar sitting on her couch. At my knock, she swung around, her lips clearly forming pouts of curses.

"Are you fucking insane?" she snarled through the widening gap of her glass door. "Mekara will unleash her wrath on you for scaring me like that. What by the burnt ashes are you doing out here?"

I invited myself in, keeping my voice down. "I was on my way to return Sophie's ring, but I think Sehrin is patrolling your back hallway."

"Shit." Flat-footed steps took her to the hidden door, head tilted as she listened for noises. "Yeah, there's a guard out there alright."

"You have to bring her to your room," I said, tugging my shirt back into place. "Please."

She crossed her arms in front of her chest, and her tail right along with it. "With a guard outside my room? The fuck I will."

"Please?" Each time she shifted her weight, I shifted mine right along with her, tipping my head, searching for her eyes. "I need to give Sophie her mom's ring back. Come on. I helped you with so much shit ever since I came to this place."

Gray lips peeled over fangs, and she let out a warning hiss. "I hate you for dragging me into this." And yet her posture eased, one hand swinging in my direction as her gaze studied me. "You look good, Adeas. Better than I've ever seen you before."

"I'm going through withdrawal. You were right, Izara. I'm addicted to that stuff."

"*Leska* told me," she said with a nod of approval, but her features darkened at the same time. "What you're trying to do here is honorable, but don't you think you're taking on more than you can handle? She told me CAT is coming for the human females. Why not wait for them? Let them handle it?"

I sat on the edge of her sleeping pod with a huff. "And how long will that take?"

"What if you get yourself killed? She's precious. You're not. If a guard catches you, they'll punish her and shoot you."

As if I didn't know. "She's suffering."

"She suffered for an entire sun cycle, surely she can survive another moon."

"It's worse for her now," I said, tapping two fingers against my chest. "We bonded, Izara. If being with a client was agony before, now it's pure torture. It's as if the link is fighting her from the inside. Same for me. I know when she's with another male because something aches inside my chest."

She stared at me for a long while, brows furrowed. "I've never heard of any Gaia link that strong."

All I had was a shrug.

What did I know about this thing, considering it had been near-extinct from our society for so long? All I knew was that I felt the way I did, with an entity living between heart and lung, screaming in disdain.

"I shared a soulbond once." A black claw pulled the side of her shirt up, revealing a puckered scar less than halfway down her ribcage. "They killed him when they took me. I still feel him sometimes, you know. Whispering to stay strong."

She thrust her head back and groaned. "Roll underneath my pod and don't make a noise."

I did as I was told and checked if the ring was still inside my pocket, waiting patiently. There were footsteps. A deep, rolling voice arguing back and forth, mixing with Izara's snarls. Doors opened. Slammed shut.

"If you think you'll burst in here and find some action between two females, then you'll be disappointed, Sehrin," Izara said. "I need her help to finish my mask because she's got the smallest fingers."

Sehrin's voice came tense and dark. "Show me that mask."

The rush of blood came to a halt inside my veins.

I slowed my breathing, flaring my nostrils wide to avoid any whistle, any wheeze, or whatever might give me away.

"You look tired, *leska*," Sehrin murmured underneath the noise of Izara rummaging somewhere. "Let me bring you some *uri* berry tea later. It'll help you sleep."

What the fuck.

My fingers heated.

I wanted to roll out from underneath that pod and punch him all over again. For a moment there, that guy almost sounded caring. And I might have bought it, if it wasn't for the fact that I'd, more than once, stitched together females he'd torn apart. I would rather kill him than let him touch Sophie.

"I'm fine." My mate's voice came strong, but her fear tingled inside my chest.

"You have one argos!" That shout was quickly followed by heavy footsteps and a door slamming shut.

I rolled out from underneath Izara's pod. "That guy's getting creepier by the sun."

"Adeas!" Body only halfway out, my mouth got assaulted by furious kisses. "How did you get in here?"

My answer drowned underneath lips pressing hungry against mine. Sophie sucked them between hers, her tongue swiping so deliciously across them before she ventured deeper.

"If you think I'll watch you two mate, then you're both insane," Izara grunted, though I detected a rise in pitch there. "Go outside. At least there he won't be able to hear you. If he comes, I'll knock the glass."

I placed my hand at the back of Sophie's head and turned onto all fours. "I missed you."

"I missed you too," she said between kisses as we both struggled to our feet. "Sehrin keeps standing outside my door, and he put another guard in the front."

Which only confirmed whatever obsession Sehrin had with my female. It wouldn't surprise me if that guy got turned on by females fighting him. Made it all the more appealing to subdue them.

"You have to be careful around him, Sophie. Don't provoke him, okay? Don't argue with him."

"What happened to your hand?" She grabbed it and lifted it up, studying a blistered, red palm. "You burned yourself?"

"Yup, on that force field around your balcony," I said with a faint laugh. "That's how I ended up in Izara's room instead."

Sophie shook her head and sighed, then quickly retrieved the healer pack from the cabinet beside us. Together, we stepped outside on the balcony, where she tossed the bag onto one of the large loungers.

220 V. K. LUDWIG

"Which one is good for burns?"

I sat down beside her, opened the bag, and pointed. "That one."

She unscrewed the tub and, with gentle motions, applied the salve to my hand. "Guess I have to spend my nights alone now until the masquerade."

My heart ached.

And for a long time after that.

"I'll find a way into your room," I said, recognizing the potential lie as the words spread bitter across my tongue. "Perhaps I should burn myself more often. I enjoy your touch."

Her smirks were the cutest thing, and I watched my fill as she closed the tub and returned it to the bag. Shyness long replaced with deep-rooted intimacy, she mounted me, her hungry kisses stoking my own appetite.

That would have been a great moment to give her the ring, if it wasn't for the way sweet moans spilled into my mouth. Sophie ground her pussy against me, making my penis swell against the thick denim. Her skin smelled of something she called mint, and her kisses tasted like the promise of a better life. A life with goals and dreams and untainted love.

"I want you, Adeas," she moaned, and suddenly the ring was all but forgotten.

"You want me?"

"Uh-huh." Her fingers raked through my hair with such demand my head jerked with her rough movements. "Mate me slow and deep."

I shoved one hand between us, knuckles rubbing over her sex while fingers fumbled my pants open. "That's how you want it? Slow and deep?"

"For now," she crooned, looking so fucking sexy with the way she threw her head back.

Grabbing her waist, I pushed her down onto my erection, teasing a groan from her before I slipped my hands underneath her shirt. I kneaded a set of small breasts, probably never to nurse a child of ours but I cared little so as long as I had her.

Sophie pulled her shirt over her head. Then, she shifted her legs to the left, to the right, slowly slipping out of her shorts. My shirt went next, her eyes not taking me in with judgement but desire. Whatever she saw, it wasn't the cuts, scars, and bruises that still covered my body, each one telling the story of a soul once lost.

"I love you, *anam ghail*," I whispered, that thing inside my chest fluttering.

And by taking my hand and placing it onto her sternum, she told me that she loved me too. Who needed words when your souls spoke to each other in their very own language?

She slipped off me, tugging my pants halfway down before she took my sneakers off. Then she kept tugging, the both of us soon naked underneath the universe, trapped within a dome of glass.

Lowered to her knees, she prodded my thighs apart, and my cock jerked in anticipation. Even before she took me in hand, her lips clasped around my crown.

"Fuck," I moaned, watching tight lips run up and down my shaft, thick veins glistening against the dim light coming from Izara's room. "Your mouth feels so good around my cock."

A slurp sounded through the late night when she pulled back. She trailed her tongue around my corona, sending intense sparks of pleasure into my testicles. Shivers followed when she cupped them, massaging my sack with her thumb.

At her next retreat, she nudged her lips tighter around my head, suckling on it with shallow strokes that sent my spine ablaze. She milked that sensitive area slowly, a drawn-out mmmh vibrating around tortured flesh whenever I sensed small amounts of seed spill into her mouth.

I dug my fingers into her hair, a little too roughly, but the thrusts I gave into that sweet mouth of hers came slow and easy. "This is so fucking good I'll curse the moment you make me release."

"No you won't," she choked out, a smile wrapping around my cock.

A tongue way too skilled to be anything but maddening ran down my shaft, edging me closer to climax with little more than air around my cock. She licked my sack, circled her tongue around one first, then the other, tempting my control. She pulled the skin between her lips, making my hand grab my cock all on its own.

I jerked myself off while she kissed the base of my shaft, her groans and whimpers too much to bear. "Suck me, Sophie. Take that cock into your mouth again and drink my seed."

That torturing tongue came back up, desperate flesh jerking against it until a hot mouth wrapped around a pulsing head once more. This was nothing like I'd ever known before. The sweetest agony.

She sucked me to the very depth of her throat, strangling on what I offered, gulping, moaning, and yet she asked for more.

I closed my eyes and leaned back, my testicles hard and swollen and so fucking ready to coat her gums in seed.

Needy, lips and tongue worked over hard flesh, eager to get a taste of me.

It didn't take much longer. A couple of thrusts and a groan in warning, then I let it all go and released my seed for her to swallow in drowned little whimpers. Stream after stream, she sucked me empty, only to keep going when nothing else came, licking me clean.

"That was amazing." My voice came out hoarse, tormented even, but it had nothing on that deep rumble coming from my chest when she impaled herself on my cock.

"Oh my fucking god," she cried out, rotating her hips on a shaft still hard, so fucking pumped full with blood I'd please her all night long in whichever way she wished. "You feel perfect."

Because I was meant to be inside her, seed her, hold her, claim her over and over again because everything about her was mine.

"Turn around on my cock," I said, holding her waist as I helped her. "Look up, Sophie. My sweet Sophie."

With her back pressed against my chest and her legs resting astride mine, I leaned back, pulling her right along with me. I rotated my hips, thrust upward, one hand caressing her breast while the other stroked her gaze upward.

"See those flashes of lights? All those stargazers and cargo vessels?" I asked, hand slipping from breast to clit, rubbing it until it turned hard against my fingertip. "That's us up there. In a few suns from now, that will be us. I'll be so good to you, Sophie, so good. I promise. On my life, I swear I'll keep it."

She took my finger and brought it to her lips, suckling

on my digit, running her teeth up and down in never-ending ripples of pleasure. "I know you will."

I grabbed her neck, pulling the back of her head against me into that groove beside my sternum where she belonged. Right above where she and I connected. I fucked and fingered her to orgasm like that while be both stared up into the universe.

And once she was sated, I returned what I'd stolen.

TWENTY-THREE

Sophie

"The table is open for bets now." White-gloved and straight-spined, the Toroxian dealer nodded.

My eyes flicked to the holographic clock over at the casino's entrance: thirty-five minutes until our escape.

My heart pounded.

My palms layered in sweat.

This had to work out! Not because they would punish me in ways I probably couldn't even imagine if they caught us, but because, for Adeas, it would mean death.

Nerves. I had to have them now.

Cool and soothing, the carved rims of the palathium chips ran along my fingers and clanked into a perfectly aligned tower. I pushed it across the black felt covering the tabletop, gambling with my life a couple of chips at a time.

The mask sat tightly against my face, red feathers covering the tension while golden glitter hopefully distracted from that relentless throb in my eyes.

I clasped three more chips and tossed them in front of

me. Someone would escape tonight, and my bet lay on us. "Torigash constellation."

"No more bets," the dealer announced, the short male standing on a pedestal at the center of the table.

At the push of a button, the wheel in front of him spun, little figurines of planets, stars, and moons clanking across its surface. They slowed. Slowed some more. Halt.

"Auromedus constellation of the tau sigma galaxy," he said, reaching for my chips. "Taigh Arosh wins. *Leska* loses."

It meant nothing.

Only a matter of chance.

I rose from my padded stool, red silk cocooning my body, bringing out all those curves nobody would ever again touch in exchange for credits.

A glance at the clock.

A wham of my heart.

In about half an hour, I would leave this hell, but I would take that devil of a mate with me. He had my soul and I had his — that in itself was heaven.

Vetusians and Jal'zar clapped as I took my loss with dignity, the motion sending a swirl of perfume and cologne through the air. All around me, the masquerade was in full swing, the entire casino decorated in grandeur only sex slavery could possibly afford.

"What a shame, my sweet *leska*." A warrior in dress uniform and black mask casually trailed his finger down my arm, the fact that he'd called me *his* suggesting he'd fucked me at least once. Obviously not a memory worth recalling. "Who would have expected that we'd see the sun of *Taigh Arosh* loose after such a winning streak."

I grabbed a flute of Cultum ice berry wine from the table beside me, letting the bubbles stir my stomach before the drink would calm my frayed nerves. "My winning streak is only just beginning."

"Ah," he breathed, one hand clasped behind his back, the other reaching toward me. "Before you rob Levear of his fortune, may I have this dance with you?"

Where was Levear anyway? I hadn't seen the boss ever since the masquerade started. Twenty-five minutes until I had to be at the kitchen.

An uncomfortable tingle swept through my veins.

Quit staring at the time!

I couldn't risk being late, but I could risk drawing suspicion even less. I'd played whore for so long, what were another couple of minutes? No need to risk our escape over a dance.

Twenty-four minutes. Shit.

Why did I keep staring?

Another deep breath.

I put the flute down and placed my hand into his. "I would love to."

He led me toward the center of the casino, where an arched ceiling ended in a glass cupola. Guards patrolled the hallways along the banister of the second floor, looking like extra-stylish bank robbers with their weapons and painted masks.

The warrior slung one arm around my middle and pulled me tightly against him, while intertwining his other hand with mine. "Are you familiar with the Kokonian Pivot?"

Repulsion raced up and down my body, that hum behind my sternum distorting into something ugly. *Not your mate.* As if I needed yet another reminder...

"Kokonian Pivot, Vetusian Sun Sway, Jal'zar Two Stomp. I can dance them all."

"Very well, *leska*," he chuckled, half a smile gleaming from the uncovered part of his mouth. "You look so stunning. I would love to spend the entire night with you."

Good luck with that. "That would be wonderful."

At the very next key of the piano, stolen from Earth, probably, I let him guide me into the Pivot. We turned and turned underneath the cupola, my eyes tracking the movement of the guards. Levear was nowhere to be seen, but that might work to our benefit. Izara, however, stood at one of the columns with a close eye on me.

I moved my legs and swayed my hips, my eyes locked on the clock while my dancing partners changed from warrior, to healer, to scholar, to... Jal'zar?

"*Kuna.*" Onyx claws dug into my hand, and a fang peeked from a snarl which bunched his gray lip against a sequin-scaled mask. "I can scent more fear on you than on the night I stung you inside the bathhouse. It's creeping from your pores so undiluted, I am tempted to hum for you to ease your distress."

A thick swallow trailed down my narrowing throat. The last thing we needed was a Jal'zar who could smell the strain of anticipation.

"I have no idea what you're talking about."

"Ever since that night, I have been wondering..." His tailclaw scratched over the silk of my dress, right above where he'd stung me, panic flaring my veins. "What if I sting you again and hum for you as is custom when a Jal'zar claims his mate? Could I force a bond onto a human soul?"

What?

A blaring alarm went off inside my skull, and I pulled away from him. "I have to leave now."

Claws dug deeper into my skin while his tail wrapped

around my waist — escape impossible. Unless I made a scene...

No scene. Stay calm.

Excuse. I needed one.

"I —"

"Now I scent your lie," he murmured. "And the way it mixes with your fear is more than I can handle, *kuna*. What has you in such distress?"

A hundred feet away from us, Izara stared at me from the corner of her eyes, head cocked in question.

A flick at the clock. Shit.

My breath lodged inside my windpipe. With seven minutes to spare, it was too early for Izara to create a distraction so I could steal myself away. Timing. It was crucial.

But I had to shake this guy.

My feet grew hot, itchy. I had to stop reacting so strongly because this Jal'zar sure smelled it. There... he just flared his nostrils. What if Adeas wasn't done preparing the escape route yet?

What was that noise?

Something hummed in the tight space between me and the warrior, and it didn't come from behind my sternum. He hummed! For me...

A strange sensation radiated from my core and spread into my limbs, turning muscles soft and skin warm. Whatever the Jal'zar did was working to calm me, but I wouldn't let him take me away.

It let my eyes lock with Izara and nodded.

Wasting no time, her heels beat the ground, and she shoved the warrior aside. "*Mikara ruk enu uri!* You speak of bonding this human whore, but refuse to take any of us Jal'zar as your *zaya*? Mikara weeps over your soul, *ulish'ok!*"

The warrior spun around, tail claw curling above his shoulder. "What I do with my soul is not a concern of yours, *kimi'tas!*"

Izara's eyes turned into purple slits. Whatever *kimi'tas* meant, she answered it with a blood-curling hiss. She thrust herself forward, claws digging into the warrior's chest while her tail claw aimed at his thigh.

"*Leska!*"

Izara's shout rang in my ears.

Prostitutes and patrons came together and rounded the emerging chaos. Above us, guards fell into a jog on their way toward the stairs. I had to get out. Now!

Slender shoulders pushed and shoved through the crowd. A mix of sweat and expensive fragrances, the tight space ripped on my shoulders and squeezed my ribcage.

I stumbled toward the back part of the casino, pencil-thin heels wobbly underneath me. Izara's screams mixed with the deep-throated shouts of guards, but I continued on my way to the kitchen.

Once there, I threw myself against the wall, taking one breath, two, three. I had to calm down, but my heart pounded so loudly it distracted from my thoughts.

I sneaked up to the kitchen door and glanced through the bullseye. Behind it, instead of ranges and counters, machines as tall as me stood sentry, the scent of *bullhabou* and grains wafting from the gap underneath.

Something heavy landed on my shoulder.

Coldness struck my core.

They already caught me?

I swung around, but that heaviness slipped down along my arm. A strong clasp around my wrist and a tug later, I was pulled through the door and into the kitchen, catching nothing but a glimpse of white from the corner of my eye.

Adeas pressed me against the wall, his fiery kiss shoving the mask around on my face. "We have to hurry."

He trembled.

Had for the last two suns since we had to stretch the Paraprofin to make it last. It was like his addiction playing peek-a-boo, reminding us that he was neither okay nor healthy. And yet he kept fighting.

I ran my fingers through his hair. "Stop kissing me or we'll never make it out."

With a laugh, he let his fingers trail to the back of my head, fumbling there until he removed my mask and tossed it behind him. "Much better. No more masks, *leska*. Sophie is much prettier anyway."

Female droids stood about and waited for whatever patrons had ordered, all human-looking because they probably served more than just meals. They spared us no attention, and Adeas pulled me behind him.

We reached what must have been a food storage, with boxes of nutrition cartridges, wooden crates holding wine bottles from Earth, and several metal containers marked in Cosmic, which I could barely read.

"This is it, Sophie. Just a few more steps and you'll be free. You're going home." He pulled me in for another kiss, this one rushed, desperate.

"*We* are going home. I'm not leaving without you."

"Yes, you will. If something happens, you keep going and leave me behind." His lips trembled so hard they slipped from mine. "But if I make it out with you, promise you won't forget about me. Swear to me that you'll remember me when I come back from rehab."

I nuzzled his cheek. "I swear."

A tear lodge from his eye, but he immediately wiped it away, handing me what looked like small foam plugs. "Put those into your nostrils. It'll filter most of the *sithadol* as you breathe through them, which is a toxic fume. Keep your mouth closed, and only breathe through your nose."

He plugged his own nose and gestured me toward the wall. "Once I lifted you up there, you push the lever on the side and climb into the vent."

"What about you?"

Without another second wasted, he wrapped his arms around my thighs and picked me up. "Don't worry about me."

Why did he make this escape about me only? How could I ever make a new life without him when he was engrained to my soul?

Spine straight, I let my manicured nails trace the outline of the vent where wall met ceiling.

A little metal hook.

Click.

The vent cover opened to the inside, and I hoisted myself into the small cubical cutout. *Push!*

Bracing my knee against the stone, my dress tore with a loud *hrkh*. The metal of the vent seared cold against my shin. I'd dealt with worse pain than that.

I crawled forward, the vent barely leaving enough room to turn. "Adeas?"

A slam, followed by an *oomph*.

My heart skipped a beat. "Adeas?"

Did he fall? Get attacked?

There was nothing for a while.

Complete silence, aside from my ragged heartbeat.

Then, stomps resonated behind me.

Another slam, followed by soles dragging over stone and... oomph. He couldn't reach the vent.

I slowly backed up. Once the tip of my heel dipped

down, I stretched my legs and braced. Five seconds later, footsteps, slam, and finally hands wrapping around my knee. At that moment, Adeas seemed almost heavy.

He moaned behind me, and I pressed my damp palms down on the metal, pulling myself forward. His weight slowly eased away from my searing joint.

No matter how I tilted my head, I couldn't see shit. "Are you okay?"

"Don't talk. Crawl straight all the way."

Right. Mouth closed.

The vent left little more room than my dress, and my stomach almost dragged over the metal bottom as I crawled my way toward freedom at funeral pace.

Wherever the *palathium* had been soldered together, sharp edges protruded. My palms dodged them just fine, but they scraped across my knees and down along my shins, cuts burning my skin. And yet I kept going, paying for freedom with pain. I was used to it.

Underneath me, the occasional vent cover showed guards patrolling hallways and staff moving along tunnels. Between the music blasting from the casino and the air handler coughing louder the closer we came to the sweat-mines, none of them noticed our sneaking around overhead.

When I reached the dark end of the square tube, I twisted my body as far as I could. Adeas' hand came into view. He gestured toward the vent in front of me at the bottom.

I once more traced the outline. This one, too, opened toward the inside, so I scooted back a little before I gave a tug.

Oh, God. That was a hundred-foot drop, at least from this viewpoint. A laundry cart stood parked right underneath it. I froze where I should have kept going, until Adeas gave a shove against my butt.

Now wasn't the time to chicken out.

I crouched toward the open vent.

My lungs faltered to a near-stop.

I dived down, down, down — *thomp*.

My body sunk into the soft depth of linen and towels, the stench of sex undeniable even through the nose plugs. The cargo crates surrounding the cart moved.

Except that they didn't.

The laundry cart was what moved, rolling slowly out of position. I had to climb out and roll it back underneath —

Clank.

Beside me, Adeas' body crashed against the metal frame with a groan before the force of the impact threw him into the sheets. Oh my god! He had to be injured.

I dug myself through fabric toward him, keeping my voice as low as panic allowed. "Are you okay?"

He clutched a hand to his side, his face a display of frowns and curled lips. His entire body trembled, screaming for that poison that had fed him for so long.

"I broke a fucking rib." And yet he waved toward the edge of the cart. "Climb out that way."

Tingly limbs pushed and pulled me over the edge, and I slipped down, heels clanking against stone. Behind me, Adeas groaned, his body clanking and thumping against the cart. Each attempt in hoisting himself over the edge failed.

"Sophie —"

"Don't you dare say it." I would *not* leave him behind.

I kicked those stupid heels off my feet, the moisture of the sweatmines settling against my naked soles. One tug on my dress, and it ripped up to my crotch.

Jumping up, I grabbed the edge of the cart. Half my

body dangled on the outside. The other half hung folded, arms reaching toward Adeas.

"Hold on to me!"

Lips pressed together, he hesitated, but eventually grabbed my arms. He pulled himself up, soles bracing against the inside of the cart. His face grew paler with each grunt.

He was heavy but I wouldn't let go.

I tossed.

I struggled.

One more wiggle and he worked himself over the edge, immediately clutching his arm over his broken rib. "Into the tunnel."

Adeas wrapped the other around me. "We're almost there."

He guided me around a bunch of those large cargo boxes we used to fill, always glancing back to make sure nobody had spotted us. Behind the boxes lay a narrow passage. An old service entrance perhaps, seemingly carved into the mildew-covered stone.

Pulling those plugs out of my nose, I tossed them to the ground. That was when I smelled it. Freedom!

It came with the tang of mold and humidity, but it diluted with each step toward the exit, filling with fresh air. We made it! We fucking made it!

"There's the stargazer." Adeas pulled his plugs out and pointed at the vessel hovering close to the stone ledge. "Yorim, start the fusion panels!"

Inside the brightly lit stargazer, a Vetusian sat on a hover chair at the far right end, surrounded by blinking holograms.

"We'll have to jump, so I'll go first and catch you. Got it?"

Did he say jump? "Yes."

I inched toward the edge.

My body froze over with hesitation, the gap between the ledge and the stargazer massive. Massive and entirely black underneath. If I didn't make that jump, I'd fall for eternity. That was what Izara had meant when she told me *Taigh Arosh* sat on a floating piece of Odheim.

Thomp!

"Start the fucking panels," Adeas shouted once more, then his voice calmed. "You can do it, Sophie." He reached a hand out for me from inside the stargazer. "I got you, okay? Look at me! Let me save you, so you can save me."

My eyes locked with his, and that invisible string hooked behind my sternum hummed with love and reassurance. This jump was nothing compared to what he and I had been through.

I took a few steps back. "Catch me."

"Always."

Naked soles braced against the cold stone underneath me. I pushed. I ran. I jumped.

Strong arms wrapped around me and pulled me inside the vessel, the cold stone against my feet replaced by ribbed metal.

"I got you," Adeas whispered, pulling me deep into his embrace, so warm, so reassuring... until he turned to stone. "Yorim?"

He stepped away from me, all warmth dissipating, placing two fingers against the side of his friend's neck. That guy didn't move, aside from the way his head seemed to slightly tilt away from the pressure.

All strength sucked from my limbs, my knees tingly as if they wanted to buckle. Yorim was dead.

"Someone shot him." Shot him? With a curse, Adeas

was by my side again, his hand searing against my wrist. "Sit down and buckle up."

"But —"

"Now!" Rough hands tossed me against the row of seats lining the wall, Adeas' eyes darting around nervously. "I have to start the fusion panels before —"

"The junkie is trying to save the whore." Where did that voice come from? Before I managed to turn, fingers wrapped around my throat from behind. They squeezed. Hard. "Problem is, *sgu'dal*, you're not hero material."

TWENTY-FOUR

Adeas

"Of all the Vetusians you could have seduced to get you out of here, you had to choose the slurring, stealing, stammering *sgu'dal*?" Sehrin jumped into the stargazer, the palathium floors underneath us vibrating on impact.

I pulled Sophie from the chair and pushed her behind me. "Not a single step closer."

He scoffed a laugh. "Or what? Look at you, *sgu'dal*. Shaking. Sweating. How long until you s-st-sta-hammer like a fucking idiot, huh?"

I reached behind me for Sophie, the motion cutting through bruising flesh and at least one broken bone. I was going to die, no doubt about that. Fine by me so as long as I would keep my promise, and Sophie would make it out.

Without turning around, I sidestepped toward the control panel with her. "Do you see the blue floating disc, *anam ghail*? Swipe over it."

"*Anam ghail*?" Sehrin cocked his head, his brows first

furrowing then arching upward along with the corners of his mouth. "*Anam* fucking *ghail*? Good enough excuse for her poor life choices, I guess."

A small hand tapped my upper arm. "What now?"

"Three interconnected red circles. Swipe over the hologram."

Deep inside my chest, between lung and heart, Sophie's fear tremored along our link. It wasn't my panic that turned my fingertips numb. It was hers.

I reached over my shoulder and smoothed whatever I came in contact with. "You'll be fine."

"No she won't." Sehrin pulled his gun from the holster, blue stripe illuminating the length of the barrel. It was charged, and he pointed it straight at me. "Don't make her a promise you can't keep. Now step aside. I'd hate to shoot you. There's no fun in it."

A breeze whistled through the open ramp coming from the blackness underneath. I had to wrestle him over the edge. With no weapon, no help, all I could do was throw myself against him. Perhaps he'd fall before he pulled the trigger. Perhaps he wouldn't.

One tremble chased the next, my skin shrinking so tightly around me each breath was a struggle. We were so close. So fucking close. I wouldn't fail Sophie now.

Fists balled by my side, I braced my soles against the ground. One step to the right to get Sophie out of his line of sight, then I thrust forward.

A snarl curled Sehrin's upper lip.

The barrel came straight at me again.

Fap!

Heat scorched through my knee. The moment my limbs came down, the joint disintegrated, caving in underneath pain while something snapped above my kneecap. A tendon?

I toppled to the ground with a scream, and Sehrin let out a malicious laugh. "Just kidding. I've been itching to pull that trigger. Good thing you stepped away from her."

"Adeas!" A torn red dress pushed into view, and a whiff of mint filled the air around me. "Sehrin, you sick animal!"

Pain tortured every nerve in my body, but it had nothing on those hot needles pricking up and down my spine. Yellow seats. Overhead handles. Holograms. Everything shook around me. No, nothing shook. Fuck! Fuck! I was rocking again. No, not now. A flurry of air. Where did Sophie go?

Sehrin yanked her to her feet by her arm, barrel pressed so hard against her cheek a shadow formed within the depression of her skin. "Another stupid move and she'll loose teeth."

"Don't hurt her!"

"Oh, it'll hurt," he said with infuriating calm. "And once she gets used to the pain, she'll come to find that there's pleasure in it. Perhaps she'll even come begging for more. Ask me to bring her so close to death she won't be able to get off on anything else ever again."

I thrust myself forward, but he dug the barrel even deeper until Sophie yelped in pain. My body froze, limbs disabled. I would give my life for her if only she escaped. But how if my life was so fucking worthless? I was so weak. So damn weak.

"Tell me, Adeas, how did you get this arrogant bitch to look at you like that, huh? When I first caught on to you guys, I figured she was just using you." He dragged his tongue over the side of her neck, ripping shiver after shiver from her. "But all those glances you stole from each other when you believed nobody was watching? If she would have looked at me like that, just once... I would have made her mine. Might still consider doing it."

"She's my bonded mate."

"Meh." He shrugged. "It'll fade once you're dead. But first, she'll suffer for that eye she took. And since I can't harm what I intend to put to good use later —"

Fap!

"No!"

"Augh!" All pain transferred from knee to upper arm, rivulets of blood rolling onto the floor.

"Get the fuck up or I'll start shooting fingers off."

I struggled myself onto my one good leg, the other only hanging there for balance. "Just take me and let her go. Do whatever you want with me."

"I'll do whatever I want with you *and* keep her. Watch." Sehrin wrapped his hand around Sophie's neck and slammed his filthy lips onto hers, kissing her until her limbs tossed.

"Stop it!" I screamed, cried, giving a sorry excuse of a hop toward them. "You're choking her you sick fuck!"

"I know," Sehrin said, his mouth hovering over a passed-out Sophie, her pillaged body draping over his arm. "Isn't it beautiful? To watch her go all soft and peaceful against me? Next time I choke her, she'll be screaming her release with my dick inside her mating cleft."

He swiped over the holograms beside him and extended the ramp, metal screeching over the stone ledge. "Walk. Hop. Whatever. Back to *Taigh Arosh*."

Pain crackled through my knee, my rib, my arm. But most of all, it raged where I kept half of Sophie's soul. I'd let her down. How could I have been so arrogant to think I could save her? Sehrin was right. I wasn't a hero. I was sick, my body and mind not capable of saving anybody — perhaps not even myself.

One leg hopping, the other dragged behind while I held onto the wall. That was how I made my way back along the tunnel. Behind me, Sehrin carried my mate, the weight of failure crashing down on me full force. I should have urged Sophie to wait until CAT got here.

"Levear's office," Sehrin said when we reached the sweatmines, where guards and a handful of workers lowered their heads. Nobody fucked with Sehrin. Nobody but us...

Everything turned blurry around me, but I didn't pass out. I had to think but could barely even look straight. I would take the blame. Tell Levear I wanted to have Sophie to myself. Mercy for her. Death for me. A fair deal, and the best outcome I could hope for.

Then we turned into his office, and my blood pressure dropped right there. That deal wouldn't happen, because Levear looked a whole lot like Yorim.

A pale body leaned crooked inside a large hover chair, pin-sized dot at the temple telling me he'd been shot.

"Change in administration." Sehrin lowered Sophie onto the blue couch in the corner. Me, he grabbed by the collar and dragged onto the ground to lean against the back of Levear's desk.

He tossed himself onto the couch next to Sophie, his fingers tracing up and down her calf. "I never asked Levear for much. Except for Sophie. But after what happened with Caroline... hmm, he should just have said yes."

With each stroke he gave over my mate's body, that

prickling along my spine extended along my arms, legs. "You killed her."

"It was an accident," he snarled. "Human females are so fragile. Do you wanna know when I decided that I wanted her?" Gun barrel clanked against a yellow, glowing pupil. "She's got fire on the inside, and I —"

"Are you planning on making me suffer by listening to your bullshit?" I scoffed. "You're doing a lot of talking. What is this? Get her into her room, then come back down and finish me off any way you like."

"Stop trying to be a fucking hero!"

At his shout, Sophie startled awake.

She sucked in a sharp breath and pushed herself up to sit, her body swaying, her eyes darting across the room. Until they locked with mine.

Her lips trembled and melted downward at the corners, her entire face scrunching up in a haunting display of fear and resignation.

Sehrin stroked over her golden hair, either oblivious or ignorant to the way her head shrunk into her shoulders. "Willing to tell me how she likes it? I actually want her to enjoy my prick."

No matter how much I commanded my legs to jump up, all I got were... trembles. I had no say over my body, as if it purposely revolted against me for starving it of that damn poison. All I had was a painfully clear mind, utterly aware of how I was failing. Right here. Right now.

"Sooophiiie," Sehrin crooned, twirling her strand around his finger, smiling at that first tear of hers. "Is that what the *sgu'dal* called you? How he got your panties to drop? Sooophiiie. Sooophiiie."

How dare he speak her name? "Shut up!"

I didn't plan. I acted.

Muscles fed by adrenaline and rage contracted underneath me. I thrust myself up, knee buckling but I didn't give a shit. Just one good hit against the temple. Temporary brain trauma. One shove with my palm against his nose. Broken bone and impaired vision. Anything would do, as long as I didn't give up.

Sehrin jumped up from the couch.

The moment his gun clicked from the chest holster, I duck and threw myself against him. Slammed right into him until he stumbled back. Sophie screamed. The couch toppled.

Something wrapped around my neck, breathing impossible. Useless feet dangled in the air - kicked it. Sehrin tossed me across the room and into the desk. Something cracked. My sides exploded in pain.

My cheek slapped against the carpet full force, burning. A ringing tortured my skull, drowning out the heavy footsteps I was certain came to finish me off. I was mistaken.

If I had any fight left in me, then it diminished the moment Sehrin followed up his laugh with a kick into my guts. It didn't kill. Only made me wish I was dead.

My entire body curled into itself.

A wheeze sucked through my tight throat.

Get up! Fight!

My body responded with defiance.

Everything trembled.

Everything shook.

"For a moment there, I was worried that things would get boring." Sehrin dug his hands into Sophie's hair and yanked her back onto the couch. "Don't you dare move stupid cunt, or I swear I'll cut your eye out."

Sophie collapsed into a shaky, crying mess and pressed

herself against the corner of the couch, knees pressed tightly against her chest. She stared at me from wet eyes, stray strands clinging to wet cheeks, tip of her nose turning red.

"Now, here comes the fun part." Sehrin kneeled down beside me, and what he did sent a flare of heat underneath my skin.

Pop.

The silver sphere touched down right in front of my nose. So close I could smell the deep blue and hear the way the powder shifted. My entire body turned light, so fucking light I must have floated.

"Fuck, you should see your eyes right now," Sehrin sneered. "Your pupils are blown already, and you haven't even snorted it yet."

"Please don't! Don't do this to him, please. I'll do whatever you want."

Sehrin laughed. "Yeah, you'll do whatever I want. But that has nothing to do with your junkie boyfriend here. Look at him, Sophie. And that's the guy you chose?"

Yeah, was I the guy she'd chosen?

My stomach convulsed. Locked up.

I'd pretended being someone I wasn't capable of being. Not yet. Would probably never get the chance of being. I would die on an overdose, either suffocating on my own snot or accidentally drowning myself.

Everything inside me screamed, shouted, that she was my mate, but what had I done? Instead of checking myself into rehab and letting CAT handle this, I'd lied to Sophie. Again. Told her I'd save her. Promised I'd get her out.

Fucking shit.

I'd broken every single promise.

Can't trust a *sgu'dal*.

"Fuck you, Sehrin!"

Did that come out at all? I tried to scream, but the words spilled out as drool dripping onto the floor. I was beaten. This was it.

"Please, Sehrin. I'll be yours. He's suffering," Sophie cried. "Don't do it, Adeas."

Just a little.

When would I get rid of that voice?

Never.

"Come on, *sgu'dal*," Sehrin whispered. "Spare me the work and overdose right here. I'll take care of Sophie. Promise."

My entire body tingled.

From the tip of my toes to the roots of my hairs, everything prickled. Proof of just how far I was from recovery, no matter how much the Paraprofin had me believe otherwise. I was just as much addicted now as I had been half a lunar cycle ago.

Everything around me spun. "Fucking asshole."

"How did you do it? Huh? Because I could tell you didn't get high for several suns. Did she fuck it out of you? Is she that good?"

A black boot carefully shoved the sphere toward me. If I as much as craned my neck that way, I could have snorted it right in. And I wanted to. Fuck did I want to suck it all in.

"You're not doing me that favor, are you?" Sehrin jumped up and punched his hands into his pockets. "Didn't expect you to be quite so... in control. I give you that."

Pupils caught on a blue vial and how it slowly, so fucking slowly, filled a syringe to the top. Beaten and defeated, I let my head collapse to the side. My body convulsed underneath sobs, too dehydrated to shed a single tear. I didn't want to die. Not like this. Any other way, but not like this.

"Please don't let her see it." Another kick into my stomach rocked me onto my back.

"No!" Sophie shouted, thrusting herself up from the couch.

One punch against her sternum from Sehrin, and she stumbled right back into the cushion. "Shut up and sit your ass down!"

He once more kneeled beside me. Betraying muscles strained toward the needle, wanting that fix, wanting that high. My heart pounded in excitement. Who would have thought dying could be so highly anticipated?

Sehrin shoved my head aside.

I swung my arms around his neck with a groan, curled myself upward with as much strength as I managed. It did nothing.

Something crackled and crunched around my broken rib, sucking all air from my lungs. There was a tug on the left side of my neck. What happened?

I turned my head toward Sophie's cries. The motion pulled on my neck. Something dangled there. Letting my fingers brush over the side of it, I found the syringe hanging.

I pulled it out. The plunger sat flush.

After so many suns without it, the drug coursed through me like liquid sunshine. It made its way into my brain, smudging my thinking one clear thought at a time. It tickled along my arteries and deep into the tiniest vessels.

I tossed the syringe aside. "Sophie?"

No answer. Just white noise.

No matter how fast my heart pounded, my breathing turned flat. My lungs slowed right along with it. No doubt my central nervous system was shutting down. I'd suffocate to death simply by forgetting to breathe.

I wheezed in a breath. "Sophie?"

Everything turned one shade darker.
My body rocked.
Something squeezed my hand.
Heaviness settled onto my body.
This. *This* was rock bottom.

TWENTY-FIVE

Sophie

"No, no, no, no... Adeas..." No matter how hard I shook him, all I got were grunts and slurs. "Don't die on me. Don't die on me, please." I slapped Sehrin's hands away from where they tried to grab me. "Why are you doing this to him?"

"I don't give a shit about him, Sophie." My fight was short-lived, and Sehrin yanked me to my feet by my arm. "Now, seeing you like this? So hurt. So vulnerable. That shit gets me so fucking hard I want to choke you all over again."

I wiggled in his clasp, fury drowning my senses. "You're a fucking psychopath, Sehrin."

"You sound like Levear." A golden, unmoving eye pinned me down, and a scarred upper lip pulled into a snarl just as his voice dropped into a menacing warning. "To be honest, the fact that you bonded yourself to this loser complicates things. But the link will fade. Over time, you won't feel him anymore."

Sehrin loomed over me, something dangerous burning

in that one good eye of his. Dark and twisted. "I'll make you my mate of choice, Sophie."

A shiver spiraled up my spine. "What?"

"Right... you've got no clue what's going on with your planet." This had to be a nightmare, but the pain throbbing in my esophagus from how he'd choked me was too biting to be imagined. "I choose you. And you, Sophie, will choose me back."

My molars crunched. "I will never be your mate. Not fated, and most definitely not chosen."

Sehrin grabbed my arm and ripped me away. He dragged me over the floor and tossed me onto the ground, the carpet burning into my knees and palms upon impact.

Less than ten feet from me, Adeas' body jerked. His spine arched, tossing him around in waves of seizures. Grunts had died into gargles and wheezing. Was he suffocating? Dying of a heart attack?

The vibration of heavy footfalls tingled my fingertips, running up my arm in quivers. Sehrin yanked my hair and pulled me onto my naked feet, but the pain barely registered. My body was too paralyzed to feel, my mind too blank to think of escape.

This was all my fault. If we would have waited for CAT, none of this would have happened. How could I have expected him to save me? Risk his life? A life he barely controlled?

My eyes burned with unshed tears, and the floor ripped out from underneath me. My mate was dying right beside me, and I was the one who'd killed him.

"Look at him." Sehrin turned my head toward dirty-white irises, fat, black pupils rolling from corner to corner. "I'm no healer, but I'd say that guy's fucking done."

"You're a disgusting, sadistic piece of shit!"

More yanking. This time by my hair once more. "Says the female who cut my eye out."

His shove crashed me against the desk, metal edge biting against my hip bones. A heavy hand pressed between my shoulder blades until my nipples turned hard against the cold surface. At the twist of my head, a vertebra cracked somewhere underneath the weight of his palm.

"It's a shame human females are so delicate," he said, his voice tinged with aggression. "That's something I learned the hard way, but I promise myself I'll go easier on you."

Will, not would, because there was no doubt punishment was but a heartbeat away. For the eye I'd taken. The scar I'd left. Each insolence I'd spat at him.

Harsh fingers clasped around my wrists, jerking my arms behind my back until my shoulders scorched. For a year, I'd pushed him too far, and his retribution would be brutal and cruel.

His weight settled against me, making my head jerk up to look at the dead Vetusian in front of me. Levear.

Heavy and suffocating, Sehrin's lips brushed against my ear, whispering, "Sophie."

Disgust filled my core, swelling like a tumor until it pressed against my organs, making everything inside me convulse. What sounded like an oath from Adeas corrupted into a curse coming from his lips.

All these weeks, I'd fought so hard, reminding myself that I was Sophie — now that I remembered, I just wanted to forget.

I am leska. I am leska.

It reverberated at the back of my skull like a silent prayer, but nothing inside me answered. Pure terror swept over me. Where had *leska* gone now that I needed her?

Needed that numb shell to protect me from whatever Sehrin would do to my body?

"Just fuck me and get it over with." Ah... there she was. A stone-cold bitch, detaching mind from body. "Then throw me back into my cage so everyone else can take what's left."

The weight retreated.

One pull on my waist, and he spun me around to face him. He pressed my legs apart with such force the rest of my dress ripped up to my bellybutton. Then he yanked on my thighs, letting my crotch hug his erection. Whatever. Just another cock.

"Do you see this thing?" He leaned in close enough his moist breath settled damp on my skin. He tapped against his bionic eye. "You cost me half my vision, and still I would have bought you from Levear the moment I had the credits. For an entire solar cycle, I got nothing from you but snarls and aggression, and then you throw yourself at that fucking *sgu'dal*? Why him? Huh?"

"I love him."

"Don't say that!" His skin turned mottled, and thick, blue veins lined his forehead. "You will love me. You will —" *Slap.* My eyes closed shut at the sound. *Slap.* No pain came. Sehrin slapped himself in the face like an insane person. "You will love me. Do you hear that? Sophie. You will love me."

Torturous pain hooked behind my sternum. I would never love him, and I would rather die here with Adeas than survive just to slip deeper than hell beside this psycho.

"What's so special about him?" Sehrin lowered himself on top of me as he fumbled his pants open. "Because he was gentle? You'll learn to like it rough. Because he whispered your name? I can do that. Listen. Sophie. Sophie..."

Something inside me snapped.

Sophie's small fists pounded unrelenting muscle, begging him to stop while *leska* told her to shut up. Didn't Sophie know that the more she fought the more it would hurt? Didn't *leska* know that she had to fight back? For an eternity, two entities fought an internal battle deep at my core, and I wasn't sure which one I rooted for.

Until I ripped my nails across his cheek.

Sehrin jerked back with a hiss, and I frantically shoved my hands across the desk behind me. There had to be something. A weapon. Something. Anything!

I clasped my fingers around the first solid thing within my reach. Cold. Stone or metal. Rough against my fingertips. With one yank, I brought it over my head and slammed it against his temple.

A dull clank, followed by Sehrin slapping whatever I'd hit him with to the ground. He wiped his hand over the bloody wound I'd caused. "I like how this is developing."

Slap.

His palm hit my cheek with such force my skin burned up like a wildfire, and traces of iron seasoned my tongue. The force yanked my head to stare at a pile of paperwork on the desk. When I turned my head back, I stared straight at the barrel of his gun.

My entire body froze into *leska*-mode.

This was it. There was no fighting this.

No escape.

And yet, Sehrin continued moaning my name, grunting it, whispering it, always bringing me back into the here and now, trapping my soul inside a body I wanted to abandon.

"I'll fuck that *sgu'dal* out of you until every part of your body hums my name."

"No!" I screamed, bucked, scratched. "Stop it! Stop!"

Tk!

A twitch skittered through his body.

His mass collapsed on top of me.

Sehrin turned entirely limp, breathing impossible aside from small gasps, and something warm drip-drip-dripped against my temple only to pool inside my ear.

I turned my head.

Then I saw it.

Izara!

An onyx tail claw stuck to Sehrin's temple, blood dripping from it as it wiggled, retreating from the brain it had just punctured.

My heart gave a jolt. "Izara!"

"Not quite, *kuna*," a deep voice rumbled.

Sehrin's corpse rolled off me and hit the ground with a loud *whomp*. In front of me stood the Jal'zar warrior from the bathhouse, ripping his scaled mask from his face. The tail claw, he wiped clean on his uniform.

"My warriors are waiting at the airlock." He picked me up and draped me over his arms, a deep, soothing rumble resonating from his chest. "You will return to Solgad with me."

"What? But... no. My mate. Please help him!"

Everything around me spun.

No. Did this nightmare never end?

This was all too much. The escape. Adeas. Sehrin. And now this Jal'zar tried to steal me away to yet another planet? To do what? Make me his whore like he'd threatened the last time?

He glanced over his shoulder where Adeas' body slowly stilled. "My soulbond will overshadow his."

That string behind my sternum ached as if it was made

of cartilage and someone dragged the teeth of a saw over it. This was insane. I couldn't take this anymore.

"Take a deep breath, *kuna*," he ordered, and the notion of his words turned my stomach upside down. "I shall sting you, hum for you, and force your soul to bind itself to mine if our goddess wills it. You will be the first of many before we claim Earth and defile their females like they have done with ours. Every sun I will rut behind you, forcing your body into pleasure no matter how much your mind wants to resist."

My heart clanked against my throat.

Blood swooshed inside my skull.

My soul belonged to Adeas. You have my soul, and I have yours. With each pound against his chest, my mind chanted it.

"Let me down!" I shouted but tossing in his arms was like throwing myself against a brick wall. "Please. Please, don't do this —"

A harrowing pain shot through my side, so familiar I let out a deafening scream. The blood in my veins heated to a point I must have melted. I hadn't known hell. *This* was hell.

My entire body curled up against a chest that had no spot where I fit perfectly, and my mind drifted into yet another pain-induced fog. He would hum for me. And regardless of if his kind could claim mine, he would make me his whore.

His chest lifted.

He was about to hum.

It began as a rattle, fluttering and pulsating against me. I braced for it. I waited. It never came.

Instead, the Jal'zar stumbled to a stop and let out an

aggressive growl. "I have one dozen warriors waiting for my return."

"Your warriors have been neutralized," someone said. In front of us stood the blurry outline of a black-scaled Vetusian.

He held the Jal'zar at gunpoint, finger on the trigger, his stance wide. He wasn't one of the guards Levear had on his payroll. Was he... a CAT officer?

"Lower the human female to the ground and step away from her," he said, his calm voice so foreign in this small hallway cramped with tension. "We will grant you safe passage if you do."

"Grant me?" the Jal'zar scoffed, his tail pulling from my side with a crackle, flinging it around, blood splattering the walls at the motion. "This female is mine, and I will take —"

His voice turned to silence.

Gravity shifted around me, and another set of arms ripped me from the Jal'zar just as he collapsed to the ground, limbs jerking and tail tossing.

"I got you, Sophie," a Vetusian who wasn't the one in nano-armor rumbled, his lips framed by a beard. "It's all over now."

"No, it's not over." I let my arm stretch out and fall behind me. "Save *him*. Save my mate."

————

Fingernails chipped in most places, red polish peeled in others, they gently dragged over Adeas' chest the way he liked it. Up on the beep of the heart monitor. Down on the huff of the ventilator they'd hooked him up to.

Face pale and lips a faint purple, he lay on the recovery pod, unconscious but alive. His lungs expanded each time the machine breathed for him, but I concentrated on the heartbeat which lay underneath. That still worked without help.

"Here." Captain Balgiz reached a steaming mug toward me. "The restaurant didn't have chamomile tea in their synthesizer databank, so I brought you peppermint instead. I hope that's okay."

I ignored the suspicion growing at the depth of my stomach, and let my fingers soak up the warmth of the mug. I'd escaped *Taigh Arosh*. And while this was hardly going to be easy, I wouldn't let my distrust in Vetusians build a new cage around my mind.

"So..." I took a sip of my tea as I pushed a stool toward him with my foot. "How long until we're leaving for Earth?"

The stool moaned underneath his mass. "Two of the other females still need tending before they're fit to travel. It won't be much longer since we have to leave here before the intercosmic community shows up with warships."

"But Adeas can't come..."

In my mind, I'd always pictured us stepping onto that stargazer together. I saw myself holding his hands, promising, pledging that I would wait for him. What were six months? Nothing, especially if you compared it to the rest of our lives.

"Not until he can breathe without assistance."

My heart sunk. "How do I know I can trust you? I won't leave him behind so the Empire can let him rot on this planet like you did with me."

"I know I failed you, Sophie." He sucked in his upper lip, and didn't return it until he'd tortured a small cut into it. "We can't undo what happened. But please consider that we have war on our doorstep, and our warriors will fight it gladly in order to return you and the others to Earth. The

258 V. K. LUDWIG

Jal'zar who tried to take you happened to be the son of a warlord."

I shivered. "He said he would make me his slave."

"And that's exactly what we need you to state. Publicly." He grabbed one of the folded blankets from the cart behind him, unfolded it, and draped it carefully around my shoulders. "The Jal'zar community is outraged. Getting a handle on abductions has cost us many warriors, and we can't risk war with them. Not yet."

He pointed at Adeas. "He ran from us that day. We underestimated how determined he was not to leave you alone, and how much he wanted to get you out of there. And sooner than we were ready to act."

"Yeah, Titean told me. He stole the Paraprofin."

There was a pause there, during which the air turned heavy with the chaos I knew would follow. I was the youngest one of the women. They would want interviews. Statements. Holograms. I wouldn't have any of that.

"Not gonna lie, Sophie, CAT left a mess behind at *Taigh Arosh*. We had no idea about the masquerade since Adeas didn't supply enough information. There will be many questions."

"I'll say whatever helps if that's what you need me to do." I slipped my hand down to Adeas', but he showed no reaction. "But I swear, if you don't bring him to that rehab facility, I'll tell the media that Jal'zar made me his mate and you killed him."

As massive as the Captain was, his weight shifted slightly away from me. "He's got a spot waiting for him. He'll go through six Earth months of withdrawal. As soon as he joins the inpatient therapy, you'll be able to visit him."

I kept his gaze when I nodded.

"You will be brought to a secret location," he said. "A

small neighborhood which you will share with the other females, with access to counseling and whatever else is required for you to overcome this."

My stomach turned. The last thing I wanted was to talk with some shrink. But if Adeas was strong enough to face his demons, then so was I.

"Sophie..." The Captain shoved on his undersized stool, frowns lining his forehead. "What made you so certain he was your mate? He ran before we got the results that confirmed it."

I tapped my sternum. "I feel him in here. Even now. To me, it's like music. To him, I think it's more like motion. Vibrations and such."

I pushed my chair closer to the pod and lowered my head against Adeas' shoulder so as not to interfere with the inhaler. A glimpse of hope coursed through me, a sensation so foreign, barely remembered, it brought tears to my eyes.

"You know, when he first ended up here, he was out for over a week," the Captain said. "He almost went into cardiac arrest twice, but do you think that fucker stopped mumbling your name? Sophie. Sophie. All the time. Drove me fucking insane because we searched and searched, but we couldn't find you."

He shifted his weight and pulled an interactive notepad from his pocket. "He drew an actual map of the entire compound. Wrote down where you are around what time. Tunnels. Service hallways. Everything. That guy... that guy..." He pointed at Adeas. "He sustained three broken ribs, a collapsed lung, a shattered kneecap, a gunshot wound to his upper arm, along with internal bruising and bleeding. That tells me he tried his damn hardest, even if we were the ones who saved you."

"You think you saved me?" I dried my tears on Adeas'

arm, a chuckle worming from my chest. "Uh-uh. My mate saved me long before tonight. Without him, you would be staring at *leska* right now."

Beside me, Captain Balgiz rose, turning away to leave before he glanced back at me. "Anything else I can do for you?"

I pulled the scrunchie from my knotted hair, which he received in his open palm. "Can you please make sure he gets this as soon as he wakes up?"

He turned the black scrunchie between his clasped fingers. "What for?"

"Don't worry," I said. "He knows what it means."

TWENTY-SIX

Sophie

I sat inside my skycar on the parking lot of Whispering
Plains, the rehab facility located in former Arizona.

So much had changed since my abduction from Earth,
and then again during the last three months ever since I'd
returned. For one, humans were finally allowed to drive in
hover traffic, which promptly caused a three percent
increase in accidents, as per Imperial News One. Mostly
caused by women, which Vetusians were quick to forgive.

I checked myself in the mirror once more, smoothing
brown bangs back into formation. Something I had only
slowly gotten used to, but with the media all over 'Sophie
with the long blonde hair', it had been inevitable.

At a voice command, the driver door opened upward. I
stepped outside, immediately catching a whiff of heat and
baked sand. The high desert offered a mild climate in these
parts which, as Melek had explained to me, helped addicts
in their recovery.

I hadn't worn heels ever since my escape from *Taigh*

Arosh. Not that I needed to. I managed stumbling up the stairs just fine inside my white ballerinas, no matter how often I'd made my way along the winding steps surrounded by shrubs and tall grasses for months now.

Once a week, I took the two-hour drive to visit Adeas. Once a week, one of the healers told me that he wasn't ready to see me yet. It stung like a knife to the heart. But it wasn't rejection that kept him pushing me away: it was shame.

Mom sometimes didn't want to see me when she'd been forced into rehab. And it was exactly those moments when I had the most hope that she would recover. Shame could be a powerful motivator for change.

But this time was different.

Melek had commed me last night, telling me that Adeas had specifically expressed that he wanted to see me.

My entire body tingled.

After almost three months, I would finally see him again. How much weight had he gained? Perhaps he'd grown a beard? Cut his hair?

I stepped inside the facility, where the draft of the AC immediately played on the hem of my white skirt. They'd reinstated his healer license on probation, and he helped at the small infirmary of this facility, taking care of the occasional injury.

I reached my hand out so the care droid at the reception could scan my DNA. "I'm here to see healer Adeas."

"Please have a seat," the droid said. "If the resident is available, one of the healers will take you to him."

I lowered myself onto one of the upholstered benches, which stood in neat rows along the wall of glass overlooking the gardens. Then I waited. And waited some more.

Seconds ticked into minutes. They added into half an

hour. Tension crawled up my spine, making me curl into myself on that lonely bench. What if he'd changed his mind?

I crossed my legs.

Uncrossed them.

Leaned forward.

It was of no help, because that tension kept needling my spine until I couldn't take it anymore.

I got up and paced around the large planter at the center, which had a roundish stone sculpture in the middle. They did a lot of yoga and meditation in this place. Being mindful. That was what they called it.

At the click of a door, I swung around.

My heart registered what my eyes hadn't even perceived yet, because it sunk.

Sunk deep and shattered.

"I'm so sorry." Melek walked toward me, each slow shake of his head like a tug on those useless, overstretched heartstrings of mine. How many more rejections could I take? "Sophie, he was so determined to see you last night. Then we had a situation over breakfast and... I thought he'd bounce back from it, but he just told me he's not ready."

I ignored how my fingers tingled.

He wasn't ready. I had to accept that.

But then my shoulders bobbed, and the whole weight of *not ready* came crashing down on me. I hadn't realized I'd been crying until my eyes burned. Why wouldn't he let me visit him? I had seen him at his worst, so just how bad could this be that he kept sending me away?

"Come here." Melek wrapped his arms around me, offering me a shoulder to cry on which I quickly soaked in tears. "It might not feel like progress but trust me when I tell you it is. This was the first time he got himself ready to see you. I think what makes it worse for him is the fact that you saw him relapsing."

"But it wasn't his choice. Sehrin injected him with it."

Melek's chest retreated on a sigh. "It's not so simple for him. He blames himself for not fighting harder."

What? He'd fought his hardest!

"What was the incident? At breakfast?"

Melek clasped my shoulders, gently prodding me away until my eyes found his. "He got so worked up over your visit, he didn't realize he pulled chunks of hair from his head. When we made him aware, he freaked out. Didn't want you to see him like that. Sophie, he's trying so hard."

"I know he is." And exactly therein lay the fucking problem because I was stuck with this disappointment and nobody to blame. "Maybe if you just brought me to him? So I could tell him that it's okay?"

Melek frowned. "We encourage them to make conscious decisions, Sophie. He decides."

He decides.

That phrase struck a chord reverberating with a memory of the first time Adeas and I had sex. I had decided then, and he'd let me. It was only fair I did the same, but fuck it was hard. So hard.

"He understands that he encouraged you to come today," Melek said, the hint of a smile tugging on his lips. "So he gave me permission to have you observe him. From afar. That way, he won't have to face a direct confrontation. Would you like to?"

"Are you kidding?" I said with something between a giggle and a sob. "Of course I want to."

At Melek's gesture, I followed behind him through one of the doors, from where he led me along a brightly lit hallway, one side entirely covered in windows.

"He's at the basketball court right now," Melek stopped in front of a door where he typed a code into the holographic control panel. "It was his suggestion that I take you to his room, since you'll be able to see him from here."

I stepped into the room, which didn't contain more than a bed, a desk, and shelves filled with at least twenty books. "This is his room?"

"Uh-huh. Like I said, it was his suggestion, so it's okay for you to be in here. My guess is he wanted you to see it." He stepped up to the window, but my feet somehow rooted to the floor. "It's progress."

My toes turned numb underneath me. A glimpse at Adeas was a mere three steps away, and yet I couldn't get my feet to move. Was that how he felt? This crippling mix of anticipation and dread?

I pointed at his bed, the edges of his blanket neatly tugged underneath his mattress. "Is it okay if I..."

"Go ahead."

Adeas had always been orderly, and I almost felt bad when I sunk onto the mattress, the blanket crinkling underneath me. Fingers trailed over fabric I knew covered him at night, and that knowledge was enough to pebble my skin. Even just sitting there, I could smell him. Clean. Like the night he'd first climbed into my closet. The night he'd first said my name.

I closed my eyes and took a deep breath, taking in the scent of my mate. And where I expected a raised brow from Melek, I only found a smile.

"He cleaned his room yesterday," he said. "Replaced his bedding. Did his laundry. He even sorted his books by color of the spine. All so he could present himself at his best for your visit."

"But he isn't at his best."

He rubbed a hand over the back of his head and let out a sigh. "Paraprofin is just as addictive as souldust. Only easier to withdraw from. We started weaning him off about three weeks ago. It's tough, but he's attending cognitive and behavioral therapy, and he's doing amazing."

"That's good," I mumbled, and yet my head sunk into my palm. "Why doesn't he want to see me? It hurts to be separated from him." I tapped against my sternum much in the same way Adeas had done when he'd told me I was so beautiful it hurt him in his chest. "It hurts right here."

"Ah, yeah, the drawback of having a fated mate. You two seem to share a connection much stronger than the average couple." And suddenly, that felt like a curse. "Feeling the love between one another is great and all, until you realize you share just as much in pain and agony." He jutted his chin toward the window. "Adeas told me pain is weakness leaving the body."

I smiled. "I told him that once."

"Then you're both wrong." He glanced over his shoulder with a grin. "Pain is strength entering your body because healing is almost never pleasant. And you are both still healing, Sophie."

He was right, of course.

Even three months later later, I still went to speak to my counselor once a week, and I didn't see that going away anytime soon. While things were constantly improving, it had taken me almost a month to convince myself I no longer had to sleep in a freaking closet.

"He's afraid of letting you down again," Melek said. "Said he wants to be absolutely sure that won't happen before you meet. And, honestly, I'd rather have that than the other way around."

I rose onto shaky legs and walked over to the window,

each step accelerating my pulse. Even before I caught a glimpse of Adeas, the *fomp-fomp-fomp* of the basketball bouncing against asphalt pricked my ears.

A few scattered mesquite trees came into view. Shrubs soon followed, dotted with pink blossoms. Sand. Lots of red soil. A basketball hoop. And then... Adeas.

My heart opened up at the sight. It expanded until breathing turned impossible, but who needed air when your chest was so swollen with love? He looked good. Still like Adeas, but his skin had a nice tan, and muscles corded along his arm as he dribbled the ball. He ran. He jumped. He dunked.

"He loves basketball," Melek said. "That guy's pretty good at it, too. I sometimes play with him after my shift before I head back home."

I wiped remnants of tears, my hand reaching for the window as if I could touch him from afar. "What else does he do all day?"

"Well, Adeas works two hours a day at the infirmary. Usually in the mornings but he always goes for a run before that. Sometimes he swims instead. In the afternoon he attends therapy. Oh and, um..."

Melek stepped away and rummaged through the bookshelf. He clasped a sheet of paper between his fingers and held it out, each pencil stroke like a caress of my soul.

"This is his favorite motive." He tapped at the drawing, gentle lines in different shades of gray. "Sophie's head resting on his chest. Oh, and when he feels particularly creative, he draws..." More rummaging, followed by another sheet. "Sophie's head resting on his chest, but... from a different angle."

Clammy fingers reached for it but stopped before they touched the paper. "They're terribly out of proportion."

Melek laughed. "His entire world used to be out of proportion."

"Do you think I could take one home?"

Melek tortured me with silence and pouting lips, until the edge of the paper stroked my fingertips. "This is against policy. Luckily, he has so many, my bet is he won't notice if one is missing. Don't tell anybody."

I took the drawing and leaned with my shoulder against the window, eyes wandering back to the basketball court. The longer I stared, took him in, the more that hook behind my sternum hummed. It vibrated with such intensity, I placed a hand atop it. Be patient.

Adeas ran, dribbled, *fomp-fomp-fomp* — then he stopped. He clasped the ball underneath his arm, his head slightly tilting, almost as if something in my direction had caught his attention. My heart bounced back full force, and for a moment, I expected him to look at me. He didn't.

He looked toward the building but never lifted his gaze. Instead, he brought his other hand to his chest. It mirrored mine, his palm resting where it hummed, where it hurt, where it hoped.

And I knew without a doubt that he sensed me there, telling me from afar that he had my soul, and I had his.

Yes, this was progress.

TWENTY-SEVEN

Adeas

"You can do this." Melek gave an encouraging pat onto my shoulder.

My palms turned clammy.

I can do this.

I have to do this!

The weight of Melek's hand turned heavier, crashing, crunching. "She came every week for four months —"

Four fucking months. Shit.

"I can't do this." I pulled away right there and turned back toward the staircase, my heart aching inside my chest. "She came every fucking week for four fucking months, and what did I do? Refused to see her each time."

And yet she kept coming back, *for me*, each time growing my shame a bit more, shrinking my courage to face her. A vicious cycle.

Cold sweat layered the back of my neck. How could I have done that to her? At times, I let her wait for almost an hour, enjoying having her close while not letting her near me. What was wrong with me? I loved Sophie. Loved her so much each second apart from her physically hurt.

As if to offer proof, my heart gave an aggressive whomp inside my chest. No. I couldn't put this off any longer.

I stopped and turned back toward the cafeteria door, where Melek remained unmoving with his arms crossed in front of his chest. Almost as if he'd known I'd turn around and do just that. Where he found that confidence in me, I couldn't say, because I had none of it in myself.

"The best moment to reunite with her was four months ago, when she came here the first time," he said with a calmness I feared I'd never ever achieve again. "The second-best moment, is right here, right now."

His words punched me straight in the gut.

Everything inside my stomach roiled, torturing me with waves of convulsions. Those wouldn't go away for days if I ran again now.

"Alright, I'm going in."

With that, I approached the cafeteria door, the electronic swoosh driving shivers up my spine. I distracted from my fear by counting steps. One step. Two steps. Three steps... Four...

My stomach bottomed out somewhere around my kneecaps, guts dangling around my legs until they locked in place.

There she was, and my entire body turned solid at the sight of nothing more but the back of her head. I could have sustained myself for a while on just this view.

For an overlong moment, I just stood there, tempted to tell myself that Sophie had left. That woman sitting there at one of the fifty-something tables? That wasn't her. Sophie had long, blonde hair. This one wore it right above her shoulders. Brown.

Sophie left. That's not her.

It would have been such a convenient lie, if it wasn't for the fact that she was the only living being inside that cafeteria. Waiting for someone. Always waiting. For me.

A glance over my shoulder revealed Melek, his face carrying that don't-you-dare-turn-around kind of look he'd studied so hard ever since he'd become my counselor.

Fuck it. I can do this.

No big deal. Just my mate. Half my soul.

I would walk straight up to her.

And I did — for maybe another ten steps.

Then all motion died into a halt, my mind tortured with every single memory of words spoken in a delusional high and promises broken while I'd chased my next score. My chest constricted so fucking bad I couldn't breathe.

I turned back toward the door.

"Why?" Sophie's voice turned my limbs to stone. "You don't wanna see me? You're running again? Fine. But at least help me understand why."

I turned around. There she was. Sophie. Standing beside her chair and staring back at me. She didn't move. She didn't say another word.

Just stood there. Waiting.

A beat of lightness inside my chest, almost as if the pain and ache suspended itself for a moment. It lifted from my sternum, making room for all those good memories Sophie and I shared. How she'd fallen asleep on my chest. How we'd eaten pasta together. How I'd washed her hair.

I couldn't say when I started to walk up to her, but I did, and each step filled my chest with warmth. Sophie was a sun all over again, shining even brighter.

I came to a halt only a few steps away from her, not

knowing what to say after such a long time, so I remained silent, listening to that joyful hum inside my chest.

She wore a white skirt with a red blouse and matching red sandals which slowly shoved over the polished concrete of the cafeteria. From her darker hair to her straighter posture to the sparkle in her eyes, this woman looked a whole lot like *leska*, but her soft gaze carried my sweet Sophie.

"I, um..." My throat tied up, clogged with all those emotions I'd only recently learned how to confront. Shame, mostly.

"Do you really want me to leave?" Her eyes turned dull, staring right at me but somehow going distant at the same time. "I'll do it if that's what you want, but not until you tell me why."

Why? Why? That word tugged at my soul, plaguing me. Fuck. If I had an answer, I would have told her months ago.

Maybe after all this time in rehab, peeling back the layers of my addiction, I did really know the answer. But saying it out loud was more reality than I could handle. Like a damn mirror showing me a guy with literally no color left in his eyes.

"You know what..." She fumbled a small, folded paper from her pocket and placed it on the table beside her, and waited until I had the guts to open my palm before she placed it there. "This is my address and my current com information. A year from now, two years... I'll be waiting. But I won't keep coming if it's too much for you."

The breeze of how she passed me tensed my muscles, her voice betraying neither anger nor blame, and that only made it so much worse. With each flop of her slippers, my knees turned weaker, that vibration inside my chest enough to collapse my ribcage.

Flip. Flop. Flip. Flop.

Tell her. Tell her! Gather your courage, you weak pain in the ass. She's worth it. She's worth everything.

I swung around, screaming my confession across the cafeteria. "Because I didn't save you. Because I couldn't be the hero I was supposed to be then. What if I can't be that hero now?"

She stopped. By the Three Suns, she stopped.

"You were shoved, scared, and slapped in front of my eyes, and I did nothing," I said, my lungs convulsing. "With the brutal way he abused you, I should have killed Sehrin. The Jal'zar was the one who did it. I should have carried you out of that place. Captain Balgiz was the one who did it. I just lay there. And... and the fact that I did nothing isn't even the worst part. After Sehrin injected me? I..." An unexpected swallow choked my voice, and it took all my strength to push through that tightness in my throat. "The moment that stuff hit my brain, I swear I forgot you were even in that room. What kind of male am I to let that happen? I was supposed to save you. Me. But I didn't. They did."

As time fluttered to a standstill, Sophie didn't move. Waiting with stalled breath, for the first time, I realized just what I'd put her through. Agony.

"You think *they* saved me?" She turned, head shaking, slow steps carrying her back toward me where she glanced up, her hands pressing against my chest. "No, Adeas. You saved me long before that night. Without you, nothing would have been left of me to salvage."

I soaked in the warmth of her palms against me. "I wanted to make sure that I could step up to my responsibilities this time. Finally be your hero."

"Finally?" She let out a small scoff. "Adeas, you were

my only friend. You saved my credits. You stitched my wounds. Washed my body. Held me. You risked your life for me more than once." A moment of hesitation, then she nestled her head against my chest where she fit just right. "And if that isn't what makes a hero, how about the fact that you're fighting your addiction? You're fighting for *us*."

I wrapped my arms around her, not fully convinced that I was a hero, but I sure wouldn't argue it. If I was enough for Sophie, then I would let her believe it... only surprise her with just how much better I would be in a year. Two years. Ten.

Forever.

"I'm sorry I left you waiting so long."

"No more apologies." She lifted her hand and showed me her wrist, a red mark decorating her skin right underneath where the scrunchie sat. "I promised I would wait, and that's what I will do. And I'll wait even longer if you need more time, but don't shut me out."

"No more shutting you out," I murmured, cupping her cheek. "I need you, *anam ghail*. You have my soul."

The way her eyes slipped to my lips made longing pound so hard at my core I couldn't think straight. "And you have mine."

I dipped down, brushing her lips gently with mine, sending a rush of excitement through my chest and teasing a moan from her. She tasted like salt and serenity, telling me one of us was crying. Perhaps both.

Sophie sighed against my mouth and slid her hand underneath my white shirt. She stroked her palm all over my body, no doubt mapping the changes I'd gone through.

Where she might have expected ribs, she found full flesh, my body healthy, stronger than even before my time as an addict since working out was what distracted me best.

"I love you so much," she sniffed, and for once, her crying didn't make me angry. She could cry all she wanted against me, because I would be there to dry her tears.

I ran my fingers through her hair and dipped my tongue into her mouth, my whole body begging to connect with hers.

I didn't realize I'd walked her back against the table until the legs screeched, resonating the empty cafeteria with what it sounded like when two people who were fated to be together reunited.

It was painful, agonizing, and every bit of what I'd feared. And it was healing and so damn wonderful I cursed myself for keeping her away for so long.

"I'm so sorry for everything I put you through," I whispered.

She grabbed my hand and placed it onto her breast, making me weigh it, knead it. "I said no more..."

Her tone was sharp but her kisses soft, each one telling me where her voice had trailed off. Stop the apologies, the shame, the guilt.

"Let the past be the past," she said. "We're here. Together."

I picked her up and sat her onto the table. By the three Suns this woman weighed nothing. Eager fingers gathered the fabric of her skirt, my body hard and ready to mate her. Feel her without any poison altering my perception of how she squeezed down on my shaft.

Sophie trailed her hand along my abs and down onto my cock, her fingertips quickly finding and tracing the outline of my head. "Not here."

I jerked back.

Right. Cafeteria.

For a moment, I'd completely forgotten where we were.

And although the room was empty, aside from two cleaning droids, the audience we had gathered outside along the windows overlooking the park made me pull her skirt back down.

Sophie glanced over at the Vetusians, at least seven residents, all hollering and clapping. "What are they doing?"

"Cheering us on, I guess." Shoving my arms underneath her legs and shoulders, I picked her up and hurried toward the door. I would never share her again.

She wrapped her arm around my neck and patiently dangled her feet as I carried her up the stairs since I had no patience to wait for the elevator. While taking mates to our room wasn't exactly in-line with the rules, Melek had only grinned when we passed him, so I took it as an exception granted.

I all but stumbled into my room, slipping out of my shoes before I lowered her onto my bed. "I haven't tasted you in so long."

She groaned at that and raised her pelvis, helping me tug her panties down, all four hands equally as frantic. But the faster she rushed to slip out of skirt and blouse, the more unhurried I became, completely enthralled by my mate.

Where Sophie had always been beautiful, she now took my breath away. Almost as if my senses, previously numbed by poison, explored her anew. And I took my time in doing so, much to her frustration, if that sigh of hers was an indicator.

Finger tracing around her navel, I leaned over and kissed a path along the side of her stomach, coming to a halt between her breasts. I turned my attention to her nipple, pink and taut, letting the tip of my tongue circle around it.

Her legs wrapped around my back and she pulled me against her. "Now you're testing my patience."

And yet she carried a grin on her lips, which I quickly sucked between mine with a thrust against her pussy. She groaned into my mouth, her pelvis grinding against me.

I backed up and slid my arms underneath her buttocks, lifting her slightly so I could run my tongue from her juicy entrance all the way to her clit.

"Again," she moaned.

And I did, but in reverse this time, suckling on her clit before I parted her lips with one swipe and penetrated her with the tip. Warm and slightly salty, her cream covered the entire pad of my tongue, turning my cock so hard I had to shift my weight onto one hip.

I kept suckling on her labia, rolling them between my lips while I freed one hand to open my pants. The moment Sophie caught the clinking of belt buckle against buttons, she pushed herself up to sit.

With no warning, small fingers wrapped around a shaft fed by thick veins. "Take your shirt off."

For the first time ever since I'd met Sophie, I didn't hesitate. I was healthy and strong, and it showed in the way her lips parted when I took my shirt off, only to say nothing. She filled the gap with my cock instead, and I let out a hiss.

"Fuck," I moaned, my thighs shaking with the way she circled the rim of my tip with her tongue. "Go easy, or I'll come right away."

The way her smile clasped her lips tightly around my cock wasn't helping either, and I fought hard to hold back. I let her suck me and played with her hair while she did, mostly for my own distraction.

"Not like this," I eventually said, gently tugging her off my shaft before I kicked my pants off. "I want to be deep inside of you, Sophie. Connect with you in any way I can."

She sat up and parted her thighs, inviting me in as she'd done once before, but asked nothing in exchange.

I trailed my hand along the inside of her leg, thumb parting pink folds. She threw her head back and moaned as I dipped one finger into her. Another soon followed, curling the way she liked it, my knuckles glistening with how much she wanted me.

Fingers wrapped around the base of my cock, guiding my head to ready her for me, stretch her. I worked myself inside her with shallow thrusts, but she quickly writhed underneath me, bucking, her head shoving over the blanket.

"I missed mating you so much," I moaned, her pussy so wet and needy I eased right into her, tight muscle sucking me deeper. "How does my cock feel, Sophie?"

"Fucking amazing," she panted, her walls convulsing around a throbbing head.

I dug my hands underneath her buttocks and pulled her onto my hard shaft, relishing the way she hissed at first but then circled her hips for more.

One tug against her sides and she arched her back for me. Angling my pelvis, I gave a few hard thrusts upward, her stomach muscles convulsing as she cried out in pleasure.

"Again!"

"Like this?" Another thrust, this one teasing such a yelp from her my sack tightened in response.

Eager to fill her, I fought to keep my movements rhythmic, penetrating her deep so I could brush my pubic bone over her clit before each retreat.

Every part of me reached out to every part of her. Each thrust into her pussy, each caress over her hip, each focused gaze, each tug on that thread between us. I felt Sophie in every cell of my body and deep into the spirit realm.

I lowered myself down close to her, kisses tracking every

part of her face. She moaned in need, small shudders and rippling convulsions around my shaft building, telling of her imminent release.

"Come for me," I whispered, hard, driving strokes bringing me deeper, claiming every part of her as mine. "Yeah, just like that, my fated one."

Her panting turned raspy until she held her breath altogether. Nails dug into my shoulders and thighs locked me in place. It was that loss of motion that chased us over the edge, nothing but our bodies tightly locked together, shoving, grinding, exploding together.

I closed my eyes, her walls clenching all around me, squeezing the first spurt of my seed into her womb. We contracted and convulsed around each other, resonating my small room with the sounds of our shared climax.

When I opened my eyes again, they locked with Sophie's, and everything came to a standstill around us. With a tug of her legs, she demanded I turn onto my back, where she immediately nestled herself on my chest.

She rested on top of me like that for a while, nuzzling me, but I sensed her restlessness, so I asked, "What is it?"

"Melek mentioned you could join the outpatient program sooner if you felt ready for it," she said, keeping her voice as casual as possible. "I went there two weeks ago and checked it out. They've got nice apartments for couples. It's restricted access only, and they have a small clinic you could work at."

I wrapped my arm around her chest and squeezed. "Are you asking me to move in with you?"

"I guess I am," she giggled.

A knock on the door sent a start through me, until Melek's voice came muffled from behind it. "You're twenty minutes past visitation."

"I'll be out in a minute," Sophie shouted back, then rolled off me to gather her things and get dressed. "Perhaps you can think about it? Discuss it with Melek?"

I handed Sophie a tissue before I climbed back into my pants, the fact that she couldn't rest in my arms longer making the idea of transferring to outpatient all the more appealing.

"I'll bring it up with him tomorrow," I promised. "I just need to make sure I won't relapse. That's number one priority."

Dressed and with her hair a tousled mess, Sophie took my hands into hers. "I'll distract you."

I couldn't help but grin. "I know you will."

After I slipped back into my shirt, I wrapped an arm around her middle, getting ready to bring her back to the reception area. But the moment we stepped outside my room, my chest clenched.

Several residents either lined the hallway or poked their heads out of their room, some winking at us, all of them grinning.

"For fuck's sake," I grumbled, swatting them away proving impossible. "This is embarrassing. It's a big deal for all males here if our match decides to mate with us, since we're only allowed to remain on Earth if we're bonded. They have no idea we did that a while ago."

But where I expected to find dread on Sophie's features, her grin put all the others to shame. "Ah, guess I'm getting that walk of shame after all."

I had no clue what that meant, though she seemed to be enjoying it greatly. Head held high, hips swaying, she crossed the hallway beside me. A warm-hearted female, showing all those *sgu'dals* that we were worth saving.

TWENTY-EIGHT

Sophie

The burger patties sizzled on the grill next to us, the smell turning increasingly bitter. "You're burning the patties!"

"Oh, shit." Adeas stopped dribbling the ball, clutched it underneath his arm, and hurried over. "Why didn't you tell me sooner?"

"Because you said you would be the one grilling today. You can't play basketball and *not* burn the food at the same time."

He grabbed the spatula, the chain link it was attached to clinking against the seasoned metal of the grill. "They're not burned. And I like them darker anyway."

"Hey, yo," Rekin called out from across the court, edge of his hand pressed against his forehead to shield his two-toned eyes from the blasting Arizona sun. "Don't just run off taking the ball with you."

Adeas couldn't help himself and dribbled the ball a few more times before he tossed it back to Rekin, who went straight for a slam dunk. And easy thing to do for most Vetusians.

Melanie, Rekin's mate, grabbed the wine bottle from beside her on the picnic table. She let it gulp into my empty glass and handed it to me before she refilled her own.

"To underage drinking!" I clanked my glass against hers. "Perhaps the very best improvement the Vetusian Empire brought to the United States."

Adeas threw me a sidelong glance, one brow lifting into a teasing arch. "Go ahead! Empty that bottle, and I'll reap the fruits of what it does to you later."

My cheeks heated. "Is that a threat or a promise?"

"That depends." Adeas flipped the patties, then walked up to me, placing one hand to the left and right beside me where I sat on the table. "What am I more likely to go through with? A threat, or a promise?"

I nuzzled his nose with mine and pulled his forehead down to mine. "You've been pretty good at keeping promises lately."

"That's what I wanted to hear."

"Except for when you promised you would fix the synthesizer," I said. "The carb cartridge keeps clogging up, and when it pops back open, it splashes the entire kitchen."

"I fix people, Sophie. Not machines."

"Rekin!" Melanie called out. "Can you take a look at Sophie's synthesizer? She said it's broken."

Rekin dropped the ball and walked over to us, wiping off sweat with his forearm before he tugged on his blue shirt. "I'm starting to hate these color-coded uniforms. There's always someone who needs something fixed. I maintain fusion panels, Mel, not synthesizers."

She let out a scoff. "Because you can take an entire

stargazer apart in under an hour, but a kitchen gadget is above your pay-grade."

Adeas grabbed one of the plates from beside me on which he arranged the patties. "I'll take a look at it later."

"Filthy lie!"

His lips pulled into a lopsided smirk I wanted to drag my tongue over. "Go get the other stuff ready."

Melanie and I slipped off the table, put out plates, and removed the covers from the cut-up onions and tomatoes. Rekin helped himself to a beer from the cooler, handing a bottle wet with condensation to Adeas.

"You know full well I don't drink." My mate was adamant about not touching any alcohol.

"Can't blame me for trying. Your track record is so fucking clean you're making the rest of us look bad."

"Alright, guys, buns are over there. Let's enjoy this barbecue before the monsoon rolls in." Adeas sat down beside me, immediately pulling me onto his lap. "Where's the ketchup?"

"You are just gross," Melanie laughed. "Honestly... how many bottles of ketchup do you go through a month?"

Adeas grabbed the bottle, shook it, and squeezed so much of it onto his patty it dripped down all around. "Two."

I gave him a little swat. "Yeah, more like four. I keep telling him he doesn't have to put it on everything."

"Everything tastes better with ketchup. I still don't get how the Empire managed to become what it is without that stuff."

Rekin made a noise at the back of his throat. "You mean an Empire at the brink of war with the Jal'zar? For the second time in a decade?"

Adeas gave a squeeze against my thigh. Everybody in

this neighborhood knew I was Sophie. Nobody knew I was *that* Sophie, and we'd been adamant about keeping it that way.

"They'll agree on new terms somehow," Adeas said. "I'm sure the Wardens know what they're doing."

"Dude, the moment the high court dismissed all charges against Zavis and announced him Warden, he took a stargazer to Solgad." Rekin took a bite of his burger and shook his head, rinsing it down with a sip of his beer. "Solgad, man. The only planet Vetusians are not allowed to step on as per treaty, and that guy grinds his boots into Jal'zar soil. Like... he was locked up for so long, and the first thing he does is go to Solgad? Why? Sometimes I wonder about those Wardens..."

I shrugged. "I would be surprised if he's still alive. Jal'zar told me he's the most hated Vetusian on that planet."

"Which is probably why he disappeared," Adeas said. "I see votes coming up for another Warden to replace him..."

"Probably hanging dead upside down for their sun to burn him alive." Just as Rekin lifted a hand as if to make an important point, he stalled mid-movement, his glance wandering back over his shoulder.

Music blasted coming from behind one of the group habitats, where two young Vetusians turned the corner.

Across from me, Rekin's hand began trembling, and he shoved nervously around on the bench. His face paled, which meant something considering this Vetusian spent so much time in the sun he'd developed a rather dark tan.

Melanie reached out to him, and Rekin immediately grabbed her hand. "The music?"

Rekin shrunk into half the male right in front of my eyes but nodded.

"Trigger!" Adeas called out.

The two Vetusians stopped dead in their track, one of them lifting a hand to his ear. "What?"

"Trigger!" Melanie got up and shouted. "The music triggers him."

"The music triggers him?" one of them called back.

"Yeah," we all shouted in unison, except for Rekin, who'd grown small and silent.

One of the Vetusians nodded and fumbled with his com, and the music soon disappeared before he said, "Sorry about that."

I exchanged a quick glance with Adeas, who offered me a half smile. Triggers remained a lifelong issue for all former addicts. For Rekin, it was a certain type of music Vetusians called *yordub*. For Adeas, it was criticism and the smell of *uri* berries since they reminded him of his ex-girlfriend.

"Sorry about that," Rekin said, tugging on the collar of his shirt, not meeting anyone's eyes.

We offered neither blame nor comfort, because the general recommendation was to let the addict learn how to deal with it on their own. Triggers, however, we all called out, and everyone was considerate of it since every single Vetusian living here was a *sgu'dal*.

The outpatient neighborhood consisted of seven group habitats equipped with around fifty apartments each. Not nearly enough to place all those women who had a souldust-addicted match, but it was a start.

Melanie assembled another burger and licked the grease off her fingers. "When are you guys leaving again? Thursday?"

"We'll leave Thursday and return Saturday the week after." I wiped my fingers on my shorts and crammed the brochure from my pocket, unfolding it between wine and lettuce. "We'll visit Aunt Debby in district three and stay the night. The day after, we'll take the transit vessel to Paris."

Rekin shook his head. "Dude, you're lucky they constantly approve your requests to leave this place. I've yet to see anything else of Earth but the rehab facilities."

Adeas and I exchanged a quick glance. Travelling. It was what we'd decided we would do. Lots of it! Perhaps we would look into adoption in a few years. Or maybe we wouldn't. We were both still young with plenty of time to figure out what we wanted.

"Exemplary conduct." Adeas tapped against the brochure. "I want to see the Eiffel Tower."

"That's a no-brainer baby," I said. "Anyway, we'll only stay for two days, and then travel to the research station outside of Gizeh since Adeas has a scholar friend there. He'll take us to the pyramids."

Adeas nodded. "On elephants."

"Camels."

"Right, camels," he mumbled between bites. "They've got funny feet."

Melanie scrunched up her face. "As if they couldn't have gotten rid of that."

"Our technology doesn't work in close proximity to the pyramids," Rekin said. "The Empire came to find out the hard way when three stargazers fell from the sky while crossing that area. Which is why they put that research station there in the first place."

"That's creepy as shit." Melanie stared at her burger for a moment, brows furrowed. "Why do you think that is?"

Adeas cleaned his fingers on a napkin before he reached for my hand. "That's what the scholars are trying to find out. Rumor has it there's something underneath the sand from before our ancestors left."

"They'll never unearth it," Rekin scoffed. "Too much sand. Too much digging. Not to mention irrelevant."

I got up and stacked my plate on top of Adeas'. "History is never irrelevant. And I'd like to learn more about the time when you left Earth since you don't have much documentation."

With a knock on the table, I excused myself and strolled over to the ball. At each dribble, that thing threatened to either punch me in the face or roll off into the shrubs.

"You've got very poor eye-hand-coordination, *anam ghail*." Adeas' voice came from behind me, who quickly handed me my glass. "Have some more wine and see if it improves."

"You just want to get me tipsy."

A devilish grin came over his features, which he rounded up with a lick over his lower lip. "And have you on my cock doing crazy things until your mind clears? Of course I do."

I grabbed the glass and held it out between us. "Maybe I should pour this wine over your head for that comment alone."

"You wouldn't dare." Faster than my eyes could follow, he dipped his fingers into my glass, sprinkling my face with drops of wine. "There! Now we're even."

Merlot running down my face, the dry bouquet of it wafting around me, I took a sip, then pressed my mouth onto his. Adeas immediately suckled on my lips, swiping his tongue over them before he dipped into my mouth.

He wrapped his arms around me, released a deep, satisfied sigh, and only said one thing. "Sophie."

A name he'd whispered once, reminding me that I

wasn't *leska*. I was Sophie. And he wasn't *sgu'dal*. He was Adeas. Names held power, and we'd taken ours back.

———

This concludes Saved. Do you have 5 minutes to spare? If you enjoyed this book, please consider leaving a review.

Made in the USA
Coppell, TX
30 August 2021

61469008R00169